The Righteous One
A Novel

Neil Perry Gordon

Dedication

To my Dad - Whose eternal soul carries the flame that illuminates my journey

Contents

Chapter 1

M yron Blass looked at himself in the mirror. The shadows under his eyes seemed to be getting darker. He ran warm water over his razor to wash off the stubble and finished shaving with a few upward strokes along his neck. The only remaining hairs were his salt and pepper eyebrows and some stubborn ones growing out of his nostrils like damn upside-down potted plants. Being completely bald made his grooming choices simpler, but he lamented that lately he was looking older than his forty-five years.

Myron grabbed a suit bag from his closet and with both hands placed it gently across his bed. He unzipped the fabric bag with the logo of BERGDORF GOODMAN emblazoned in gold letters on it, and carefully removed the garments. Putting on a new custom tailored suit for the first time from the Men's Store at Bergdorf's was a moment that affirmed in his mind that he was a man to be reckoned with.

Downstairs in the foyer, he took one last look in the mirror, and tugged up on the knot of his gold and navy striped tie. A peek through the sidelight window by the front door showed that his driver, Benjamin, was waiting for him. He ran the tips of his fingers down the lapel of his jacket and watched the nap of the suede shift into a lighter shade of brown. Then he ran it back up again and restored it to its original deep luster.

Myron stepped through the elaborate carved wooden front door adorned with polished brass hardware and out onto the curb. He took a look up and down the impeccably landscaped and well-appointed street and smiled and tipped his fedora to Benjamin, who stood by his perfectly detailed, black 1960 Cadillac Coup de Ville.

"Where to, sir?" Benjamin asked, offering a charming smile and holding the rear car door open.

"Morning Benjamin, let's go see Pops," he said.

Myron stared out the window as Benjamin drove across the causeway to City Island. He loved the countryside approach. The elevated bridge to the island provided a majestic view of the fishing boats anchored in the harbor. His father had lived here for the past twenty years since his mother passed. Myron wanted his father to move in with him, but he refused.

"What am I going to do? Watch TV all day?"

"Come on, Pops, it would be nice having you around."

"Nonsense. If you want to see me, you get in that fancy car and drive over."

The car pulled up to the weather beaten, waterfront home on Horton Street. Myron stepped out of his car and cursed at the damp mist drifting over from the saltwater bay, laying a moist coating upon his suede jacket.

As usual, the front door was unlocked. Myron entered and shouted, "Pops, where are you?"

There was no answer, which was also not surprising. *He's probably out back*, Myron thought. He walked through the kitchen and out the back door, and there was Solomon Blass, sitting in an old lawn chair on a narrow and awkwardly tilted boat dock, with a fishing rod in his hand.

The moment Myron took a step on the dock, Solomon rose, put down the rod and said, "Let's take a walk."

"Okay, Pops, whatever you say."

Solomon grabbed his cane hanging off the back of his chair.

"How you doin'?" Myron said.

"Myron, I need to talk to you about a dream I had."

"A dream? Sure, tell me about it," Myron said as he followed Solomon along the rocky shoreline of City Island Harbor.

Solomon lifted his index finger into the sky and said, "I dreamt I was back in Warsaw with the Tsvi Midal. Leo was with me and we were working a shtetl in Galicia. We had a few girls in the wagon ready for the ride back to Warsaw when I saw the *tzaddik*. He looked right at me with these sparkling blue eyes. I couldn't draw my gaze away. He was young, no more than a teenager." Solomon stopped and turned to his son, grabbed his shoulders and pulled him in tight. "He looked at me and said, as clear as if he was standing in your shoes right now, '*I have returned*'."

There was a moment of silence before Myron asked, "Who has returned, Pops?"

"I just told you, the *tzaddik*."

"A *tzaddik*? What's a *tzaddik*?" Myron said shaking his head.

Solomon clutched his cane and pointed it at his son and said, "It is said that the *tzaddikim* are the hands of Hashem, gifted with the ability of providing a bridge into the Creator's world. There are only thirty-six *tzaddikim* that live upon the earth at any one time."

Myron shook his head. "And what does this have to do with us?"

Solomon's eyes opened wide and he whispered, "The final battle is upon us. My time in this body is coming to an end, but your survival will depend on destroying the *tzaddik*."

They walked back to the house in silence and ended up in the kitchen. Solomon sat down, and said, "The *tzaddik* will seek to destroy me and everything we built. He must be stopped."

Myron turned his palms upward, shrugged and said, "Okay, Pops, what do you want me to do?"

"Bring me the rabbi. He'll know."

"Sure, Pops, right away."

Chapter 2

Moshe Potasznik sat behind his work table, trying to finish replacing a sole, when the bells hanging on the shop's front door jingled. He removed his eyeglasses, set down the knife that he used to cut leather into shape, and went to greet the customer.

"Good morning sir, how may I be of service?" Moshe asked.

"Are you Moshe the Cobbler?"

"I am," Moshe answered, thinking this was plainly obvious.

The man reached into a pocket of his gray overcoat and pulled out a card.

"My employer, Mr. Lieberman, would like to speak with you," he said, handing Moshe a card.

Moshe offered a gentle smile and accepted it. He slipped his eyeglasses on and read:

ARNOLD LIEBERMAN
NEW YORK CITY COUNCILMAN
2400 GRAND CONCOURSE
THE BRONX, NEW YORK
CY8-6000

Moshe looked at the card, and then stared out the window of his shop to the building across the street. "Isn't that the, um...?"

"The Paradise Theater? Yes, Mr. Lieberman owns the theater, his office is on the third floor," said the man.

Moshe realized he was still pointing out the window and turned back to face the visitor. "And what does Councilman Lieberman want with me?"

The man, slightly taller and much slimmer than Moshe, took off his gray felt fedora and placed it on the counter. From inside his gray overcoat he reached in and pulled out a handkerchief and wiped the sweat off his brow. "It's stifling hot in here."

"It's a warm one," Moshe agreed. "Can I offer you some cold water?"

"Yes, that would be great."

"Just give me a second, I have a pitcher in the fridge," Moshe said, and walked into his workroom.

Moshe wondered why the owner of the Paradise Theater, where he just saw the movie *Spartacus*, starring Kirk Douglas, would want to see him.

He offered the glass of water to the man dressed in all gray.

"Thank you, Moshe," he said, and guzzled it down.

"Please tell me your name, sir, and why does the councilman want to speak with me?"

"People call me Gray," he said gesturing his arms like a performer to emphasize his gray wardrobe.

Moshe scanned the man from head to toe; from his gray leather shoes, which Moshe noted were in a serious need of a shine, to his gray slacks poking out under his gray overcoat. He wore a gray dress shirt, a gray tie, and sported a nice full head of gray hair. Even his eyes sort of looked gray.

"I can see," smiled Moshe.

"Mr. Lieberman has not shared with me the reason why he wants to see you, Moshe. I am nothing more than a humble messenger."

"When would he like to see me?"

"Oh, right now," Gray said, gesturing to the front door.

"In the middle of the work day?" Moshe asked.

"This shouldn't take too long. Please come now," he said, gesturing to the door.

Moshe looked out onto the busy sidewalk and wondered how many customers would be disappointed at finding the shop closed. But curiosity moved him to grab the shop keys from the hook, turn the sign to CLOSED and lock the front door.

The Paradise Theater was not only Moshe's favorite movie house in The Bronx, it was also considered an architectural marvel in all of the city's five boroughs. Over the marquee that announced the current showing was a Seth Thomas clock, where at the top of each hour in a recessed alcove, Saint George appeared and slayed a fire-breathing dragon.

The main lobby's ceiling featured three recessed domes, each one decorated with hand-painted murals representing various themes of movie-making. But what Moshe marveled at most was the beautifully carved marble statue of the Winged Victoria positioned upon a marble fountain, where a pool of water reflected shimmering images of the three domes above it.

Moshe once read in a program that the auditorium was designed to represent a sixteenth-century Italian baroque garden. During a showing, if Moshe sank low enough into his seat, he could see the ceiling filled with twinkling stars shining through a painted array of clouds that somehow appeared to be floating slowly by.

Gray held open one of the large, just-polished brass doors leading into the main lobby and gestured toward the elaborately decorated wrought iron railing that wrapped along the carpeted spiral staircase. "Please, Moshe, this way."

Moshe climbed up the two levels to the very top floor. He glanced to his right and saw upon the landing a set of padded doors leading to the upper levels of the theater. This was a familiar sight when he and his wife Leah ended up in the nose-bleed seats a few times, when the theater was at its capacity.

Gray directed Moshe through an inconspicuous door and inside to a reception area that lacked the ornate architectural designs of the theater's public spaces. A woman with curly red hair was busy typing at a desk. She briefly looked up and said, "Go right in, he's waiting for you."

"Thank you, Agnes," said Gray.

Moshe offered Agnes a smile, which went unnoticed as she quickly returned to her task on the typewriter.

"You must be Moshe the Cobbler?" Arnold said the moment Moshe took his first step into the office.

"The last I looked," Moshe said offering a quick wit.

"It's nice to meet you," Arnold said, reaching out to shake his hand.

Moshe clutched Arnold's hand and looked into his gentle brown eyes, set off by bushy eyebrows and smooth as silk skin. He imagined that Arnold probably indulged himself with a barbershop shave each morning.

"Thank you, Gray. Please close the door on your way out," Arnold said.

Gray offered Moshe a brief wave and left.

Arnold walked over to a large window. Moshe watched him as he stood there for a moment, gazing out. *He is dressed as a councilman should be*, thought Moshe. He wore a brown business suit that seemed to be tailored to fit his hefty frame, and from what Moshe could make out from a brief glance, expensive shoes.

"So you may be wondering why I asked you here."

"Now that you mention it…" he said, with a casual flip of his hand.

Arnold sighed and said, "What I am about to tell you, you may find, um, strange."

Moshe shrugged. "I've seen plenty of strange things in my lifetime, Councilman."

"Please, Moshe, call me Arnold."

Moshe nodded.

Arnold walked over to his leather chair behind his desk and sat down. "Please sit."

Moshe tried to sit, then realized he had forgotten to remove his work apron which still had a few tools tucked inside the large pouch.

"Sorry, do you mind?" Moshe gestured to the desk.

"Tools of the trade?" Arnold said.

"Please, Arnold, tell me why I'm here," Moshe asked, placing his apron down.

"I've been studying with a rabbi who you probably know."

"And who would that be?"

"Rabbi Shapira. I believe his father was your rabbi from your birthplace in Krzywcza," he said.

"You know Rabbi Shapira's son?" Moshe asked.

Arnold nodded, smiled and said, "He's teaching me Kabbalah."

Moshe barely remembered the rabbi's son. He was at least ten years older than Moshe, and left his family to study at the Rabbinical school in Lviv when Moshe was still a young boy.

"Maybe I met the rabbi's son a few times," Moshe said, and wondered what this had to do with him.

"Well the rabbi remembers you." Arnold leaned in and said, "I've been looking for you for over ten years, Moshe, and all this time, you were right across the street."

Moshe shrugged, gave a slight tilt of his head and asked, "And why would you be looking for me?"

"Rabbi Shapira told me of your story. How you were born in the Galician shtetl of Krzywcza, and about your family's daring escape from the first World War. What he didn't know was what happened to your family when you made it to America."

Moshe thought about the old rabbi. The last time he had seen him was forty-five years ago when his father, Pincus, and Pincus's friend Jakob had rescued him, his mother, Clara, his sisters, Jennie and Anna, and his brother, Hymie.

"That was a long time ago. What interest is my life to you?" Moshe asked.

"I don't mean to be disrespectful, Moshe. But what I learned from the rabbi, and why I have been looking for you all these years is because I know that you are *tzaddik*," Arnold said.

Moshe froze at hearing these words. He had not been called *tzaddik* since he was a teenager living on the Lower East Side, just after his family immigrated to America. He remembered well the events, both in Krzywcza and in New York, of his abilities of easing those in distress and being able to foretell tragic events moments before they occurred. The last one was when his father Pincus died the next day after his mother Clara passed away. But that was over fifteen years ago.

When Moshe asked how he found him, Arnold said, "That is the most amazing part. I searched every record I could find on families who emigrated from Krzywcza before 1920 with no luck. Then, just a few weeks ago, I met someone at shul who heard about my research and asked me if I ever heard of an organization called the Landsman Society. He explained that these organizations were support groups set up by immigrants from the shtetls of Eastern Europe, as a way to help one another create new lives for their families in the New World." He paused, and looked at Moshe.

Moshe nodded and said with a smirk, "And that's when you found the Landsman Society of Krzywcza."

"Exactly!" Arnold said, pointing a finger at Moshe as if he had just won a prize. "Your father was its founder, Pincus Potasznik. Rabbi Shapira remembered that Pincus was a cobbler. So I was finally able to put two plus two together and presto, Moshe the Cobbler."

With his palms lifted upwards, Moshe asked, "So, what do you want from me?"

"Moshe, you're *tzaddik*, one of only thirty-six in all of the world. You may not have practiced your gifts in a while," Arnold lowered his voice and said, "but we need you now."

"Need me for what?"

"There's a Jewish gangster living right here, in the Bronx. His name is Myron Blass. He leads an organized crime outfit that has been infecting the community. I had some business interactions with him years ago," he said, and paused with a guilty-looking grimace.

"I used to run a small sports book. It was mostly a hobby. That's how I got to know Myron. Of course I had to give it up when I decided to run for the city council seat for the Bronx 15th Congressional District. I had thought Myron was just a small-time bookie, but when I was elected I learned about how far-reaching his criminal organization really was."

Moshe felt himself blush slightly that he didn't know who Councilman Arnold Lieberman was. But then again, he didn't pay attention to local politics.

Arnold continued, "I also learned that the brains behind the organization was Myron's father, Solomon. They're involved with massive real estate deals, a sports book, and have several politicians in their pockets. When I became councilman, Myron even approached me right in this office," he said sounding exasperated.

"What's so unusual? Sounds like typical gangster behavior that I read about nearly every day in the News," Moshe said.

"You're right, if that was all it was—except a few weeks ago I was sharing a story with Rabbi Shapira about Myron, and his father Solomon. The rabbi asked me if I was speaking about Solomon Blass, the old man, which indeed I was.

"The rabbi said that he had seen him at several Kabbalah lectures recently asking questions about Kabbalah's supposed dark side. He thinks there is something sinister with the man. When I told him about Solomon's history, he had gone as far as calling him *rasha*," Arnold said.

Moshe squirmed uncomfortably in his chair. Memories flooded his mind about his abduction as a teenager by the hands of the renowned palmist Dora Meltzer. She was accused of being *rasha*, which Moshe learned was some sort of evil counterpart to the *tzaddik*.

From what he remembered about his encounter with the palmist, she thought she could, through some magical ceremony, steal Moshe's connection to Hashem. Of course, she never had the chance to do so because of the last-minute rescue by his parents.

"So what does this have to do with me?" Moshe asked.

"The *rasha* must be stopped, and it can't be done without you."

"What do you mean?" Moshe asked flipping his palms upwards.

"According to Rabbi Shapira, only *tzaddik* can stop *rasha*."

Moshe shook his head and closed his eyes. When he opened them he leaned forward and waved his right hand and said, "I don't know what you are saying to me."

"Moshe, if Solomon Blass is indeed *rasha*, then you need to stop him, and only a *tzaddik* can do this. He and his son have already done irreparable harm to the Bronx."

"I think you're talking to the wrong man, Arnold," he said looking at his watch. "And I really need to get back to the shop."

"Of course, I understand. But why don't we get to know each other and at least become friends?"

"Sure, that sounds fine," Moshe said, anxious to end the conversation.

"Great," Arnold said, slapping his palms together. "Please come for dinner at my home and bring your wife. That's a good way for us to get acquainted since we are neighbors," Arnold said, pointing out through the window.

Chapter 3

Kabbalistic wisdom had helped Solomon to master ways of coping with the stresses of life by considering them blessings. The concept behind this practice was that all blessings emanate from the Creator and since the Creator is an endless source of goodness, even life's most challenging moments can be understood as a path to evolving one's eternal soul.

He understood that man's most basic needs were what the Kabbalists labeled as Desire and the sole object of this need was nothing more than one's pursuit for happiness. The achievement of this is accomplished by lifting the Curtain of Darkness that we live behind in order to discover the Light. Once we are connected to this Light, we no longer have fears that cripple us psychologically.

But in order to connect to the Light, we must learn how to face the Opposition, the source of life's challenges. The uninitiated at first cringe at this term. However in order to achieve authentic spiritual growth, the Opposition must not be feared, instead it must be accepted as a blessing from the Creator.

After years of practice, Solomon was able to master these lessons and put them into practice. But after some time, he wanted to go deeper and reach a higher spiritual level. That was when he twisted the righteous intent of the mystics.

He discovered, through his life experiences, that it was true that the universe was built on the idea of balance. Where there was the light, there must also be darkness. Where there was the meek and fearful, there must also be the strong and the fearless, and where there was the Obedient, there must also be the Opposition.

Supporting his efforts to build upon his connection to the Opposition, for as long as he could remember, Solomon had an ability to see future events in his dreams.

He remembered the first time he knew he was dreaming. He was speaking to his father who died a few weeks before, in the fire of the Great Synagogue of Warsaw.

"Papa, you and Mama died in the fire," Solomon said.

"I've come to tell you that I will always be here for you, in your dreams," his father said.

"Am I dreaming now?"

"You must learn how to be awake in your dreams, son."

These words from his father fueled his awareness of being awake in his dreams. He soon learned that once he knew he was awake, he could actually do what he wanted.

At first he used the knowledge for amusement. Flying was a favorite activity. He would stretch his arms out like a bird and soar high above the earth. He also discovered the joy of having sex in his dreams, which resulted in changing his bed linens often.

Then the guides started to appear. He had no ideas where they came from, but they had an agenda. The first visitor came the night before he was to board a steamship and sail to America, from the Port of Hamburg.

While he was standing in a long line waiting to board, with his small valise in his hand, he felt someone tap him on his shoulder. He turned around, and saw a small man wearing round spectacles, and a long black coat.

"Don't get on," the stranger said.

Solomon said, "I'm going to America."

"The ship won't make it. It will collide with another ship and sink. All these people will drown."

Solomon looked up and down the long line of men, women and children. "Shouldn't we warn them?"

But the visitor was gone, and Solomon realized he was dreaming.

The next morning when he awoke he walked down to the dock and saw hundreds of people lining up to board the ship. He decided not to board that day and bought a ticket for the next voyage to America. When he arrived in New York a month later, he read in the newspaper about the tragic sinking of the SS Berlin. All two hundred and eighty passengers and crew perished at sea.

Over the years, his dreams continued to provide useful information on outcomes of events that he could exploit. The easiest ones were knowing the results of sports scores. He would go to bookies and make bets even when the odds seemed crazy. But he would win, every time. Soon the bookies stop taking his bets, so Solomon started his own sports betting business.

He knew about land deal opportunities and political outcomes that made him a rich man. Of all of the moves he made, the most dramatic was dreaming about the sudden, and accidental death of his wife Ruth.

Solomon met Ruth at a social gathering at a friend's home a few years after he arrived in America. Ruth emigrated from Russia a year earlier and was still struggling with finding her place in the New World. Solomon was not only attracted to her stunning beauty, but also to her vulnerability. He wanted a woman to depend upon him, and Ruth became that woman.

They married a few months later, and the following year, Myron was born.

The dream occurred six months before Myron's eighth birthday.

He was sitting across from a beautiful woman who was holding on tightly to his right wrist, while running her finger gently across his open palm.

"I can see a terrible car accident involving your wife. She won't survive."

Solomon tried to pull his hand away, but she wouldn't release her grip.

"Your ability of foresight is a gift, Solomon. You should honor the giver," said the palm reader.

"Who is the giver?" Solomon asked.

"The giver is the rasha," she said.

The next day, Solomon purchased a $1,000,000 life insurance policy on Ruth, naming him as the sole beneficiary. Six months later, a car skidded on the ice and slammed into Ruth as she was walking on the sidewalk, killing her instantly.

For many years Solomon stumbled upon his prophetic dreams like a child finding a nugget on a treasure hunt. He was pleased to discover an occasional gem but was unable to consistently capitalize upon it. But that all changed when he met Rabbi Henryk Appel and was enlightened how to exponentially wield his dreams into greater power and treasure through the understanding and manipulation of Kabbalah's dark side.

It was ten years earlier in the neighborhood diner and he had taken a seat on one of the red vinyl upholstered barstools. Sitting next to him was a man dressed like a rabbi, who was fishing out bits of potatoes from his soup. Solomon asked, "Tell me, Rabbi, why do you eat alone?"

The rabbi put down his spoon in his bowl of soup, shrugged and said, "I always eat alone."

"You have no family?"

The rabbi exhaled and said, "No, just me."

Solomon stood up, walked over to an empty booth, and said, "Come, Rabbi, sit with me."

The rabbi stood, took his bowl of soup, and joined him.

"My name is Solomon Blass," he said, reaching across the table between them.

"Henryk Appel," the rabbi said, and shook Solomon's hand.

The two men sat for hours. The rabbi told Solomon his story.

He had been a Rabbinical student from the ancient city of Safed, the birthplace of Kabbalah. "But I wasn't in good standing with the faculty because of my fascination with Kabbalah's dark side," the rabbi confessed quietly, and looked around the diner making sure he wasn't overheard.

Solomon stopped sipping at his coffee as his interest was piqued.

"I barely finished my first year when I was asked to leave the seminary."

With nothing keeping him in Israel, he decided to seek his calling in America. He arrived with only a valise in hand. A friend from Israel told him of someone at a well-known seminary in Manhattan.

"Go see Rabbi Joel Rabinowitz, he's on the faculty. Maybe he can find you a position," his friend advised.

Upon his arrival in New York, he went to see this man at the Rabbinical Seminary, where he did land a part-time teaching job. But that soon changed to full-time, when his course, *Embracing the rasha,* became one of the seminary's most popular.

The faculty was not pleased with the content of his course, but since he was bringing in desperately needed funds to the struggling school they allowed the course to be offered.

Rabbi Appel pontificated that it was the *rasha* that created the natural balance to the *tzaddik,* and that one could not exist without the other.

"It has been said that the *rasha* is the evil counterpart to the *tzaddik.* So if the *tzaddik* is the extended hand of Hashem, then what is the *rasha?*" he would ask his students on the first day of class.

After a few feeble attempts by the students to answer, he said, "The *rasha* is the hand that slaps the *tzaddik's* away. Is it not the meek that seek out the soft comforts of the *tzaddik?* If you want to be strong, independent leaders, and ultimately better rabbis, you must understand and embrace the *rasha.*"

To the seminary's disdain, many young men connected to this toxic message.

"It is the *rasha* that is the honest one, because he acts out of his true nature, while the *tzaddik* creates this façade of a false ideal of accepting what the Opposition offers us as a *blessing* and a way to live one's life. Does it make sense to live a life as the Obedient follower, accepting life's challenges as the way things are supposed to be, or do we fight back? Perhaps another way to interpret this wisdom is to say that yes, we can accept life's tests as a blessing from the Creator, but it is how we react to these tests that will determine how we grow and ultimately enhance our soul."

Eventually, as the seminary grew and became financially stable, the faculty gathered its collective nerve and dismissed Henryk Appel. This was the second time he was fired by those who disagreed with his message of romanticizing Kabbalah's dark side.

That meeting was the beginning of a long and complex relationship between Solomon and the rabbi. That first day in the diner, when Solomon told the rabbi he was an eager student of Kabbalah and that he was looking for a teacher, he offered Henryk an opportunity to be his private rabbi.

"You should know that I'm not really a rabbi. I was thrown out before I was ordained."

"Sounds like you escaped before your passion was extinguished. You will teach me all there is to know about the ways of *rasha*. My office is upstairs in this building," he said, pointing to the ceiling of the diner before continuing, "I'll set you up in your own office, and don't worry about the money, I'll pay you more than any synagogue or seminary in the city would."

Chapter 4

"Come on, Leah, we're going to be late," Moshe pleaded to his wife.

"Don't rush me," she snapped.

Moshe locked the front door and helped Leah down the steps. He had already pulled the car out of the narrow driveway and parked it on the street. Moshe opened the front door and helped settle his wife into her seat.

"Be careful with my hair. I just went to the beauty parlor," she barked at her husband.

"Okay, Leah," Moshe said taking a closer look at her perfectly coiffed crown of newly colored blonde hair. "It looks beautiful."

Even as Leah approached her sixtieth birthday, she looked several years younger. Her eyes were as blue as the first time they met, her skin just as smooth and she still sported a shapely figure.

"Yes, I think the hairdresser did a good job this time. Not like last time. Last time I wanted to kill her, don't you remember?" Leah said, carefully patting her stiff hair-sprayed bun.

"I do remember, Leah," Moshe said as he closed her door and rolled his eyes.

With her vision continuing to deteriorate, Leah had become more dependent upon him. Leaving the house frightened her, and the prospect of taking a tumble down a flight of stairs was debilitating. Even with Moshe's ability to calm those in pain, he apparently had no effect upon his wife who seemed to have grown numb to his touch over their forty years of marriage.

Moshe was visited by Gray the day before at the cobbler shop with a dinner party invitation for him and Leah at Mr. Lieberman's home in Riverdale. The last time he was in this exclusive community in the northern Bronx was when he attended the closing of the sale of his parents' former home.

As they pulled into the driveway of 46 Fieldstone Road, Leah shrieked, "Oh my, Moshe, is this the house?"

Moshe glanced over to his wife and smiled at her sudden ability of good eyesight.

"This is it," he said, looking at the enormous stone mansion covered with crawling ivy and featuring black-iron framed windows that looked like they came from a European castle.

Standing and welcoming them at the open front door was Arnold Lieberman.

"Greetings, Moshe and this lovely young woman must be your daughter, Leah."

Leah let out a yelp. "I love this man!"

As they entered the well-appointed home, Arnold introduced his wife Sadie.

"It's a pleasure to meet you, Sadie," Moshe said.

"This is the most beautiful home I have ever seen," added Leah.

"Thank you, Leah," Sadie said.

Arnold stepped aside and Moshe was able to see, standing alongside the staircase leading to the upper floors, a man with a long beard, dressed in a white shirt, black pants, and a yarmulke resting on his thinning crop of silver hair.

"I know you haven't seen each other since you were children, so allow me to present Rabbi Shapira."

Moshe couldn't believe his eyes. It was as if the Rabbi of Krzywcza was standing before him. This was the son, but the resemblance to his father was remarkable.

"What a surprise," Moshe said, shaking the rabbi's hand.

"It's been a while, Moshe," said the rabbi, running a hand through his long salt, and pepper beard.

This mannerism triggered a flood of memories that reminded Moshe of the rabbi's father and made him smile.

After dinner, Leah and Sadie shared stories about their grandchildren, while Arnold escorted Moshe and the rabbi out onto the back porch.

"I'm happy that you came, Moshe," Arnold began, as the three men took a seat on the white wicker furniture overlooking the landscaped backyard.

"Thank you for the invitation and surprising me with your special guest," Moshe said looking at the rabbi.

"I don't know if you know this, Moshe, but I was at your Bar Mitzvah," the rabbi said, nodding.

"Were you? I'm sorry, but I don't remember."

"And no wonder, the shul was packed with every Jew in the shtetl that day, all to witness your Bar Mitzvah. That was a special day for everyone."

The rabbi turned to look at Arnold and continued, "It was just after the mass murder of the wounded soldiers at the synagogue. People were despondent and needed hope. It was Moshe's presence and his ability to comfort those close to death that inspired my father to make his greatest sermon of his seventy years as a rabbi."

"That I do remember," Moshe said.

The rabbi leaned forward, putting his elbows on his knees, and whispered, "Have you had any more of your um... episodes?"

Moshe stood up and walked over to the white wood railing wrapping around the porch. He looked out onto the impeccably groomed landscape for a moment. Then he turned to look at the rabbi and Arnold waiting for a reply and said, "The last episode I had was the day my father passed."

"That was over fifteen years ago, Moshe," the rabbi said.

Moshe nodded.

"You have had no premonitions since that day your father died?"

Moshe just shook his head.

"What about your touch? Your ability to comfort others in times of grief."

"There's a glimmer of that from time to time, but that too has mostly withered," Moshe said, shrugging.

Arnold glanced over to the rabbi, who was nervously running his fingers through his long beard and asked, "Rabbi, what do we do?"

"Are you asking how to revive a *tzaddik*?"

Arnold nodded vigorously.

"This is beyond my knowledge," the rabbi said.

"Excuse me, gentlemen, for saying this, but I like my life the way it is, being just a cobbler," Moshe said.

"But you're not just a cobbler, Moshe, you're also *tzaddik,* and unless you can regain your connection with Hashem, many people will suffer," the rabbi warned.

"This sounds crazy."

"You remember what I told you about Solomon Blass?" Arnold said.

"That he is *rasha*," Moshe said.

Both the rabbi and Arnold nodded.

"Do you know that I've had experiences with *rasha* before?" Moshe said.

Arnold turned to look at the rabbi, then both gawked at Moshe.

"It was when I was fifteen years old. Her name was Dora Meltzer, a palmist."

"A palm reader?" Arnold said, sounding amused.

"Father first met her on the steamship when he immigrated to America. She was offering readings to the passengers. She told him that his son, meaning me, had special abilities. Years later, when the rest of our family arrived in America she found me and kidnapped me." Moshe paused, smiled a bit, leaned in and looked around to make sure no one else could overhear and then whispered, "She was my first, you know…" he said with a sly smile and an upward shifting of his eyebrows.

Arnold's jaw hung loosely, enjoying the sudden scandalous story.

"Father said she was *rasha*. She drugged me and brought into this synagogue on the Lower East Side. There were these signs of the zodiac painted on the ceiling that I could see from where I was laid down upon the bimah." Moshe used his hands to demonstrate his prone position.

"She was going to perform a ceremony with a rabbi who she believed was versed in the dark arts of Kabbalah. She wanted to drain the *tzaddik* out of me and transfer it into her somehow. But at the last minute, I was rescued by my parents. I don't know what happened to Dora. I believe she went to prison for a few years."

"That's an incredible story, Moshe," Arnold said.

Moshe shook his head and said, "If you ask me, I think it's all farfetched nonsense. A long time ago I may have had something, but now it's gone. All of it is just memories that have faded away, until you appeared. This idea that some *rasha* is enriching himself by having the ability to see into the future is ridiculous."

"It's not so ridiculous, Moshe, and I can prove it. How would Myron know the outcome of a vote before the City Council even voted on it?"

"What do you mean?" Moshe asked.

"Just last month Myron and Solomon bought an old abandoned apartment building in the South Bronx for a song. A few days later the council voted on claiming the building under eminent domain for the new expressway. They ended up doubling his money in just a few weeks," Arnold explained.

"And please explain why this is such a danger?" Moshe asked.

Arnold rubbed his chin. "The issue is not an unfair advantage of profiting off their knowledge of future events. It's how they can gain leverage over the entire political system in the city. It is one thing knowing of events before they occur, but what happens when you combine that with a skillful ability of wielding power? Imagine how the voters will react to a politician who can accurately predict future events? Then try to consider if Solomon and Myron were able to trade their knowledge with a Mayor or a Governor in exchange for financial opportunities and power?"

Moshe looked at Arnold and then at the rabbi and said, "I'm sorry, but I still don't understand what this has to do with me."

"We need to match the power of the *rasha*, and the rabbi says that is only possible with a *tzaddik*," Arnold said.

"Well, like I said, my abilities are gone and there is nothing I can do about it, even if I wanted to."

Rabbi Shapira rose from the rattan chair and stood next to Moshe. He placed his left hand on Moshe's shoulder and while stroking his long beard he said, "There are only thirty-six tzaddikim in the world at any given time. Finding you, Moshe, was a stroke of luck. As *tzaddik* you are called upon to fight the *rasha* when needed. This is the will of Hashem."

"What does anyone know of the will of Hashem?" Moshe said, lifting his arms into the air.

The rabbi kept a hand on Moshe's shoulder and looked at him and said, "There have been times in history where *tzaddik* have been called upon for such a task."

Moshe flipped his palms upwards, as a gesture to challenge the rabbi and said, "Okay, tell me."

The rabbi continued stroking his beard while he thought for a moment. Then he began, "It can be said that Moses was *tzaddik* and the Egyptian pharaoh Ramses was *rasha*."

Moshe laughed. "Now come on, Rabbi, I am no Moses."

"Of course not," the rabbi said and held up his hands, acknowledging the poor example. He pointed a finger into the air and said, "I did hear a story about a woman who lived in the Warsaw Ghetto during the war. She was able to ease the pain of her fellow Jews just before they passed. Just like you, Moshe."

"Can a woman be *tzaddik*?" Moshe asked.

"Of course, why not?" the rabbi said with a smile and a tilt of his head.

Moshe shrugged and rubbed the back of his neck, nervous that his options of refusing were dwindling the more the rabbi spoke. But he knew that he did indeed have a gift, though it had been a while since there was a need to call upon it.

The Righteous One 27

"I don't know if I can do this," Moshe said, and paused. "But just say I agree. How would I go about restoring my abilities?"

The rabbi looked at Arnold, then back to Moshe, smiled and said, "You and I would need to travel to the ancient city of Safed in northern Israel, the birthplace of Kabbalah."

Chapter 5

Rabbi Henryk Appel told Myron that turning ninety years old held an important significance according to Kabballah. "All Jewish men achieving this milestone become the hand of Hashem. But for the ones with the *gift* such as your father, his powers become enhanced."

Maybe this explains the increased accuracy of Solomon's prophetic dreams, Myron considered. As long as Myron could remember, his father had had an uncanny ability to foresee events. When Myron asked how he knew of things before they happened, his father said, "I see it in my dreams."

When Myron turned eighteen, his father sat him down and shared his biography. Solomon was born in 1870 in Warsaw, Poland. At the time when he was turning eleven, the Jews were being falsely accused of the assassination of the Russian Tsar, Alexander II. This triggered a large-scale wave of riots against the Jews, which became known as the *Pogroms*. In Warsaw, a riot ensued and twelve Jews were killed, many more were injured and several women were raped. Among the dead were both of Solomon's parents. Solomon told Myron that he had dreamed of his parents' murder two days before it occurred.

This left Solomon, at the age of eight, an orphan. Fortunately, his father's brother, Uncle Hersch, was able to take him in. Uncle Hersch was a carpenter who worked on the Great Synagogue of Warsaw. Once the construction was completed in 1878, the administrators asked him to stay on and help manage the new facility. As part of his compensation he was given a place to live in a small cottage located on the grounds of the largest synagogue in the world.

For ten years, from the age of eight until eighteen, Solomon lived in the cottage with his uncle and attended the synagogue's school for the youths in the surrounding Jewish community. These young boys were privileged to learn from some of the greatest teachers in the city.

But what interested Solomon the most were not the formal classroom courses. Instead, he loved the afternoon *public conversations*, as they were called. These were where the best minds of the synagogue spoke of the mysterious and mystical side of Judaism, known as Kabbalah. Solomon was fascinated with the hidden messages behind the words of the Torah.

He latched on to and became friends with Jan Baran, a rabbinical student and the son of a prominent rabbi who shared Solomon's enthusiasm for the mystical messages of the sacred texts.

Through Jan's influential father, the boys were invited to attend private lectures at important rabbis' homes where the topics discussed were too controversial for the public conversations. This was where he first learned about the thirty-six *tzaddikim* and their balancing dark force, the *rasha*. When the rabbis spoke of it, they did so only in whispers, so as not to attract evil, and thus Solomon and Jan grew up knowing and fearing its dangers.

Solomon wondered if his prophetic dreams meant that he had a spiritual connection to the Creator.

Jan asked, "Have you had more prophetic dreams since your parents' murder?"

"I've had more, but they were not very exciting. But that changed when I was thirteen, when I had a dream that I was at the circus. The tent was huge, hundreds of people filled the stands. Show horses and dogs were in the center-ring performing amusing tricks. People were pointing and laughing and I too was enjoying the show. Suddenly I found myself inside a nearby horse stable watching a stableman smoking a cigarette. He took one long drag and flicked the glowing butt on to the straw-covered wooden floor which instantly caught fire and quickly spread. I then found myself watching from afar as the tent exploded into flames. I could hear the people inside screaming and the animals screeching in pain as they burned alive." Solomon paused to take a breath.

"Did this actually happen?" Jan asked.

Solomon nodded. "Indeed it did, a few days later. Two hundred and sixty-eight people were burned to death, eighty people were injured and over one hundred were missing or couldn't be identified. They were probably burned to ashes."

"That's incredible. Have you had more dreams since?" Jan said.

Solomon nodded. "Just last week I dreamt about the death of the Grand Rabbi Sirkis. Not only did I dream of his death, Jan, I saw him standing at the bimah during early morning service, and falling to the ground, clutching his chest with the congregation surrounding him. Exactly as it occurred."

Jan slapped his hands together and said, "Solomon, you do have a gift. Perhaps you are *tzaddik*?"

"That's crazy," Solomon said, but thought that he would want to learn more about it. He talked Jan into visiting with a rabbi known to have the ability to recognize *tzaddik*. "Maybe he can tell me if I'm one," Solomon said.

The streets of Warsaw were covered with a fresh snowfall as Solomon and Jan took off on foot one early winter morning to meet Rabbi Saks. The word was that Rabbi Saks could instantly identify *tzaddik* after a short conversation.

The boys entered the apartment building and walked up the winding staircase to the fifth floor. They found apartment *E* and knocked on the blue painted door. The door creaked open, and standing before them was an elderly man dressed in a white shirt and black pants.

"What do you boys want?" the rabbi barked.

"Excuse me, are you Rabbi Saks?" asked Jan.

"I am, and who are you two?"

"I want to know if I'm *tzaddik*," Solomon blurted out.

He stared at Solomon and said, "Do you know how many boys like you knock on my door with the same question? Why should I…" the rabbi paused, rubbed his red-rimmed eyes, took a closer look at Solomon, then raised one eyebrow slightly. Finally, he nodded and said, "All right boys, come in."

Solomon looked at Jan hopefully as they entered.

The apartment had a stale, crusty odor that hung like a storm cloud, and was packed with hundreds of volumes of books piled in stacks of various heights.

"Sit down," the rabbi said pointing to two wooden stools.

Solomon and Jan sat next to a small table on which sat a dinner plate with an uneaten piece of a cold potato that a few cockroaches were now feasting upon. He picked up the plate, scattering the pests, and tossed it into the sink with other unwashed dishes.

"Why do you think you're *tzaddik*?" the rabbi asked.

Solomon sat upright and told the rabbi about several instances where he saw the future in his dreams, including his most recent one about the death of the Grand Rabbi Sirkis.

"That is most interesting," the rabbi said.

"Do you think he is *tzaddik*?" asked Jan.

The rabbi stroked his beard and studied Solomon for a moment, then he said, "I've never heard of *tzaddik* of having such a skill, but I have read cases of *rasha* exhibiting this ability. Perhaps you are *rasha*?"

Solomon felt like he had been hit in the face. He whispered, "Are you saying that I'm *rasha*?"

The rabbi gently patted Solomon's hands and said, "Of course not. But you should pay attention and make sure you stay on the righteous path and not get distracted by the dark side."

Solomon looked at Jan, then back at the rabbi and said, "Thank you, Rabbi."

"Go now, but stay in touch and let me know if you have any more of these dreams," the rabbi said, and escorted the boys back out through the blue front door of his apartment.

Chapter 6

Later that night, after offering his farewells to his dinner guests, Arnold sat down at his desk. He was encouraged by Rabbi Shapira's idea of traveling to Safed with Moshe, but the rabbi's last comment worried him.

"There is no other way to restore Moshe's connection to Hashem, unless we go to Safed. But you should know, Arnold, that only *tzaddik* can help Moshe."

Arnold threw his hands in the air and said, "It took me ten years to find Moshe and that was by chance because I met you. How would you be able to find another *tzaddik*?"

The rabbi smiled, stroked his beard and said, "I know many rabbis in Safed and with their help, and Hashem's, we will."

This did little to relieve Arnold's anxiety. Myron and his father Solomon needed to be stopped. Just this past year they had the uncanny knowledge of being in the right place at the right time, again. How had they known to buy land in Locust Point six months before the City of New York announced its plan to build the Throgs Neck Bridge? All five properties they bought flipped for huge gains since they needed to be demolished as a public right-of-way for the new bridge.

But the most disturbing rumor Arnold heard was that Myron shorted the stock of Trans World Airlines before its flight 266 collided in mid-air with United Airlines flight 826. The TWA plane was inbound to LaGuardia Airport and crashed in a field in Staten Island, while the United aircraft crashed in Brooklyn, narrowly missing a school. All 134 people aboard both planes died, along with six people on the ground, while Myron collected another huge payday.

The first time Arnold met Myron was at an Irish pub on Webster Avenue one early fall evening. This place was known for taking bets on games and where Myron Blass held court in a booth at the back of the establishment.

An occasional drinker, Arnold never ventured much into bars and certainly never into an Irish pub. But earlier that day a friend told him of this guy who was taking bets on the 1958 World Series between the New York Yankees and the Milwaukee Braves. As a big Yankee fan, Arnold wanted to place a bet. He was instructed to go to the pub, take a seat at the bar and ask the bartender if he could speak with Myron.

As he was waiting for the okay to approach the booth in the back, a man sitting next to Arnold struck up a conversation while he was watching a football game on the television set perched on a high shelf over the bar.

"I gather you're here to see Myron?" said a crusty looking older man with a week's worth of unshaven stubble, growing over pinkish discolored skin.

Arnold turned to him and nodded.

"Placing a bet on the Yanks?" he asked.

"I am. How did you know?"

"Game seven is tonight. Not too hard to figure," he chuckled.

"I suppose you're right." Arnold smiled.

The man leaned in. Arnold could smell cigars and scotch on his breath. "The only way to play this game is to take the bets, not make them," he said, sliding his glass down to the bartender for a refill.

"What do you mean?"

"Do what he does," the man said, tilting his head to the back of the bar where Myron was sitting. "That's the way to make real money."

"How do you do that?" Arnold asked.

"When you get your moment with Myron, tell him you want to start making a book and run it through him. If he agrees, he'll set you up in exchange for a piece of the action," the man said.

"That was how it started. I only wanted to do the sports book thing as a hobby. But only when I got elected did I learn the full extent of what Myron and his father were really up to," Arnold told Rabbi Shapira as they drank coffee one afternoon at the Fordham Diner.

"Are you sure about these predictions?" the rabbi asked.

"I'm sure. People talk about them," he said and then whispered, "That's how he knew about the bridge construction project, and the planes colliding."

The rabbi placed his hand on his cheek and said, "Arnold, how do you think he is able to make these predictions?"

Arnold shook his head. "I don't have a clue. Maybe it has something to do with this connection to the dark side of Kabbalah?"

"Perhaps my suspicions were right, and he is *rasha*."

Arnold looked at the rabbi, rubbing the back of his neck. "What does this mean?"

"Perhaps this ability of foreseeing the future is an indication that he is *rasha.* I have heard of such stories," the rabbi said pointing a finger into the air.

"We need to find out how he does this," Arnold said.

The rabbi nodded and said, "The *tzaddik* is our only chance to stop the *rasha*."

Chapter 7

Like many Jews, Moshe had always wanted to visit Israel. But he had never ventured beyond New Jersey since he arrived in America with his parents and siblings after their harrowing escape from their home in Krzywcza during World War 1. Now he was about to tell his wife Leah about this absurd idea of traveling to a small city in northern Israel in order to locate an unknown rabbi with the hope of restoring a questionable spiritual connection with Hashem. Most likely she would complain, but Moshe knew after all these years that she would eventually give in and wish him well.

When he first met Leah he was twenty-two years old and running his dad's cobbler shop. His father Pincus came in occasionally, but Moshe handled the day to day operations. People loved Moshe and his cobbler shop was drawing customers from all areas of the Bronx.

On a warm summer day, near closing time, a woman barged into his shop. She flung the shoes on the counter and said, "You must be Moshe the Cobbler."

Moshe looked up and saw a young, pretty blue-eyed woman with auburn hair, standing with her hands on her hips, staring at him.

"I am," he said standing up.

"You know, Moshe, I took two trains to get here. Don't ask me why my mother can't use the cobbler right down the street from our apartment. No, she says. I must go see Moshe the Cobbler. So, Moshe, what makes you so special?"

Moshe shook his head nervously and said, "Nothing makes me special."

Leah looked around the piles of shoes filling up the shelves. "You work alone?"

Moshe nodded. "It's just me."

"Fine, here," she said, handing a pair of women's shoes to him. "She would like these re-soled."

Moshe reached out to take the shoes from Leah. His fingers briefly slid along hers in the exchange. This caused a sudden shift in Leah's belligerent attitude. A calmness washed over her face and she smiled.

When he wrote the ticket for the shoes he asked Leah for her phone number. After he wrote it down he looked up at her and asked, "Is it all right if I give you a call?"

"I would hope so. How else would I know when my shoes are ready?"

Moshe took a breath to gather his nerves and said, "No I mean, call you for a date."

Leah tilted her head and smiled. "Sure, Moshe the Cobbler, that would be nice."

Within six months of that first encounter, Moshe had proposed and the following year they married. They had two daughters, Barbara and Elaine. At the age of seven, Barbara contracted Polio. Though he tried many times, Moshe couldn't ease his daughter's suffering. He would stay by her bedside for hours. But her symptoms of fatigue, fever and muscle quivers were not relieved by his touch.

Moshe wondered why he was able to ease the suffering of dying soldiers moments before they passed, but not with his own family. He once was able to communicate something divine, but that was now gone.

The plan for when Moshe was away in Israel was that Leah would stay with Elaine and her husband Walter. He had no choice but to close the cobbler shop, and pray that his customers would understand and come back when he returned.

Leah, as predicted, had second thoughts about the trip.

"Moshe, you're going to have to explain this again. Why are you going to Israel?"

"Leah, I already explained this to you three times."

She took a deep breath, placed her hands on her hips, exhaled and said, "Tell me again."

Moshe knew that he had couldn't avoid telling Leah the real reason for going to Safed. "Apparently, Rabbi Shapira thinks that I'm *tzaddik*. You've heard that before. Maybe when I was young I had something special, but it has faded."

Leah smiled and nodded.

"They want to take me to Safed and see if my ability can be restored."

"And why would they want to do that, Moshe? What do they want from you?"

Moshe sighed. "They want me to stop a *rasha*."

Leah shook her head. "What in the world is a *rasha*?"

"It's the evil counterpart of a *tzaddik*. This gangster has this ability of seeing into the future, and the rabbi thinks he may be one."

"Moshe, what business is it of yours to try to help this councilman and rabbi with a fight against some gangster? You're a cobbler, not a policeman," she insisted.

"The police are helpless against them. If it is true what they say about Myron and Solomon Blass, I may need to stop them."

Leah placed her hand on her cheek and said, "Have you lost your mind?"

Moshe looked at Leah and grasped her hand and said, "Leah, I am not just a cobbler. I am also *tzaddik*."

"No, Moshe Potasznik, you're also *meshuga*."

Chapter 8

Myron and the rabbi walked into the lobby of the office building at the same time.

"Good morning, Rabbi," Myron said, as they stepped into the elevator and the doors closed behind him.

"Good morning, Myron," the rabbi said.

"Thanks for coming in. I know this is early for you," Myron said referring to the six AM meeting he called for.

The rabbi nodded, his bloodshot eyes acknowledging his struggle. When the doors opened to the top floor of the building both men stepped out. Straight ahead stood double doors marked with a brass plaque that read - BLASS ENTERPRISES. They stepped inside the well-appointed reception area.

"Good morning, sir," said the pretty secretary at her desk.

"Good morning, Shirley," Myron said, handing his hat to her.

Both men entered the office.

"Please close the door and sit, Rabbi. We need to talk," Myron said, gesturing to the chairs in front of his desk.

The rabbi leaned his briefcase along the front wood panel of Myron's desk, sat down and waited for Myron.

Myron stared silently at the rabbi, causing him to stir uncomfortably in his chair. Then he finally spoke. "I visited with my father this morning."

"How is Solomon doing?" he asked.

"He is as strong as ever. I swear that man will outlive me."

"That's good to hear," said the rabbi.

"But something has changed. Since turning ninety he tells me he is dreaming less frequently, but when he does the dreams are more profound, more meaningful."

The rabbi nodded. "Ninety is the age when we are all become an extension of the Almighty. Those with your father's abilities, even more so."

"He had a dream," Myron said, and paused and looked into the rabbi's eyes.

"What did he dream?"

"All he said to me was, *the tzaddik has returned.*"

The rabbi's jaw slacked open for a moment before he said, "The *tzaddik* has returned? What does that mean?"

"Why are you asking me? You're the rabbi," Myron said as he glanced down at his messages on his desk.

"This is very curious," the rabbi said.

"Give me a few minutes to go through my messages, and I'll take you out to see Pops."

"Sure thing, Myron."

Chapter 9

This was Moshe's maiden voyage in an airplane and his bouncing knees were visible proof of his nervousness as they waited to board the El Al flight inbound for Ben Gurion Airport in Tel Aviv.

"Relax, Moshe. I've made this trip many times," Rabbi Shapira said.

Moshe exhaled and said, "I'll be fine."

During the long overseas flight to Tel Aviv, Moshe and the rabbi spoke for hours.

"How much do you remember about my father?" the rabbi asked.

"I have many fond memories. Your father meant a lot to me, and my family," Moshe said with a gentle smile.

"He said he had never met anyone like you in his life and that's saying a lot, Moshe, since he lived until ninety-nine years old."

"I was just a boy when I saw him last."

"Not just a boy, Moshe, you are also *tzaddik*." The rabbi smiled, and then continued, "How did you feel when you found out that you are one of thirty-six *tzaddikim* on the earth with this special connection to Hashem?"

"It felt back then, and actually still feels today as if you are speaking of someone else, not me."

The rabbi said softly, "But how do you explain what you did to ease the suffering of those dying soldiers in the synagogue?"

"I cannot explain it. What did your father tell you?"

"He spoke of it briefly, just before he passed. He described that terrible day and how you comforted the wounded men, many of whom were gasping for their last few breaths."

"I was not the only one caring for them."

"I know that, but father told me how your touch, moments before death, connected these poor men to Hashem and allowed them to pass in peace."

Moshe just nodded, not knowing how to respond.

"He also told me the story of Captain Berbecki and his Russian soldiers," the rabbi said.

"That day is emblazoned in my mind," Moshe said pointing to his forehead. "The captain was angry that the rabbis of Galicia declared a holy war against the Russians, encouraging the young Jewish men to fight in the war. We became easy targets for retribution. They barged into the synagogue and ordered at gunpoint the wounded Jewish soldiers, who were sprawled out upon the pews and on the floor, to line up outside in the snow against the synagogue wall, where they were executed. Shot dead in cold blood," Moshe said with a long exhale.

"I'm sorry, Moshe, to bring up such a troubled memory." With a warm smile, the rabbi added, "But there were also good stories. Like your Bar Mitzvah."

Waiting for them when they landed at Ben Gurion Airport was a man who Rabbi Shapira greeted warmly. Moshe first noticed how Aaron resembled his cousin. The men looked to be about seventy years old and both sported long salt and pepper beards.

But where the rabbi's eyes were a dark brown, Aaron's sparkled an emerald green, which seemed to complement his upbeat personality.

"Moshe, this is my cousin Aaron. My mother and his mother were sisters."

They shook hands and Aaron said, "It is an honor to meet you, Moshe. My mother spoke of you often."

Aaron led them to his car in the airport's parking lot.

"Here we are," Aaron said, pointing to his Israeli made, 1960 Sussita.

With the luggage in the truck, Moshe climbed into the back seat.

Aaron twisted to look at Moshe and said, "It's an honor to have you in our country, Moshe. Just relax, I'm a very good driver. I'll have you in Safed in about three hours."

As Aaron navigated the traffic in Tel Aviv and eventually beyond the city limits, they headed northbound along the coast. Moshe gazed out of the window onto the turquoise Mediterranean Sea dotted with palm trees and smiled, thinking of the blackish waters of Orchard Beach in the Bronx, where he and Leah swam in the summer.

"Moshe, wake up. We're almost there," the rabbi said.

Moshe stirred from his sleep in the back of the Sussita as it chugged its way up a steep incline leading into Safed. Moshe turned to look out the back window and said, "Safed is up in the mountains, I didn't realize."

"It's the tallest point in all of Israel," said Aaron. "Did you know that there are four holy cities in Israel, each embodying an element of nature. Jerusalem is earth, Tiberias is water, Hebron is fire, and Safed is, of course, air."

"Makes sense," Moshe said as they continued to climb and snake through narrow roads barely wide enough for their car.

"I hope you won't mind being my guest, Moshe. My apartment is not very big, but it's on a quiet street and you'll have your own room," Aaron said.

"Oh, of course. I am grateful. Thank you."

"But we should stop for something to eat. You must be starving after such a long journey," Aaron said.

"That would be great," the rabbi said.

Aaron pointed a finger in the air and said, "I know the perfect place."

Chapter 10

Myron and Henryk found Solomon waiting for them on his boat dock.

"It's about time. Sit down," Solomon said pointing to two decrepit folding lawn chairs.

"What is it?" the rabbi asked.

With both men seated, Solomon leaned forward, looked back and forth at his son and the rabbi and said, "I've dreamt about the *tzaddik* again."

"Tell us about it, Pops."

"He wasn't young, like in my first dream," Solomon said shaking his head. "Maybe he was in his sixties."

He pressed his hands onto his knees to help himself to stand up and looked out onto the waves barely lapping upon the rocky shore and said, "My dream was about three men, two of whom were traveling to Israel. The third man, who remained behind, was someone I recognized," he said, wagging a finger at Myron. "It was that guy who used to run the sports book with you. You know who I mean. He owns the Paradise Theater and is now a councilman."

"You're talking about Arnold Lieberman?" Myron said.

"That's him. The other one was called Moshe."

"Who's Moshe?" Myron asked.

"Moshe was the *tzaddik*," Solomon said.

Henryk flipped a hand in the air and said, "And what were they doing?"

"Moshe and this third man boarded a flight to Israel," Solomon said.

"And why would they be going to Israel?" said Myron.

Henryk pointed his finger in the air and said, "The question to ask, Myron, is why would a *tzaddik* be going to Israel?"

"What do you think, Rabbi?" Solomon asked.

Henryk paused a moment, nodding slightly several times as if he was calculating the possibilities and then said, "Perhaps they are going to Safed."

Solomon pointed a finger at the rabbi and said, "I bet you're right."

"I don't understand," Myron said, shrugging.

"Safed is the birthplace of Kabbalah. The *tzaddik* could be planning to consult with the great minds of Kabbalist wisdom," Henryk said.

"To what end?" asked Myron.

Henryk looked at Solomon and said, "Perhaps to challenge the *rasha*?"

Solomon felt the air sucked out of him as Henryk's comment catapulted him back to his youth in Warsaw, to the day when Rabbi Sirkis had voiced his suspicion that Solomon was a *rasha*. Before he could stop himself, he clapped his hands together and yelled, "No! The *tzaddik* must be stopped."

"How do you propose we do that?" Myron asked.

Solomon pointed to his son. "You'll go to Safed."

"How will I find him?" Myron asked.

"Go and see Arnold Lieberman. I'm sure he knows something," Solomon said.

"Solomon, do you know who the third man was?" asked Henryk.

"I don't know. All I can tell you is that the councilman called him rabbi."

The matinee showing of *Ben Hur* starring Charlton Heston had just started when Myron and Henryk entered the theater lobby. A skinny teenage boy politely asked for their tickets, and then yelled at them to stop when they rushed by and proceeded up the staircase to Arnold Lieberman's office.

They marched past Agnes who begged them to stop and barged into Arnold's office. Arnold stood up from his desk and said, "Myron, what a nice surprise."

"Arnold, we need to speak with you."

"Of course, please sit down," Arnold said, gesturing to the chairs.

"What can you tell me about the *tzaddik*?" Myron asked, glancing over to the rabbi.

"That's a strange question. Why would you think I know anything about a *tzaddik*?"

"Arnold, you know who I am. Stop with the bullshit, and just tell me what you know," Myron said.

Arnold shifted nervously in his seat. "I really don't know what you're talking about."

Myron smiled and said, "My father seems to think otherwise. But if you don't want to talk, that's all right. As I'm sure you know, we have our own effective ways of digging up information."

In the car on the way back to his office, Myron knew Arnold was lying. His father's dream was all the proof he needed. But it was obvious Arnold wasn't going to give up anything easily.

"Myron, how do you know Mr. Lieberman," Henryk asked, breaking his chain of thought.

"He came to see me a few years ago wanting to start a bookie business. He used to bring in good money, that is until he became a councilman and quit. I never had a problem with him—until now."

"What are you planning to do?" Henryk asked.

"I'm going to have Arnold followed."

Chapter 11

Arnold peered out through his large office window overlooking the Grand Concourse and saw Myron and the rabbi getting into their car and driving away. There was little time. Myron Blass was not one you wanted to anger. He knew that if Myron wanted to extract information he had an assortment of unpleasant and painful ways in his gangster's toolbox to get what he wanted.

A disturbing thought occurred to Arnold. Myron had insinuated that his father, Solomon, was suspicious of the presence of a *tzaddik*. *What if Solomon foresaw my discovery of the tzaddik and Moshe's and the rabbi's imminent trip to Safed?*

He turned from the window and walked toward his office door. He decided that he must go to Safed and warn Moshe and the rabbi that they may be in danger.

"Agnes," he called out, as he stepped into the reception room.

"Yes?"

"Is it too late to get on the flight with the rabbi and the cobbler?"

Agnes looked at her watch. "There's no way. They're taking off in an hour."

"Book me on tomorrow's flight to Tel Aviv," he said, grabbing his hat.

"Excuse me?"

"Agnes, what's so hard to understand? Get me a seat on the next flight to Israel and please don't tell anyone. Understood?"

"Sure, okay, Arnold."

When Arnold got home to pack he told his wife, Sadie, that he was going to visit his brother in Miami.

"Is everything all right?" she asked, placing a worried hand on her cheek.

"Yes, of course. I just need to go see Sammy about a few things. It's nothing to worry about," he assured her.

Arnold knew it was best not to tell her the truth. Under the slightest duress, she would easily give up his travel plans to Safed. Agnes, on the other hand, would take a bullet before she would share any of his secrets.

The flight from New York to Tel Aviv gave Arnold time to think about what he had stirred up by exposing the *tzaddik* to those skilled enough to notice. Maybe it was a crazy idea thinking that someone like Moshe, such an unassuming and gentle man, could battle the evil Solomon and his contemptible son.

With the dinner meal served and the lights turned down for passengers trying to sleep on the redeye flight to Israel, Arnold reminisced how this all began. Ten years ago, he met Rabbi Shapira at an event at his synagogue in Riverdale. Rabbi Shapira had arranged for the famous Kabbalist, Rabbi Babi Sali, to visit the Riverdale Synagogue during his New York City tour.

Arnold remembered how excited he was to meet the heralded Moroccan rabbi. The synagogue held a banquet in his honor. Rabbi Baba Sali was a thin and frail man, with dark deep-set eyes. Even with his fragile-as-glass looks, he

The Righteous One 53

portrayed a man of immeasurable wisdom, as he scanned the room from his seat of honor upon the dais.

The synagogue's cavernous ballroom was set up with dozens of large round tables and, by chance, sitting next to Arnold was Rabbi Shapira. After the ceremony, which included a few words by the esteemed rabbi of honor, Arnold asked Rabbi Shapira if he would like to get a coffee with him at the Fordham Diner.

"Is it true that Rabbi Babi Sali is *tzaddik?*" Arnold asked as he reached for the sugar.

The rabbi leaned forward, with his elbows on the laminate table top, looked around at a few patrons at other tables and whispered, "Keep it down. It's best not to speak too openly about this."

Arnold nodded, feeling as if he was just let into a private club. He whispered, "I understand that there are only thirty-six *tzaddikim* on the earth at any one time."

"This is true," the rabbi said, barely audible.

"Do you know who these people are?" Arnold asked.

"I only knew of one," the rabbi said.

"Who is that?"

"There was a boy, who my father knew in Krzywcza. He escaped during the war with his family to the Lower East Side. He never told me his name, but he said his father was a cobbler. My father told me how he offered comfort to the wounded soldiers just moments before they passed. He said he witnessed the hand of Hashem."

Arnold patted his cheek and said, "You think this man is still alive and living in New York?"

"It's possible." The rabbi shrugged.

"We need to find him," Arnold said.

"No, we must not interfere." The rabbi wagged a finger.

"Why not?"

"The Zohar says that *tzaddik* must remain anonymous."

"What about Rabbi Baba Sali? He is certainly not anonymous."

"That's because he's not of the thirty-six."

"But he is known as *tzaddik*," Arnold said, squinting his eyes and expressing confusion.

"He is *tzaddik* because of his age. All good and studious observers of our faith become *tzaddik* when we reach ninety years of age."

That was when Arnold's obsession with finding the *tzaddik* began. It took a decade of researching newspaper archives in the library, taking courses on Kabbalah and speaking to countless intellectuals, writers and educators before he finally had a breakthrough.

Through many months of research, he discovered the documents of the Landsman Society of Krzywcza at the New York Public Library. In timeworn, handwritten documents he read about the society's founding member Pincus Potasznik, who had a cobbler shop on Grand Street in the Lower East Side.

With a renewed sense of optimism Arnold scoured the area, asking merchants if anyone remembered Pincus the Cobbler. After weeks of dead-ends he wandered into a carpentry business called Rubenfeld's. A man wearing an apron was seated at a lathe, carving out a decorative leg for a chair. He looked up as Arnold approached.

"Can I help you?" the carpenter asked.

"Are you Mr. Rubenfeld?" Arnold asked.

"Indeed I am. How may I be of service?"

"I am trying to find someone who remembers a cobbler who had a business on Grand Street around the year 1910."

"Well, that's before my time, but perhaps my father may know."

"Your father?" Arnold said, sounding upbeat.

"Yes, he's the original Rubenfeld. He's ninety-five years old and his memory is not great. But for some reason he remembers things from long ago."

"Would it be possible to speak to him?" Arnold asked.

Later that afternoon, Stanley Rubenfeld took Arnold to meet his father, Hersch. Not only did Hersch Rubenfeld remember Pincus the Cobbler, but they were also cousins.

"We were from the same shtetl," Hersch said. "When he arrived here, he came and found me and asked for help starting this Landsman Society. I had to explain that I was too busy to assist him and that made him very angry. We never spoke after that," the old man said.

"Do you know what happened to him?"

"Pincus became famous after he gunned down the gangster, Leo Gorpatsch. It was in all the newspapers."

"Pincus the Cobbler, killed a gangster?" Arnold asked.

Hersch nodded, and smiled.

"Do you know what happened to Pincus?"

"The family moved up to the Bronx years ago. His son Moshe took over the business."

That was when Arnold found that the *tzaddik* was right across the street from his office on the Grand Concourse in the form of Moshe the Cobbler.

Chapter 12

Moshe had never seen a place as beautiful as Safed. His childhood memories of the Galician village and surrounding countryside where he was born were few and fading. For the most part of his sixty years Moshe lived in the Bronx, which was nothing like this city carved into the rolling hills and cliffs.

From the back seat of the car Moshe observed tall buildings made of white limestone crowded around the spiderweb of roads and alleyways. Open shuttered windows displayed arrays of colorful flowers in window boxes and glimpses of long purple wisteria wrapped itself across wooden beams over inviting patios.

After parking the car, they walked through an alleyway to a small outdoor cafe that was squeezed in between two buildings. Moshe, Rabbi Shapira and Aaron were served hummus and pita bread.

"This is how we eat," Aaron said, showing Moshe how he used the pita bread as a utensil.

Moshe scooped the pita into the hummus, and tasted the creamy dish of mashed chickpeas, seasoned with paprika, lemon and olive oil.

"Delicious," Moshe agreed, and quickly grabbed another piece of bread.

After lunch, they walked down a narrow path and came out onto a plaza that led them to the entrance of a synagogue.

"This is the Ari Ashkenazi Synagogue," Aaron said, gesturing to the ancient building of white limestone blocks, with two sets of large windows, deeply recessed into the building's façade. Aaron led the men through the large wooden doors hanging off black wrought iron hinges.

As they entered, Moshe grabbed a yarmulke from a small unadorned wooden box placed on a table. Aaron was wearing a beautiful embroidered yarmulke and the rabbi had on his black fedora hat. Moshe cringed inwardly at the fact that he had to borrow a yarmulke from the shul, but his life in America was not one as an observant Jew.

Once inside, Moshe knew he was not in an ordinary synagogue. Aaron had told him at lunch that the synagogue was established by Sephardic immigrants from Greece in the sixteenth century. It was destroyed in an earthquake in 1837 and wasn't rebuilt until twenty years later. During the 1948 Arab-Israeli War a bomb exploded in the nearby courtyard. Shrapnel flew into the synagogue packed with people seeking shelter. Miraculously, no one was hurt.

Moshe gazed at the unusual series of limestone archways that formed the hallways leading into the sanctuary. He stepped inside and stopped in his tracks. Towering before him was the Torah Ark. As his head tilted back to take in its magnificence, his mouth fell open, absorbing its holiness.

"This was carved from olive wood in 1857," Aaron said, gesturing to the series of columns rising from the floor to twenty feet overhead. Each column featured colorful, carved depictions of flowers, fruits and vines intertwined among other symbols of stories from the bible.

"This is the most holy of places for the study of Kabbalah," said Rabbi Shapira.

"Are we here to speak with someone?" Moshe asked looking around at the people coming and going.

"No, I just thought this would be a good place to start your journey," Aaron said glancing over to the rabbi for support.

"The truth is, Moshe, we don't know where to go, or who to see about your condition," said the rabbi.

"Perhaps you're wrong about me. I don't feel anything unusual and I doubt I still have a connection to Hashem," Moshe said, adjusting the borrowed yarmulke to prevent it from slipping off his head.

"My father, and your rabbi, was sure of it, Moshe. He recognized the signs and I have no reason to doubt him. We are here in the spiritual city of Safed to find a way to rekindle the flame inside you," the rabbi said as he placed both hands on his hips and leaned back to admire the Torah Ark.

Chapter 13

Myron bit into an olive as he stared out the window from his first class seat, hoping the martini he was sipping would help him sleep at least a few hours on the redeye to Israel. He needed to slow down his thoughts. He kept rehashing what his father had said to him earlier when he stopped by on his way to the airport to say goodbye.

"I need to speak with you."

Even though he was short on time, his father insisted that he visit him before leaving for the airport.

"It's important," he told his son on the phone.

When Myron arrived, Solomon shared a story of how he had met Leo Gorpatsch in Warsaw as teenagers working for a local Jewish mobster named Berek Weis, whose business was offering high-interest loans to those who had nowhere else to go. Berek employed teenage boys like Solomon and Leo to pick up his payments from clients who borrowed money from him.

Shortly after Solomon and Leo both turned eighteen, they were summoned to Berek's office.

"Berek had an office in the back of a butcher shop," Solomon said.

"I know, Pops, with the sawdust on the floor," Myron interjected.

When the boys walked into Berek's office, a man was sitting in a chair with his back to them.

"Ah, come in, boys. I want to introduce you to someone."

The man sitting in a chair twisted around to look at the boys.

"This man is visiting from a place called Argentina. His name is Mr. Martin Roitman," Berek said.

A thin man wearing a bright robin's egg blue suit, with a sunflower yellow tie, stood up and offered a large and charming smile. "It's nice to meet you, boys. Berek has told me wonderful things about the two of you."

Neither Solomon nor Leo had heard of the country Argentina. They had also never met someone quite like Mr. Roitman, with his charm, and his funny accent.

"It's a pleasure to meet you. Mr. Weis has told me how resourceful you boys are," he said with elaborate gestures that involved sweeping his arms from side to side.

Solomon tilted his head, trying to understand the man's lyrical delivery of his words.

"Mr. Roitman has a wonderful opportunity for both of you to make good money," Berek said.

"How would you boys like to travel around the country and recruit beautiful young Jewish women to come work for rich men in my country?" Mr. Roitman asked.

Solomon looked at Leo, and they both shrugged.

"Sure, sounds good, what does it pay?" asked Leo.

"You will make more in a week than you were making here in two months," Mr. Roitman said.

The boys looked at each other and let out a laugh.

That was how they started working for the Tsvi Midal, an operation that lured young Jewish girls and young women from shtetls, to work as sex slaves for wealthy Jews in Argentina. Mr. Roitman gave the boys an advance to buy suits, and instructions on how to travel from village to village. He told them to place posters in local synagogues that advertised *a rosy future for young Jewish girls.* Frightened parents, most financially desperate, would send their daughters away in hopes of a better life for them.

Part of their job was for Solomon and Leo to bring the girls to a large house in Warsaw's business district, where they were taught the prostitution trade by several older women who initially befriended the girls, nurturing them in a maternal way. This endeared the frightened girls to them and eventually earned their trust. Gradually, they were introduced to a few men, who took part in the training and understood the delicate process.

The girls were told that these lonely men were looking for nothing more than companionship. *It's only an innocent night out with a gentleman so he can enjoy himself with a pretty girl on his arm,* they preached.

Over the eight weeks, the expectations of the dates increased from hand-holding to kissing, then to fondling, oral sex and eventually intercourse. Escape was not possible for the girls, since the only option was on foot to home hundreds of miles away. Those who did try to run away were soon caught, beaten and returned back to the brothel with visible deep purple bruises on them.

After the two months of training, they were taken by train to Hamburg where they boarded a steamship to Buenos Aires, Argentina. Once they arrived, they were assigned to large brothels, some housing as many as sixty to eighty sex slaves.

After telling the story about his friend Leo and the Tsvi Midal, Solomon finally got to his reason for having asked Myron to come. "Leo was shot dead in The Donnybrook on Clinton

Street during a business meeting, and do you know who killed him?" Solomon asked his son.

"I don't know, Pops," Myron said shaking his head.

"It was a cobbler, named Pincus Potasznik."

"A cobbler killed Leo Gorpatsch?" Myron asked.

"That's only part of it. Pincus had a son named Moshe, who is also a cobbler."

"Okay, Pops. What does all of this mean?"

"Moshe the Cobbler's shop is across the street from the Paradise Theater."

"Are you serious?" Myron asked.

Solomon nodded and said, "It means that the Moshe in my dreams is the son of Pincus the Cobbler, the one who killed Leo. Moshe the Cobbler is the *tzaddik* and is going to Safed. He is the one coming to me in my dreams. We have to stop him."

Myron tried to contemplate the significance of the father of a *tzaddik* murdering the childhood friend of a *rasha*, nearly a half-century ago. Besides his father's eerie ability of predicting future events, Myron never witnessed anyone else with these so-called *powers from the mystical realm of Kabbalah.* Apparently, now that was about to change, as he was heading directly to its source—Safed, Israel.

Chapter 14

On the morning of the second day in Safed, Moshe awoke hours before sunrise as he struggled with the effects of jetlag. While Aaron and the rabbi slept he decided to take a walk. The experience of traveling to Israel had so far been a blur. Everything had happened so fast. Just a few days ago, he was a simple cobbler from the Bronx and now he was in one of Israel's four holy cities, searching for a way to understand what it meant to be called *tzaddik*.

There was no doubt that there was some spiritual connection he felt he had when he was young. There were the incidents of when he would fall ill, just before a tragic event occurred. Moshe remembered people explaining this phenomenon by calling him an *empath*, which he understood to mean a person with an ability to sense and feel the emotional state of another. But that didn't really describe what he experienced.

The most significant connection he felt with Hashem was when he was able to calm those in pain, just through his touch. He never forgot that day in the shul in Krzywcza, with the wounded soldiers. Men cried out in agonizing pain, with no medical care to relieve their suffering, and they were magically eased just by his touch, ultimately allowing them to pass on peacefully.

After his family escaped from the ravages of the war and emigrated to America, his abilities diminished over the years. It was true that his customers commented often on how wonderful it was to visit him at his cobbler shop.

"You always make me feel better, Moshe," they would often say.

But that would hardly qualify as divine intervention, he lamented.

Aaron's small apartment was not far from the Ari Ashkenazi Synagogue. But that was all Moshe knew of the neighborhood. Unlike the box-like grid layout of the streets in the Bronx, Safed was a meandering web of roadways that morphed into alleyways, and back into streets, barely wide enough for cars or trucks to pass through.

Moshe soon found himself on a street with several art galleries. It was still hours before they would open, but he enjoyed looking at the paintings and sculptures in the window displays.

As the sun began to brighten the white roads and buildings of Safed, Moshe walked into a large park with views overlooking the valley below. He realized that he had wandered too far from Aaron's apartment and would need help finding his way back.

He saw an elderly man sitting on a bench looking right at him. He was wearing a long black robe with a shiny black ribbon sewn along its edge. On his head sat a circular black hat with a black tassel hanging off its top. His beard was white, except for a golden yellow patch just under his mouth.

The man gestured to Moshe to sit down next to him.

"It is good to see you," said the man in Yiddish.

"It is good to see you too," Moshe replied to the unusual greeting.

"I know why you are here."

"You do?" Moshe asked with wide eyes expressing his surprise.

"I recognize you."

"Have we met?" Moshe asked.

"Oh no, we never met. But you're *tzaddik*."

Moshe stared at the man, and asked, "Who are you, sir? And how do you know I am *tzaddik*?"

"I am who you are looking for. My name is Rabbi Yitzhak Rubin," the rabbi said with a warm smile. "And I've studied the ways of the mystics my entire life."

Moshe shook hands with the rabbi, and said, "My name is Moshe Potasznik."

"Ah, Moshe, I am happy to meet you. We should get started. There is a lot of work we need to do before it's too late."

"What do you mean too late?"

"Danger is lurking. Once the *tzaddik* has surfaced, the *rasha* will come."

Just then Aaron's voice called out, "Moshe, is that you? We've been looking everywhere for you for the past hour."

Moshe looked down the path and saw Rabbi Shapira and Aaron walking toward them.

"Rabbi Rubin?" Aaron asked, his arms spread wide in a question.

"Yes, we just met," Moshe said.

"What an honor it is to see you, Rabbi," Aaron said.

"You know the rabbi?" Moshe asked.

"Of course. He is the leading authority of Kabbalah in Safed," said Aaron.

"Come now, gentlemen, we have no time to waste," said Rabbi Rubin, as he stood and led the three men down the pathway and out of the park.

Chapter 15

Arnold placed his suitcase in the trunk of the rental car and took a look at the map. The attendant drew a line straight up the coast to the city of Acre. Then the line turned inland toward Safed.

"It's about three hours, depending on traffic," he told him.

He folded the map and took a seat behind the wheel of his questionable rental car. It took a few turns of the key in the ignition for the engine to turn over. He shifted the gear into reverse and backed out of the space. First gear took a moment to engage and he was moving forward.

As he drove through the rental car parking lot, he caught the eye of a man staring at him. He slowed down to watch the man through his rear view mirror quickly get into a car and pull out behind him.

Arnold stopped to give the attendant at the gate his paperwork. He glanced again in the mirror and saw the man behind the wheel. The shadows made it difficult to make out much, except a red beard.

Without concern, Arnold pulled out of the rental car lot and headed north, following signs to Haifa.

About thirty minutes outside of Tel Aviv, Arnold found himself in dire need to relieve himself. He found a service station on the outskirts of a town called Netanya. After he took care of his business he washed his hands in a sink that barely offered a trickle of water and walked back to his car. As he reached for the door handle, he saw a car parked on the side of the road. Even with the glare reflecting off the windshield he was able to make out that the driver had that same red beard. He stopped to stare and wondered if this was just another coincidence, or perhaps he was being followed.

There was only one way to know. Arnold got into his car and instead of heading north toward Haifa, he drove through the small streets of Netanya. He alternated looks between the road and the rear view mirror and as suspected, the man with the red beard was indeed following him.

He wondered if this man was sent by Myron to follow him. But whoever it was, the last thing he wanted to do was to lead him directly to Moshe and Rabbi Shapira. Arnold took a deep breath and white-knuckle gripped the steering wheel and headed back north along the highway.

Even though the January weather was cool, beads of sweat trickled down his forehead. He rolled down his window, allowing the wind to cool his anxiety and looked again in the rearview mirror and saw the red-bearded man looking back at him. *I need to lose him, before I get to Safed.*

Then he saw the sign for the city of Haifa. *That's it*, he thought. *I'll shake free of him there.* He desperately maneuvered the tight streets and roadways of Haifa, trying to shake his tail and every ten seconds checked out the rearview mirror for the red-bearded man. He hadn't reappeared. It had been several minutes since he lost him in the winding streets of Haifa before Arnold exhaled and felt himself relax a bit. He even dared a smile and looked at himself grinning in the same mirror he was obsessing over just minutes before. He then pressed the accelerator to the floor and sped onward to Safed.

Chapter 16

Rabbi Rubin and Moshe sat together in the study of his small second floor walkup, off a confusing array of alleyways in the heart of Safed.

"Do you live here alone?" Moshe asked glancing around at the apartment.

"I'm afraid so. My wife passed many years ago, and my eight children are scattered across Europe and America, except for my youngest daughter who lives in Galilee. She tries to visit me on Sundays," the rabbi said with a slight smile.

Moshe listened, and wondered how a man of Rabbi Rubin's age was able to take care of himself. The apartment, though small and cluttered with towering piles of books and yellowed newspapers, did not look dirty. Actually, Moshe thought, there was an odd sense of order to the place, which suggested that the rabbi actually referred to these volumes and publications for his studies.

"I would like to know about your life, Moshe. I assume that you are not an observant Jew."

Moshe briefly touched his uncovered head and said, "I am ashamed to say that I am not."

"Don't be, Moshe."

Moshe leaned forward and asked, "Rabbi, back in the park you said you recognized me."

The rabbi smiled. "Moshe, I've studied Kabbalah for over seventy years from the most renowned scholars here in Safed, and my teachers have learned from their masters, going back two-thousand years to the time of Rabbi Shimon Bar Yochai. Back then this land was under the brutal regime of Roman rule which Rabbi Shimon publicly spoke out against. The Roman governor responded by issuing a death warrant for the rabbi. Because of that he went into hiding in caves not far from here, where he learned through divine inspiration the secrets of the Torah. These secrets revealed the wisdom of the universe, and he collected these secrets in a book called the Zohar," he said, pointing to a leather bound volume sitting on his desk.

Moshe picked up the book and looked at the worn out inscription of Hebrew letters on its cover.

The rabbi continued, "You ask how I recognized you. Those that are born *righteous* are encircled with a field of energy. I can see it as clearly as I can see the sunrise each morning," he said, polishing the lens of his eyeglasses with an old worn cloth.

"But I do not understand how I can be *tzaddik* when I do not actively practice Judaism."

"That is a very good question," the rabbi said holding a finger in the air. "Before I answer, let me first ask you something."

Moshe nodded.

"Do you still consider yourself a Jew?"

Moshe exhaled deeply. "Of course I do, Rabbi. Even though I don't go to shul, except on the high holidays, my belief in Hashem is strong. Oh, and I forgot to say that I am also Kohen," Moshe said referring to the Jews who claim to be descendants of Moses's brother Aaron.

The rabbi clapped his hands together and said, "Ah, a Kohen and *tzaddik*. Moshe, you must not neglect who you are any longer. Your lack of devotion may have caused your connection to Hashem to be broken."

Moshe rubbed his chin and said, "I understand, but is it too late for me? I'm sixty years old."

"Hashem has chosen you, and thirty-five others, as an extension of his powers. As long as you still have a breath in your lungs, it is not too late. But you should know that *tzaddikim* have no extraordinary powers of their own. They are merely a conduit of the creator's hand as a way to help those in need. But without devotion to Hashem, such privilege is dimmed, as you can attest."

Moshe nodded and said, "What do I need to do?"

"Give yourself to the study of the Torah, and ask for Hashem's forgiveness."

"That's all?"

"The act of contrition is the easy part. Obeying Judaic laws in daily life, however—that takes work. There is much to learn and to practice. Not just here while you're in Safed, but when you travel back home to America, as well. You must also understand, Moshe, that even with such a reawakening of your devotion, there can be no assurances of reconnecting to the Almighty."

"I understand, but that doesn't explain why I had the gift when I was younger. My devotion was nothing more than it is now."

"One cannot understand every mystery, Moshe. Apparently there was a need at that time that outweighed your lack of devotion. Apparently that need has risen again."

Chapter 17

The best part about Charlie's Oyster Bar was that Solomon could walk there in minutes. Regardless of the weather, he would go every afternoon. Ralph, the owner, who bought the bar from Charlie a few years back, kept a table by the front window reserved for Solomon, thanks to his regular presence and generous tips for the past six years.

As Solomon walked to Charlie's along the dirt packed road, he felt his stomach begin to churn. He had never experienced such unease before and hoped that a stiff drink or two would soothe him.

He had once thought of his dreams as his Excalibur, the legendary sword of King Arthur that wielded magical powers. That exuberant feeling had only been enhanced when he turned ninety. It had actually felt like a rebirth. But then he'd started having these disturbing dreams about the *tzaddik*, which not only caused his stomach to be upset, but also gave him a short fuse.

He pondered that the cause of his anxiety was that these dreams only announced the appearance of the *tzaddik*, and not the reason for it. Perhaps future dreams would enlighten him as to why a threat to his very existence was now haunting him.

That afternoon, Charlie's was busier than usual. So busy, in fact, that Ralph had not realized that a young couple, visiting the island for the day, took a seat at Solomon's reserved table.

With patrons stacked two deep at the bar, Solomon entered. Every head turned to look when Solomon swiped his cane across the wooden table where the young couple sat. Beer bottles scattered, and the bar hushed in complete silence.

"What the hell are you doing sitting at my table," Solomon demanded.

The couple, probably on a date, and no more than twenty-five years old, jumped to their feet, their clothes soaked in beer.

"What the hell, old man?" yelled the young man.

"Who are you calling old?" Solomon barked, and lifted his cane, threatening to strike again.

Ralph ran over to settle the dispute.

"I'm sorry, Solomon. I didn't realize someone was sitting here," Ralph said.

"Ah, no harm done. Just clean up this mess, and bring me a whiskey," Solomon said.

The couple walked out of Charlie's without paying.

"Sorry about that, Ralph. Just put the damages on my tab," Solomon said.

With the bar crowd starting to thin out, Solomon ordered his third whiskey.

"You all right?" Ralph asked. "I've never served you more than two drinks."

"I'm fine," Solomon said gesturing to Ralph to pour.

"Okay, Solomon. You just seem upset," he said, topping off the tumbler.

"Yeah, I'm upset."

"You want to talk about it?" Ralph said, sitting down on the stool next to Solomon.

Solomon shook his finger at Ralph and said, "I am no one to trifle with."

"No, you are not," Ralph agreed with a warm smile.

"You, and everyone in here are living in the dark," Solomon said, gesturing to the lingering patrons.

Ralph turned to look at his customers enjoying themselves.

"You all live a life of darkness. Any fulfillment or happiness is fleeting, while I live a life of endless joy, and infinite knowledge. While you wallow in a miserable existence, I have lifted the curtain and can see the light."

Ralph stared at Solomon for a minute. He stood up, patted Solomon on his shoulder and said, "You have a strange way of showing it, my friend."

Solomon got to his feet and stumbled a bit until Ralph steadied him.

"Can I walk you home, Solomon," Ralph asked, offering Solomon his cane.

"Nonsense, give me that," Solomon said grabbing his cane.

"Okay, just be careful. I don't want to find you lying in the bushes on the roadside tomorrow when I come to work."

Solomon flipped a hand, dismissing Ralph's comment, and walked out the front door. His cane provided the extra support he needed to make his way home. Just as he arrived at the walkway leading to his front door a black car pulled up. Two large men wearing black suits got out.

A third man, tall, thin and well-dressed, approached Solomon and said, "Good afternoon, Mr. Blass. Please get in the car."

"Fuck you," Solomon blurted and lifted his cane in an attempt to strike the man.

He felt someone from behind him grab his arm and halt his swing in midair. A moment later he was shoved into the back seat of the car, in between the two large men.

"What the fuck is going on?" he yelled.

"Just settle down. You'll find out soon enough," said the tall thin man seated up front.

Chapter 18

Myron stopped at the first pay phone he could find in the terminal at the Ben Gurion Airport. He had arranged with a private detective in Tel Aviv to tail Arnold once he left the airport, and report on his final destination when Myron arrived. He also asked the detective to provide him with a gun when they met. Myron felt naked without carrying a piece on him, but knew bringing one on an international flight was not a good idea.

When he reached the detective's office a woman answered.

"Hello, this is Myron Blass, I've arrived in Tel Aviv. Have you heard from Dov?"

"Ah, Mr. Blass. I have been expecting your call. Dov has indeed called in. He said you are to proceed to Safed and meet him at the Hotel Canaan, where a room has been reserved for you."

Myron knew that Arnold was hiding something when he questioned him at his office. He had him followed and sure enough, Arnold was seen boarding a flight to Tel Aviv the next day. Apparently Moshe and the rabbi had already gone, and Arnold was on his way to warn them about Myron's visit to his office.

Myron rented a car and headed up the coast towards Safed. He needed to decide what he was going to do when he reached Safed. Apparently his father considered this so-called *tzaddik* a threat that needed to be neutralized.

Myron had tried to comprehend the mysteries of Kabbalah, but could never grasp its meaning, or practical use in everyday life. His father would tell him that only someone versed in Kabbalah could see beyond the one percent of what everyday humans experience. He told Myron that there is a curtain that we live behind, and once this curtain is lifted we then can discover the remainder of the ninety-nine percent of life, where the Light shines bright, and fills us with extraordinary happiness.

Several hours later, Myron arrived at the Hotel Canaan and checked in. Along with his room key, he was handed an envelope with his name written on it. He opened it up and read:
I'LL MEET YOU IN THE HOTEL LOBBY AT 8 TONIGHT - DOV.

An hour before his meeting with Dov, Myron did his best with the clumsy handheld spout in the smallest stall he had ever tried to shower in. He changed into a casual shirt and navy blue sports jacket, and walked down the six flights along the narrow winding staircase leading to the lobby.

He was a few minutes early, but Dov Levi was waiting for him.

"You must be Mr. Blass. It is a pleasure to meet you, sir. My name is Dov," he said, reaching out with his hand.

Standing before him was a young Israeli man wearing a tight shirt that amplified a muscular physique. His blue eyes were set off by his red hair, and tightly cropped red beard.

"It's a pleasure to meet you too, Dov," Myron said and shook hands with the man.

"I know of a place where we can get some dinner and talk. Would that be all right with you?" Dov said.

"Please lead the way." Myron gestured to the entryway.

Café Max was built into a cave. Myron marveled at the freeform rock walls decorated with strings of lights and candles flickering about. A young man playing guitar sat on a stool upon a small platform.

"The food is decent, and the music is nice," Dov said.

Myron scanned the place, and said, "I like it. Good choice."

Dov told Myron that he served in the Israeli Army and was a Captain in the Sinai War against Egypt in 1956.

"I've since retired, and started my own detective agency," Dov said.

Myron leaned in and asked, "Do you have the gun?"

Dov opened the flap of an army issued backpack and handed it to Myron. "It's one of mine. There's ammo in there too."

Myron hooked the backpack onto the back post of his chair and asked, "Have you found Moshe and the rabbi?"

"Not yet, but I know Arnold Lieberman is here, and I assume, according to your story, so is Moshe. Safed is a small place, Myron. They cannot stay hidden for long."

"So you followed Arnold here, to Safed?"

Dove shook his head and said, "I lost him in Haifa. But where else would he end up? If, as you say, they are searching for some Kabbalist rabbi, then Safed is the obvious place."

Myron put down his glass and stared at Dov. "You lost him? Are you kidding me? I paid you to follow him and tell me exactly where they are—not guess," Myron said, slamming his open palm on the table. The sudden bang reverberated off the rock walls, and the few patrons turned their heads to check out the commotion.

"It's okay, Myron, relax. I'll find them. It's not going to take me long," Dov pleaded.

Myron stood up, pointed a finger at Dove and said, "You're done," and stormed out of the café.

"Myron, wait," Dov said.

Myron turned as he walked out the door, giving Dov a glare of disgust.

Chapter 19

Arnold saw Safed's white stone buildings reflecting the morning light. *What a beautiful city*, he marveled, as he drove in from the west. The last time he visited Safed had been six years earlier, when he attended a conference on Kabbalah at the Ari Ashkenazi Synagogue.

Arnold surprised himself by finding the synagogue easily and parked his car nearby. As he walked up the steep incline to the pathway leading to the landmark building, he recalled being told that the synagogue was built in memory of the great Kabbalist Rabbi Isaac Luria who died in 1572. *This seems like a good place to inquire whether anyone has seen Moshe and Rabbi Shapira*, Arnold thought.

Arnold entered the synagogue, which was full of young rabbinical scholars milling about. He wandered the administrative halls unnoticed until he came upon an open office door and peeked inside. A man was sitting behind his desk busy punching numbers into an adding machine.

Arnold knocked on the door.

"Excuse me. Sorry to bother you," Arnold said.

The man looked up and said, "How may I help you?"

Arnold took a few steps into the office, and said, "My name is Arnold Lieberman. I was here six years ago for a conference, and I was wondering if you could help me find someone."

The man leaned back and gestured to the empty chair. "Okay, Mr. Lieberman, please sit down."

"Thank you, sir," Arnold said, and reached across the desk to shake the man's hand.

Arnold looked at the name plate on the desk which read: GERALD ABRAMOWITZ

"Mr. Abramowitz, I am looking for two of my associates who just recently arrived in Safed from New York. One is Rabbi Shapira and the other is a cobbler named Moshe Potasznik."

"What do you want from me?"

"I need help finding them," Arnold said, and began to realize how ridiculous he was sounding.

"I'm sorry, Mr. Lieberman, but I am just an accountant. I don't know how I can help you find your friends."

"I'm sorry to waste your time," Arnold said, rising from his chair. Then he saw a photo displayed on the desk of the accountant posing with the renowned kabbalist Rabbi Yitzhak Rubin.

"Is that Rabbi Rubin?" Arnold asked, pointing to the framed photograph.

"Yes, you know of him? I've met the rabbi several times. He lives here, in Safed."

"Can you direct me to where I can find him? Perhaps he can help me locate my friends."

Later that afternoon, Arnold found Moshe and Rabbi Shapira sitting at an outdoor café speaking to Rabbi Rubin.

"I found you," Arnold said, spreading out his arms joyfully.

"Arnold, what are you doing here and how in the world did you find us?" Rabbi Shapira, said, surprised.

"I'll tell you later," Arnold said and turned to the rabbi and reached out to shake his hand. "It is an honor to meet you, sir."

"Please sit, Arnold, the rabbi was about to tell us something important," Moshe said pointing to the empty chair.

"What is it, Moshe?" Arnold said.

"After Moshe and I spoke, I did some thinking and spoke with some of my colleagues," Rabbi Rubin began.

"And what did they say?" Arnold asked.

The old man clasped his hands together, shook them back and forth and said, "I'm afraid that Moshe will not be able to relight his connection to the Almighty. For some reason, which only Hashem knows, Moshe is no longer *tzaddik*."

Chapter 20

The car pulled up to a townhouse on the corner of Fifth Avenue and 124th Street in Harlem.

"Where the hell are we?" Solomon asked as he was ushered out of the car and up the steps to a large brownstone and into an entrance foyer. He looked about in awe at the dramatic interior of the Roman style columns towering alongside a sweeping staircase leading to the upper floors.

"This way, Mr. Blass," instructed the tall, thin man.

Solomon entered into a dimly lit, well-appointed room decorated with antique furnishings. Standing in front of a large, mahogany desk was a man in a perfectly tailored suit.

"Mr. Blass, thank you for coming," said the man, extending a hand.

"Who are you, and why the fuck am I here?" Solomon said, refusing to shake hands.

"There's no need for profanity. Please sit, and I'll tell you everything."

Solomon sat down without taking his eyes off the man's nose. It looked the nose of a boxer who lost more fights than he won.

"My name is Mikey Coppola. I'm a businessman just like you and your son Myron."

"So what? Tell me why I'm here?" Solomon asked again.

"You and your son have made quite a reputation up in the Bronx."

Solomon said nothing. This was not the first time he had been approached by an Italian curious about his success.

"I'm not going to ask you about your methods, but you have an uncanny ability of picking winners. Have you and your son ever considered expanding beyond the Bronx?"

"No, we're happy with what we have," Solomon said.

Mickey rubbed his chin before he spoke. "I appreciate your caution. But wouldn't it be easier for us to be partners rather than competitors?"

Solomon shook his head. "You know, Mr. Coppola..."

"Please call me Mickey," he interrupted.

Solomon nodded. "Okay, Mickey. I've had many similar proposals from your ilk over the years and I've never agreed to one. Why would I now?"

"I don't appreciate your tone. This is just a discussion about a business opportunity. No need to get testy."

"Now you listen to me, Mickey," Solomon said wagging his finger at Mickey. "First of all, you can address me as Mr. Blass. Second, I have every right to be testy. It's not like I came here on my own free will. So if you and your goons here don't mind, I would like you to take me home now, or do I need to call a taxi?"

Mickey leaned back in his chair, spread his arms out wide, and said, "Okay, Mr. Blass, I want no trouble. But all I ask is that you discuss this with your son, Myron. You should be thinking about his future. How will he carry on, when you are not around anymore?"

This statement carried more weight than Mickey could have known. It tapped right into Solomon's underlying and persistent fear that Myron would flounder without Solomon's ability to make strategic decisions based on his foresight offered in dreams. Solomon slumped back in his chair, thinking, *Maybe he's right.*

"All right, Mickey, I'll discuss it with my son, and get back to you. Can you have someone take me home now? I'm an old man and need my rest."

"Of course, Mr. Blass," Mickey said, flicking a finger at the tall, thin man.

Chapter 21

Arnold, Rabbi Shapira and Moshe huddled around the table staring at Rabbi Rubin after his startling announcement that Moshe was no longer *tzaddik*.

"I don't understand. How can Moshe suddenly stop being *tzaddik*?" Arnold asked.

"It's not sudden. The last time Moshe had an episode was when his father passed. That was over fifteen years ago," the illustrious rabbi said, patting Moshe's clasped hands resting on the café table.

"But what about what you said about how I could salvage my abilities if I dedicated myself to being a studious and devout Jew?" Moshe asked.

Rabbi Rubin nodded. "I know what I said, Moshe. But I think I was just trying not to hurt you. The truth is, I don't see how it is possible."

"I suppose this was a waste of time. I'm sorry, Arnold," Moshe said.

"Wait a second, what if you're wrong? Why should we give up?" said Arnold looking at Rabbi Rubin.

The rabbi tried to sit a little taller in his chair and said, "Our body is a vessel for our soul, and when we die, our soul is reborn into a new body. This continues through many incarnations, until our soul connects to the spiritual world. This takes devotion and work to rise above the basic egotistical desires of man. The soul of *tzaddik,* however, has already made this connection to the spiritual world, but must continue to strive in his lifetime to keep this connection strong, or as we can now see, it could be broken. Apparently, this is what occurred with Moshe."

Arnold looked at Moshe and asked, "What do you have to say about this?"

Moshe exhaled a long breath. "I never asked for this gift and was never told that I needed be an observant Jew in order to keep it. What I experienced was something that just happened. I'm sorry, Arnold."

"It's not your fault, Moshe. I suppose we should make plans to head back home," Arnold said.

"But what about the *rasha*? What will we do now?" asked Rabbi Shapira.

All eyes turned to Rabbi Rubin who just shrugged.

Arnold exhaled a long breath and said, "I'll make the arrangements. We will leave tomorrow."

Later that night, Moshe lay awake in the small bedroom in Aaron's apartment. The open window provided a pleasant breeze, but that didn't relieve his anguish. How could he be so ignorant? He knew he had a gift that only thirty-five others in the world also had. Now he was being told that he was no longer *tzaddik*.

But what was worse was how he found a way to disconnect his soul to Hashem. Rabbi Rubin said that the soul of *tzaddik* has made the connection to the sacred world, while all others must continue to be reborn into a new soul in order to achieve this ultimate spirituality.

Moshe placed both hands on his face and started to cry. As tears rolled down his cheeks, he realized that the last time he lived his life where his daily practices included observing Judaic law was his childhood years leading up to his Bar Mitzvah. His life since then has been at best one where he could call himself a Jew in name only. He had been given a gift from the Creator that he had squandered.

Moshe looked up to the heavens, lifted his arms into the air and thought, *How is it possible to carry this shameful burden for the rest of my life? It was one thing to disappoint a loved one, a friend, but to neglect Hashem, this is unimaginable.*

Chapter 22

The next morning Myron wandered along the streets of Safed. He stopped for a coffee at a small café and struck up a conversation with a waiter.

"So tell me, where would someone go to learn from the top Kabbalists in Safed?" Myron asked the young man, who just shared with Myron that he was studying Kabbalah.

"That would be the Ari Ashkenazi Synagogue," he told Myron.

Myron thanked the waiter and after a short walk, found himself standing before the illustrious building. That was when he saw Arnold Lieberman walk out of the front doors and head in the opposite direction of where Myron was coming from.

Myron reached into his jacket pocket and touched the small handgun that Dov had given him. Spotting Arnold was a stroke of good fortune that Myron couldn't pass up.

He followed Arnold through the winding streets until he came to a staircase that led to a second floor apartment. Arnold climbed the steps, turned the unlocked doorknob and entered the apartment.

Myron followed quietly up the staircase and stood behind the closed door. The open window alongside it allowed Myron to clearly hear the conversation going on inside.

"We're all set. We have a flight out tomorrow morning. Aaron, if it's okay with you, can you drive us to Tel Aviv this afternoon? We will spend tonight at the Tel Aviv

Hilton and catch a taxi in the morning to the airport," Arnold said.

"All of a sudden I don't feel so good," an unfamiliar voice said.

"What's wrong, Moshe? You look terrible."

Moshe is here, Myron thought. He reached into his pocket and pulled out the handgun. He slowly turned the doorknob and stepped into the apartment. Seated at the round table were four men gawking at Myron's sudden appearance.

"Myron, what are you doing here?" asked Arnold.

"Get up, and stand against the wall," Myron ordered, waving the gun.

Arnold, Moshe, Aaron and Rabbi Shapira slowly rose from their chairs.

"You must be Moshe," Myron said observing beads of sweat rolling down Moshe's pale face.

Moshe looked over to Arnold. "You know this man?"

"This is Myron Blass, the son of Solomon Blass. Come now, Myron, put the gun down, there's no reason for violence," Arnold pleaded.

Myron pointed the handgun at Moshe. "I came here to stop you, and that's what I'm going to do."

"No, don't," the rabbi said, and stepped in front of Moshe the instant Myron pulled the trigger.

The gunshot rang out loudly in the small apartment. Rabbi Shapira clutched his chest where the bullet entered. Blood oozed between his fingers and he collapsed to the floor.

Moshe quickly kneeled down beside the rabbi who was now lying in a growing puddle of his blood.

"What have you done?" Moshe said.

Myron looked at the gun, then back at Moshe, and mumbled, "I didn't mean to shoot him."

Moshe lifted the rabbi's head onto his lap and clutched his hands. "I'm with you, Rabbi. You'll be okay."

The rabbi's eyes became glassy and watery. He squeezed Moshe's hands. Then it happened. As Myron stood over them, he watched the pained expression on the rabbi's face melt away into one of contentment. He could even say that he witnessed a brief smile.

Could it be that there was some divine force that Myron could actually see travel through the hands of Moshe and into the passing soul of the rabbi?

Upon his last breath, the rabbi said the words that shook Myron to his core. "Moshe, you are still *tzaddik*."

Chapter 23

On a Saturday afternoon, Myron met his father at Charlie's Crab House. The place was nearly empty, as it typically was at the end of the summer season.

"Hi, Pops," Myron said as he entered the restaurant.

"What's going on with you? You look terrible. Are you nervous about the trial?" Solomon said.

"Wouldn't you be? I murdered a man in front of witnesses."

"You need to pull yourself together, Myron. There is something I need to speak with you about."

Myron picked up the cloth napkin from the table and patted beads of sweat off his bald head and asked, "Can I get a drink first, Pops?"

"Sure, Myron," Solomon said and signaled Ralph to bring over another scotch by holding up his tumbler.

A few minutes later Ralph came over with the drink and said, "How you doin', Myron?"

"I've been better," said Myron.

"Enjoy," Ralph said with a forced smile and returned to the bar.

Myron quickly downed his glass of scotch in one swallow and said, "All right. What do you want to talk about, Pops?"

"While you were in Israel, I was forced into a car on my way home from Charlie's. It was Mickey Coppola's goons. They brought me to his home in Harlem."

Myron's eyes widened and his jaw fell open. "What did he want?"

"He wants a partnership."

"Really? I'm sure you told him to fuck off," Myron said.

"I did at first, but then I reconsidered."

"You did? Why?" Myron asked spreading his hands out wide.

"After you killed that rabbi in Safed, I had no choice but to make a deal with Mickey. That's how we got his lawyer to represent you. Hopefully, he will get you off from getting fried in the electric chair."

Myron nodded, placed a finger on his lips and then pointed towards his father and said, "But now we owe Mickey Coppola."

"For now we do. But I'll give him something big as payback. Then we'll be square."

"But what are we going to do about the *tzaddik?*" Myron asked.

"Tell me, what did you see in Safed?" Solomon asked.

"After I shot the rabbi, he clutched his chest and fell to the floor in excruciating pain. Moshe just reached out, and touched him." Myron paused and shook his head. "Pops, it was magical. The rabbi looked at Moshe in total peace. There was no more suffering. It was if Moshe allowed the rabbi's soul to peacefully depart from his body."

Solomon nodded, listening to his son. Even if Moshe the Cobbler was really *tzaddik,* Solomon still did not know how the *tzaddik* could be a threat to his existence. Moshe's ability to ease the passing of the soul meant nothing to Solomon. Unless there was something else he had not yet come across. Perhaps his dreams would provide an answer.

Chapter 24

It was a sunny day, three weeks after he came home from Israel when Moshe took Leah to Orchard Beach in his 1956 seafoam green, Chevy Impala. He loved going to the beach after the hectic summer season was over.

"Sit here on the bench, Leah. I'll go set up the chairs and blankets, and come back and get you," Moshe said.

"Okay, Moshe, just don't forget I'm here," Leah yelled, as he walked along the sand toward the shoreline.

Unable to wave, since he carried two chairs, a beach bag, and an umbrella, he acknowledged her command with an exaggerated nod.

After he set up their spot, he helped Leah across the unsteady sand and into her beach chair. He sat down beside her and tried to relax. So much had happened since coming home. The first thing was the funeral for Rabbi Shapira, at the Riverdale Jewish Cemetery.

The entire affair caused quite a stir in the community. The Daily News sent a reporter to interview Moshe at the cobbler shop. The last time Moshe had a story written about him was when he and his friend Max witnessed a gruesome murder when they were young boys in Krzywcza.

The article denounced Myron Blass as a small-time hoodlum, who murdered a respectable rabbi while they were both visiting Israel. Since the accused and the victim were U.S. citizens, Myron was extradited back home to stand trial for murder, and the rabbi's body was returned to New York for burial.

Representing Myron in court was the criminal defense attorney Frank Lugano, who was well-known for representing famous Mafiosi. How Myron was able to hire such an effective lawyer was a mystery to Moshe. But for whatever the reason, it did the trick. After only a few hours of deliberation the jury found Myron Blass not guilty.

When the news was announced that the rabbi's killer was not going to prison, Moshe's customers wanted to know what happened.

"This is outrageous, Moshe, how does a murderer walk free?" he heard over and over.

All Moshe could reply was with a shrug of his shoulders and a deep frown.

It became difficult to get his work done and he ended up staying late into the night in order to catch up. After a few weeks of this, Moshe had enough and asked Leah if they could spend a day at the beach.

Of all the people who knew Moshe, Leah knew him the best. She had witnessed many versions of the man, but remained devoted and supportive, even with her recently failing eyesight that drained her enthusiasm for most things outside the home.

"Moshe, tell me what happened in Safed," Leah said, adjusting her large straw hat that featured on its crown a bright-yellow plastic sunflower.

"Leah, I really don't walk to talk about this now. Can I please relax?"

"So everyone gets an explanation, except for me?" she said, looking out into sea lapping the shore.

Moshe sighed. "No of course not, it's just that I am exhausted."

Leah lifted her sunglasses and gave him a look that needed no words. After forty years of marriage, Moshe knew when he needed to give in.

"Okay, just give me a minute."

Leah smiled triumphantly. Moshe sheepishly smiled back. After all these years, he couldn't resist her bright blue eyes, which were still just as beautiful as they were when they first met.

Her family immigrated from Romania to America in 1905, when she was just a year old. Leah was the youngest of ten children, five girls and five boys. Her father Benjamin loved Moshe from the first day he met him.

"This is the man you should marry," he told his daughter.

"Your father never approved of anyone so quickly. Becky and Anna had hard times earning his blessings for their fiancés," Leah's mother, Sarah, told her.

That was when Moshe had the *touch*. No matter who it was, he had an ability to instill a calmness, even to the most agitated.

On one their first dates, Moshe was walking Leah home along Union Avenue when they came upon a disturbed homeless man screaming for anyone to listen how he had been screwed out of his family's inheritance.

Passersby stared and seemed frightened at the man hovering next to his belongings packed into a metal shopping cart by the entrance to the elevated train station. Leah clutched Moshe's arm as they passed. But then a strange thing happened. The man jumped in front of Moshe and Leah and pointed his finger inches from Moshe's face.

"Why don't you help me?" he pleaded.

Leah pulled at Moshe. "He's crazy, keep walking."

But Moshe stood still and looked into the man's watery eyes. He placed his hands on the man's shoulders, and said, "I understand."

The man clutched Moshe in a tight hug and started to cry.

"Moshe, what are you doing?" Leah cried out.

"It's okay, Leah," Moshe said.

The man released Moshe and smiled. "Thank you," he said, and sat down on the pavement, seemingly at ease.

Moshe opened his wallet, took out a ten dollar bill and handed it to the man.

"God bless you, sir," he said.

As they walked away, Leah turned to look at the man who was still sitting on the pavement and was now cheerfully greeting people as they passed by.

"What happened back there?" she asked.

Moshe shrugged and said, "He just needed some attention."

"No, that was more than attention. You did something to him," Leah insisted.

"Come now, Leah, it's all good," he said, wrapping his arm around her shoulders.

Leah looked at him and smiled.

"Moshe, are you listening to me?" Leah was saying loud enough for a couple sitting nearby to look over.

"I'm sorry. Yes, I am listening."

"Are you going to tell me what happened in Safed?"

Moshe clutched the armrests of his beach chair and said, "I met this famous rabbi who knew I was *tzaddik*, even before I said a word to him."

"How did he know?"

"He said that I was encircled with a field of energy."

"A field of energy? Where? I don't see it," Leah said looking at Moshe from different angles.

Moshe flipped his hand at her. "Stop it, Leah."

Leah smiled.

"After we spoke and I told him my story he said that to regain my connection to Hashem I would need to become an observant Jew. But later on, he changed his mind and said that no matter what I did, I was no longer *tzaddik*."

"How is that possible?" Leah asked shaking her head.

"But things changed when Rabbi Shapira was shot."

"What do you mean? What happened?"

"Right before Myron Blass barged into Aaron's apartment, I fell ill. It was the same feeling I had just before Dad died."

"Then he shot the rabbi," Leah murmured.

Moshe lowered his voice to say, "He gave his life in order to save mine."

"Oh my, Moshe," Leah sighed.

"Then there was…" he paused and looked at to the sea. "It's hard to explain. All I can say is that I felt a connection."

"What do you mean?"

"I was on the ground with the rabbi's head resting on my lap. He was moaning in agonizing pain and clutching his chest where the bullet entered. Blood was seeping out in between his fingers and puddling around him. I was stroking his hair when it happened. It was as if my fingertips sent an electrical charge into the rabbi's soul. His pain seemed to just melt away. His eyes and face relaxed, and then it was over. He passed."

"What do you mean an electrical charge. Where did it come from?"

Moshe smiled, stood up from his beach chair, and leaned over to give Leah a soft kiss on her cheek. "It was from Hashem."

Chapter 25

Arnold felt his heart pound hard against his rib cage as he scaled the City Hall steps. He had been in the same room as Mayor Douglas before, but this was going to be the first time they would meet privately, face to face. The scandal of the Myron Blass acquittal for the murder of Rabbi Shapira sent a chill throughout the entire city and the mayor wanted to know what Arnold knew about it.

During the subway ride to lower Manhattan Arnold rehashed what occurred on his trip to Safed. There was no way he could tell the mayor everything about it. How would an Irishman understand the Jewish mystical world of Kabbalah? He figured what would be of the most concern was not the reason why they went to Safed, but how in the world did Myron Blass get Mickey Coppola's attorney to represent him and beat the murder charge.

Arnold, on the other hand, was not so surprised. He knew what Myron Blass was capable of. His brief sports book relationship gave him an insight into the man, but he never thought he would be capable of murder.

All in all, he felt good about his sudden rise of relevance in the world of New York City politics. Arnold knew that the mayor would be impressed with his firsthand knowledge of the newly formed relationship between the Blasses and the Copollas.

After sitting in the mayor's reception room for nearly an hour he was shown in. As he stepped into the office, the first thing Arnold saw was the tremendous desk floating in the middle of the room, like a battleship occupying a small harbor. Sitting behind the desk was the three-hundred-plus pound mayor, who seemed in scale with his oversized furniture.

"Arnold, so good to see you again. Please come in and take a seat," the mayor said.

Arnold sat down facing the imposing desk and adjusted himself to sit up taller just to see over the stacks of books and folders blocking his view of the mayor.

"No, not there. Come, Arnold, let's talk," he said, standing up, and gesturing to the sofa pushed up against the wall on the other side of the room.

"Tell me what you know about this upstart Myron Blass. How the hell did he get Frank Lugano to represent him?" the mayor asked.

Arnold nodded. "That's a good question, sir. Myron and his father Solomon have kept their businesses in the Bronx. As you know, Frank Lugano is Mickey Coppola's attorney. It looks like there may be a new relationship between these two families."

"What do you know about the father? I hear he's an old man living on City Island."

"Yes, he just turned ninety. But I wouldn't discount his abilities because of his age. I know both the father and the son, and without the skills of Solomon, Myron is nothing but a smalltime gangster."

"Arnold, I would like for you to keep an eye on them, and report to me directly about their activities. Especially now, if they are hooking up with Mickey Coppola."

On the subway ride back up to the Bronx Arnold wondered where all of this was headed. Solomon had apparently made a deal with the Coppola crime family, which resulted in Myron beating the murder charge. This would be considered a significant favor and Mickey would expect something equally grand in return.

But if they were indeed working together, the results could have devastating consequences for law and order in the city. Could the only counterbalance to their power be the cobbler? And even after Moshe's epiphany in Safed, would he have the ability to fight a crime machine like the Coppolas?

As the train rose from the tunnel to the elevated platform, the sunlight beamed through the smut-covered windows and shone upon Arnold's face. He leaned back in the seat and closed his eyes, taking in its warmth.

Things were moving quickly. He imagined a simmering cauldron and with each passing day a new potent ingredient was dropped in, bringing it to a near boil. Arnold took a dose of pride in knowing that he played a role in creating this brew, but he also prayed that he wouldn't one day regret it.

Chapter 26

Myron tapped his foot nervously as his driver Benjamin sped down the Major Deegan highway. This would be his first meeting with Mickey Coppola. A few times he caught a glimpse of the notorious mobster sitting in the gallery as a spectator at his murder trial. He knew that the jurors saw him too. Every time Frank Lugano addressed the jury, Myron marveled at the sudden shift in people's reaction. An elderly woman avoided eye contact with Lugano when he spoke, probably hoping that she would disappear. There was this young man, perhaps in his twenties, whose face turned several shades whiter as if his life was being threatened at gunpoint each time Frank Lugano approached the jury.

There were several rumored stories of jury tampering at previous trials, where the Coppolas had an interest in the outcome. But so far, nothing was ever proven. That was because just the sight of the infamous gangster Mickey Coppola frightened people enough, without the need of making actual personal threats.

Benjamin parked the Cadillac in front of Antonio's, an Italian restaurant on Arthur Avenue in the Bronx. Nothing Mickey did was done without reason and selecting a restaurant in the Bronx did not go unnoticed by Myron. Perhaps this was his way of showing Myron his intention of taking control of his territory.

Sitting outside were two of Mickey's men. They were smoking cigarettes and playing cards on a small table barely large enough for the game with an ashtray overflowing with cigarette butts.

Benjamin quickly jumped out of the car and opened Myron's door. Myron led with his expensive, and just polished shoes as he exited his car. He took a moment to stand and let the two goons playing cards take in his magnificence. Certainly they would be impressed with his suede suit and polished alligator shoes. But they hardly paid him attention, except for a brief glance and a friendly nod. He returned the wisp of an acknowledgment and entered the restaurant.

"Mr. Blass, you're here. Please, come and join us," a voice rang out as soon as Myron stepped inside.

Myron needed a moment for his eyes to adjust to the dimmed interior of Antonio's. Walking towards him was Mickey Coppola with an outstretched hand.

"Thanks for coming," Mickey said, shaking Myron's hand.

"My pleasure," Myron said, removing his fedora and gently stroking his bald head.

Mickey took a step back, spread his arms out wide and said, "You are looking very dapper. I love the suit, and will you look at those shoes! Are they alligator?"

"Indeed they are," Myron said, lifting his foot a few inches in the air to allow his pants to fall back for a better view. *He can't be that bad—he noticed my shoes*, Mickey thought.

"I'm impressed. Come, let's eat. Do you know Antonio? He makes the best eggplant parmigiana in the city."

Standing behind Mickey was a large man wearing a white apron, stained with shades of red tomato sauce. "It's nice to meet you," Antonio said, thrusting out his beefy paw.

"Come, let's start with wine," Mickey said, gesturing to the round table covered with a white table cloth.

With both men seated, Antonio poured red wine from a carafe.

"Have you ever had wine from Montepulciano?" Antonio asked.

"Can't say that I have," Myron said tasting the wine.

The two men watched as Myron sipped.

"Delicious," he said, placing the glass down.

"If you will excuse me, I'll prepare your lunch," Antonio said.

Mickey leaned in and said, "I own the place now. Antonio had a little trouble, so I helped him out."

"You own Antonio's?" Myron asked.

"It's a good place for us to do our business."

"I suppose so," Myron said, looking at the empty restaurant.

"There's a room in the back if privacy is needed," Mickey said with a wink.

As the two men enjoyed the wine, Myron felt it was a good time to share his father's dream. "I want you to know that my father and I are grateful for Mr. Lugano's brilliant defense. Who knows where I could have been without it."

"Sitting in the electric chair," Mickey said, gulping down some wine.

"Yeah, right," he said and took a sip of wine to ease his nerves. "So, as a thank you, I have some information to share with you that could prove... um, lucrative."

Mickey lit a cigar and motioned with his hand for Myron to continue.

His father had a dream a few days ago about a police raid on a brothel in lower Manhattan. While this was not

Mickey Coppola's territory, he knew that this was useful information to put into his hands.

"He'll know what to do with it," Solomon assured his son.

When Myron shared that in a few days a brothel on Houston Street would be raided, Mickey asked, "How do you know this?"

"We just do. I assume you will know how to capitalize upon it," Myron said.

Mickey took a puff on his cigar and exhaled, allowing the smoke to rise above the table and hang for a moment before evaporating. Then he said, "Indeed I do, Myron. Indeed I do."

Chapter 27

Even with the day at the beach with Leah, Moshe had a hard time letting go of the Myron Blass acquittal. His customers even remarked that he was curt, which was out of character for the always pleasant Moshe the Cobbler. But the outcome of the trial was too much for him. *How could the jury, after hearing from Arnold and himself as eyewitnesses, still believe Myron's attorney that the shooting was accidental?* He was so angry that he closed the shop an hour early. He needed to cool off and thought a walk in St. James Park would help.

Once in the park, he calmed down. The sun was nearly setting, but there were at least thirty more minutes of daylight. With both hands clasped behind his back and his eyeglasses hanging off a cord around his neck and swinging back and forth, Moshe walked the pathways encircling the park.

There was so much to make sense of. He recognized the dangers of someone like Myron Blass. He had seen evil like this before when he was much younger. It was back in Krzywcza during the war when Captain Berbecki led the Russian army into their synagogue and demanded to take Rabbi Shapira into custody. Moshe stepped forward and offered that the captain take himself instead. Moments after Moshe was taken, orders were given to line up the wounded Jewish soldiers outside against the synagogue wall, where they were shot dead by firing squad. Later that same day, his mother Clara had to give of herself sexually to the Russian captain in order to secure her son's release.

Moshe had no idea where this was headed, and certainly no idea how it would all end. No longer was he just a cobbler hoping to retire to Florida in a few years. Now he was a weapon against evil, which he thought was so bizarre that he dared not speak about it to his wife, or to his two daughters.

Moshe sat down on a bench and watched a few young boys kick a ball across the field. Dusk was turning to night, and the boys were being called for by their mother to come along, as it was time to go home for dinner.

As Moshe turned to see where the voice was coming from he noticed a man lying under some bushes. It looked as though he was going to sleep there for the night. Moshe rose from the bench, climbed over the railing that separated the walkway from the foliage, and approached the man.

This was not the first time he felt an urge to aid the homeless. Leah would often complain that whenever they came across a "bum in the street" as she would call them, Moshe would want to engage with them, either by reaching generously into his wallet or by just by simply touching the man to see if his connection to the Almighty would provide some improvement to their life. "It's the least I can do," Moshe would say.

Still fresh in his mind was the mystical moment he shared with Rabbi Shapira at his passing. If he indeed had renewed his connection to Hashem, perhaps this encounter may offer additional proof.

As were many of the others he observed and helped, this man was dressed in dirty, threadbare clothes. Moshe could smell his pungent body odor as he got closer. His head was resting on an old army-style duffle bag which was overstuffed with rags spilling out of its opening.

"Leave me alone," shouted the man. He voice was graveled, sounding like he smoked too much.

"I'm not here to harm you," Moshe said, as he crouched down.

"What do you want from me?"

Moshe could now see the man's eyes. They were bloodshot and glassy. His face and arms had spots of dried bloody scabs, where he must have picked at some skin condition too many times.

"When was the last time you ate?" Moshe asked.

The man showed Moshe a small piece of a sandwich that he must have pulled out of the wastebasket in the park.

"Why don't you come with me and let me buy you a decent meal? There's a diner on the corner. You could use a burger and a cup of coffee," Moshe said.

The man hesitated a moment then nodded and emerged from the bushes. Now Moshe could see the rags the man was wearing. Layers of faded clothes covered his body, most of which were so old that they were unraveling into threads that hung off him like garland on a Christmas tree. His worn-out shoes left several toes exposed.

"Before we get you something to eat you'll need new clothes, follow me," Moshe said leading the man out of the park and into Alexander's Department Store, on the corner of Fordham Road and the Grand Concourse.

"Just stay close," Moshe said, walking through the grand sets of brass doors.

Shoppers turned and gawked at the homeless man walking through the perfume and fragrance kiosks on his way to menswear.

Thirty minutes later, Moshe and Jack were sitting at the counter of the Fordham Diner. Jack was wearing a new shirt, pants and shoes along with new undergarments. Moshe watched Jack's reaction to each sip of coffee. It was as if he was drinking a specially brewed elixir that was seeping into his soul.

"Good?" Moshe asked.

Jack nodded, and took another bite of his cheeseburger, ignoring the trail of meat juices and ketchup running down his chin.

"Why are you doing this for me?" Jack asked.

Moshe shrugged. "It looks like you need a helping hand."

Tears welled up in Jack's eyes.

"Tell me what happened to you?" Moshe said, reaching across the table to squeeze Jack's shoulder.

Later that night, Moshe told Leah that he hired someone today to help out at the cobbler shop.

"Wonderful, you finally listened to me. How did you find him?"

"We sort of found each other," Moshe said.

"Who is he?"

"His name is Jack McCoy. He's from Texas. He's worked with leather before on a ranch. He'll pick up the work quickly, I'm sure."

"So he just walked into the shop, and asked for a job?" Leah asked, still confused.

"Not exactly, we met in St. James Park."

"You hired a stranger in the park?"

"I suppose I did," Moshe said, trying to contain a smirk.

"You're hiding something, Moshe. Tell me, what is it?"

"Like I said, his name is Jack, he's from Texas and he was living under a bush in the park."

"What?" Leah said.

"Leah, he was homeless. I bought him new clothes at Alexander's, and a meal at the diner. He had some bad luck the past few years and needed help. So I am helping him."

"I can understand giving him some money for a meal. But Moshe, you are giving him a job, too?"

Moshe nodded.

Leah continued, "So, let me ask you another question. Where is this Jack fellow going to live? Will he be commuting from the bushes at St. James Park?"

"Not exactly. I rented him our basement."

Chapter 28

Solomon sat at his table at Charlie's Oyster Bar, watching the New York Giants play the Chicago Bears. He knew from his dream that the Giants were going to win 21–20. So earlier that day, he put his money on the Bears, since the Giants were not going to beat the three-point spread.

The game was late in the fourth quarter when Mickey Coppola walked in the bar.

"There you are, Solomon, you're a hard man to get a hold of. I've been calling you for the past two days," Mickey said, taking a seat on the stool across from Solomon.

Solomon spread his hands out wide and said, "Here I am."

"I wanted to thank you for that tip on the brothel raid. Jacky DeMeo owes me big time."

"Glad I could help out," Solomon said.

"I'm curious how you knew about this. Who's your source at the Tenth Precinct?"

Solomon took a sip of his drink and smiled. "Why are you here, Mickey?"

"Okay, keep your secrets," Mickey said, and signaled to Ralph, the owner, to pour him a drink. "Whatever Solomon's having is fine," he said, and turned back to Solomon. "I came to talk to you about Myron."

"What about him?"

"He makes a nice first impression. He carries himself well. The other bosses are also impressed with him."

Solomon agreed that Myron dressed to the nines, and was well spoken, but enough to impress important people, that sounded like a stretch. But perhaps his son deserved more credit than he gave him.

"All the family bosses meet occasionally to discuss matters that affect us all," Mickey said and threw back his drink in one swift gulp before he continued, "We are concerned about the mayor's new initiatives. It's been hurting our businesses, so we're looking for a candidate to back in the election this fall."

Solomon shook his head, and asked, "Okay, what has this got to do with me?"

"We want to groom Myron to run for mayor."

"Mayor of what?" Solomon asked.

"What do you mean of what? Of New York City, what do you think I am saying?"

Solomon shook his head. "Mayor of New York City? You can't be serious."

"He is the sizzle, but you're the steak, Solomon."

"What the fuck are you talking about?"

"Myron is the pretty boy and you're the brains. You get it now?" Mickey said sounding annoyed at needing to explain the obvious.

"Have you lost your mind? You want Myron to run for mayor? He's not qualified to hold such an office. Who will vote for him?"

"You leave that to me."

"I'm not doing it," Solomon said, grabbing his cane and standing up.

"Sit back down," Mickey said, giving Solomon a sharp push backwards and forcing him to sit down.

"What the fuck, Mickey," Solomon objected.

"You listen to me, you old fuck. I saved Myron from the electric chair. Do I need to spell it out for you? I own you and Myron."

Solomon didn't need a dream to see this was coming. His son's stupidity had backed him into a corner and Mickey Coppola was going to milk this for all its worth. But Myron as Mayor of New York City? This would certainly be a humbling and embarrassing defeat for Myron. But at this point it was probably time to stop protecting his son.

Solomon sat at the table alone after Mickey left. A roar at the television caught his attention. The game had just ended. Apparently, he missed seeing the Giants kick a field goal. But he did see the final score, which was Giants 24–Bears 20. The Giants had beat the spread, meaning Solomon lost his bet.

He grabbed the table with both hands. The shock of hearing the score nearly caused him to fall off his barstool. As both teams walked off the field Solomon realized that his dream of the final score was wrong.

When Solomon got home and lay down upon his bed, all he could think of was the final score, and what that meant, which was that a dream had failed him. This had never happened before. *Could this be the end for me?* he wondered.

Chapter 29

The records room was in the sub-basement of the Forty-fourth Precinct in the Bronx. Arnold and his secretary Agnes faced row upon row of musty old records, stored in rusty metal filing cabinets. A strange odor that they could almost taste enveloped the windowless storage area.

Arnold was told by the mayor on a phone call that he had unlimited access to any of the records the precinct had in its procession.

"Get me something we can use on the Blasses," the mayor demanded.

"Let me see what I can find. Perhaps there is something that can explain the roots of this new partnership."

"Good. And one more thing. A few days ago our boys downtown had a raid of a brothel go south. Somehow this super tight-lipped sting operation leaked. The plan was to send in an undercover detective as a john and provide cause to raid the place. But what happened instead was when the detective arrived, none of the girls would accept money in exchange for sex. The detective looked foolish, and the sting never proceeded. How they got the heads-up was a mystery. See if there's any connection to Coppola or the Blasses," the mayor said.

"What are we looking for?" Agnes asked, scanning the files in an opened filing cabinet drawer.

"I'm not sure. The mayor wants to find dirt on Solomon or Myron. We need to find a reason to press them legally. But they always seem to be a step ahead of the law."

"But what about that cobbler, Moshe? Wasn't he supposed to help?" Agnes asked.

"You're not supposed to know about that."

"I've been working for you for over twenty years, Arnold. You think I don't see or hear things?" Agnes said with a smirk.

"I suppose you do," Arnold agreed. "Sadly, I don't think that the *tzaddik* can help. The trip to Safed did ignite something inside him, but what if it's not enough to stop a mobster, like Solomon? Maybe there's another way through something we find here," he said, glancing at the multiple rows of five-foot high filing cabinets.

Hours later, Agnes pulled a file and showed it to Arnold. "I think I found something."

"What do you have?" Arnold said, walking down the corridor formed by the arrangement of the cabinets.

Agnes brushed back a lock of her red curls and pointed to something inside a faded yellow folder as Arnold approached. "This is a transcript of a surveillance at Solomon's home on City Island taken two years ago. It's a conversation between Solomon and his son Myron."

"Can I see?" Arnold said. He read aloud.

SOLOMON BLASS: What took you so long?

MYRON BLASS: Traffic, sorry Pops.

SOLOMON BLASS: All right, just sit down.

MYRON BLASS: Sure, okay.

SOLOMON BLASS: I had a dream last night about Leo.

MYRON BLASS: Leo Gorpatsch?

SOLOMON BLASS: We were fishing out on the Sound.

MYRON BLASS: What did he say?

SOLOMON BLASS: He said that our enemies are not who we think they are.

MYRON BLASS: Who are they?

SOLOMON BLASS: That's the troubling part. He didn't say.

Arnold looked up at Agnes and shrugged.

"What does that mean?" she asked.

"I don't know. Are there any more transcripts in the file?"

"Let me see. Yes, here is another one," she said, handing it to Arnold.

SOLOMON BLASS: Did you read the paper this morning?

MYRON BLASS: So it finally happened. I was wondering why it took so long. You told me about this almost a year ago.

SOLOMON BLASS: Big deals like this takes time. But we did well. I see that Singer agreed to buy Container Corp for eighty-six dollars per share. What did we buy it at?

MYRON BLASS: I bought ten-thousand shares at twenty-four, when you told me about your dream.

"Oh my god, Agnes. I think Solomon knows things will happen through his dreams."

"His dreams predict the future?" Agnes asked.

Arnold looked at her and drifted off into thought, before he added, "How else does he know about all these things before they happen?"

"These transcripts mean that the police know about this. Why don't they do something?"

Arnold shook his head and said, "It's not a crime to dream, Agnes."

"But then how could he be stopped? He would know what's coming ahead of time and prevent it from occurring."

Arnold let out a long sigh. "I don't know. But I suppose you're right."

Chapter 30

"How can I run for mayor? I've never held an elected position in my life," Myron said.

"You'll work with a political consultant to get you up to speed on the issues," Mickey said.

"But why would anyone vote for me?" Myron asked, confused.

"You think people vote for the most qualified candidate?"

Myron shrugged. "I assumed so."

"They vote for an image, a fantasy. That's what we'll create. You have the outer package, we just need to refine the inner one. Like what you'll say in speeches and answers you give to interviews."

"But to run against Mayor Douglas? I've seen him on television. He always appears composed and professional. What if we end up in a debate?"

"Let me worry about that. You just follow the program, we'll do the rest," Mickey said.

"I don't know, Mickey. This sounds nuts."

Mickey flicked a few ashes off his cigar and glared at Myron for a moment before speaking. "Let me say this to you once. Like I told your father, I own you. You'll do what I want and quit bitching about it. You understand me?"

Myron took a breath, and let it go with a nod. "I understand. When do we get started?"

"Good, now go and get back to the party. Mingle and introduce yourself around. There are some important people here today to meet you. I'll catch up with you soon. I have a few things I need to attend to first," Mickey said.

Myron stood up from the tufted upholstered chair sitting in front of Mickey's desk and turned to walk out. Standing in his way was one of Mickey's men. Myron looked up to the wall of a man, then turned to Mickey for an explanation.

"It's okay, Billy," Mickey said as Billy stepped aside, allowing Myron to leave.

As Myron left the well-appointed office and searched for the doorway leading to the festivities in the backyard, he thought about what his father had told him.

"As crazy as it sounds, Mickey is going to ask you to run for mayor and I don't see much choice for you but to embrace it. Perhaps something good can come from it."

Myron couldn't imagine what that good could possibly be, but as with most things in his life he would just see where life led him, and at this moment it was leading him to Mickey's beautifully landscaped backyard that featured a magnificent view of the Long Island Sound. A large tent was set up where people were being served drinks and appetizers while listening to the sounds of a live band playing "In the Mood" by Glenn Miller.

Myron tugged down on his suit jacket and adjusted his tie. He knew he looked good, as people's heads turned to see him walking across the lawn. He ordered a scotch and wandered over to the water's edge to take in the view and calm his nerves with a drink. *Today will certainly be a multi-drink afternoon,* he decided.

He smelled her, before he saw her. At first he thought it was the rose bushes blooming nearby. Then standing next to him was a young woman.

"Hello, Mr. Blass," the woman said.

Myron turned, and saw her. He took a step back to look at her. "Hello," he managed to say.

"I'm Niko, Mickey's daughter," she said, offering a stunning smile that accompanied her brilliant green eyes.

"Mickey's daughter?" Myron said, offering his hand.

She shook his hand. "I've heard Father speak of you."

Myron turned his head toward the house, looking over to see if anyone was observing their conversation.

"You seem nervous, Mr. Blass," Niko said.

"Your father has that effect on people."

"Don't be. Come, let me show you something," she said and led him down a meandering staircase made of large quartz stone steps.

Myron watched Niko's hips swing back and forth. Her yellow dress flowing softly over her gentle curves. Her bare legs extended with each step downward. The majestic view of the landscape no longer drew his attention.

"Here we are. Isn't it beautiful?" she said, gazing at the waves splashing upon the boulders along the rocky shoreline.

"Magnificent," Myron agreed.

"Tell me, Mr. Blass, are you married?"

"No, I'm not, and please call me Myron."

"You're not married? Such a handsome man. How is this possible, Myron?"

Myron could feel himself blush. This young woman was playing with him. He would love to have her. *But she's Mickey's daughter. This would not end up well.*

"I don't know. I guess I never found the right woman. Perhaps we should get back to the party," he said, pointing back up the stairs.

"Of course, come, let's go," she said, grabbing his hand and leading him back up the stairs.

A few steps short of the top, she turned and kissed Myron on the cheek and said, "Let's keep in touch, Myron. You can find me at the Stork Club. It's Daddy's place. I work there on weekends."

She turned and ran off like a little girl. Myron stood there watching. His heart pounded lustfully for the young gorgeous woman. But he could not allow himself to give in to the temptation. An affair with Mickey Coppola's daughter was certainly a fool's game.

Chapter 31

Jack's strong hands helped out Moshe with one skill that was getting harder as he aged—the cutting of the leather soles into shape.

Except for the beginning years with his father, Pincus, Moshe always worked alone. Now that Jack was assisting him he no longer worried if he needed to run an errand or even just use the bathroom during business hours. Jack was reliable and brought a cheerful attitude toward each day.

Jack told Moshe that he came from a small town outside of Austin, Texas, called Johnson City.

"You have any family?" Moshe asked.

"Both my parents died in a fire when I was thirteen. Pretty much I lived on my own for about ten years. I got a job working on a horse ranch. That's why I have a feel for the leather. They had me repairing saddles. Then last year a friend of mine was heading to New York City for a job interview and asked me if I wanted to tag along. I dabbled a bit as an artist and thought maybe I could be discovered. But the real reason was, I had nothing better to do, so I went."

"What happened to him?"

"He went back home, and I decided to stay. My art was not as good as I hoped for and with no money, things spiraled down quickly, and I ended up living on the streets. Eventually, I made it up to St. James Park, where you found me."

"Well, you got a second chance, Jack. My wife thinks I lost my mind hiring you and renting out my basement. Don't make me regret it."

"I promise you, I won't, Moshe," Jack said.

"You're looking good, now that you're cleaned up," Moshe said.

Jack ran his fingers through his blond hair and looked down at his new clothes and smiled. "I feel good, Moshe. Thank you."

Just then, the front door opened and in walked Gray.

"Good afternoon, Moshe," Gray said.

"It's good to see you, Gray. How can I be of service?" Moshe asked.

"Have you hired an assistant?" Gray asked, seeing Jack behind the counter sweeping the floor.

"This is Jack McCoy. Jack, this is Gray."

Jack walked over and shook Gray's hand. "Pleased to meet you, sir."

"Moshe, could you spare a few minutes and visit with Mr. Lieberman?"

"Let me guess. He wants to meet with me right now."

Gray smiled and opened the front door for Moshe.

"Very well, Jack, you're in charge. I'll be back shortly."

"I got it covered. Don't worry, Moshe."

Moshe looked at Jack and nodded. "Let's go, Gray."

When they reached the doors to the Paradise Theater, Gray said, "I have a few things to do. I'll catch up with you later, Moshe. Just head upstairs. Mr. Lieberman is waiting for you."

Moshe nodded and headed inside.

"Good afternoon Moshe," Agnes said as he walked in.

"Hello, Agnes, how are you?" Moshe asked.

"I'm well. Go right in, he's waiting for you."

"Ah, Moshe, thank you for coming. Please come in. Can I get you something to drink? Perhaps a schnapps?" Arnold said, pointing to the glass bottle sitting on the small bar nestled in between bookshelves.

"Sure, why not."

Arnold walked over, picked up a glass, and held it to the light. He shook his head and grabbed a cloth napkin, polishing away a few spots. "That's better."

He poured two drinks and handed one to Moshe.

"L'chaim," they toasted.

"There are a few new developments I want to tell you about," Arnold said, sitting on the chair next to Moshe.

"What's is it?"

"I was doing some digging in the police archives and I came across this transcript of a conversation between Solomon and Myron," he said handing the pages to Moshe.

Moshe put on his reading glasses and read the document. He looked up to Arnold and said, "I don't understand what this is?"

"It's a conversation between Solomon and Myron. Apparently Solomon is a prophetic dreamer. He can foresee future events in his dreams."

Moshe stroked his chin. "That's hard to believe."

"Think about it, Moshe. How did Myron know to find us in Safed?"

"Are you saying that Solomon foresaw our trip in his dream?"

"Makes sense, doesn't it?" Arnold said.

Moshe nodded slowly. "You're right, there's no other explanation. So now what? Is there a way to stop Solomon from dreaming?"

Arnold stood up, looked out the window at the traffic below on the Grand Concourse and said, "No I don't think so, but at least it's something."

"I suppose," Moshe said rising from his chair.

"Wait, Moshe, there is one more thing. There is a rumor circulating around City Hall that Mickey Coppola is grooming Myron Blass to run for mayor in next year's election."

"That's crazy. The guy who tried to murder me is going to run for Mayor of New York City?"

"I agree, it's ludicrous. But what if it's true, and he actually wins. What then?"

"Arnold, I really don't know. Can we discuss this another time? I need to go back to work."

"How's it going with that Jack person?" Leah asked.

Moshe was drying the dishes with his back toward Leah.

"He's good with his hands and remembers to smile at the customers. I'd say that's a good start."

"How much rent is he paying?"

Moshe put down the damp dish cloth and turned to face his wife. "Leah, he has no money. Let him work for a while, then he will pay us twenty-five dollars per week."

"That's it? You can't rent anything as nice as we have for that cheap."

"Okay, but we never rent it out anyway, so it's all found money."

"I don't like it, Moshe. I'm telling you now, this won't end up well," she said.

"It will be fine, Leah. Stop worrying. I'm going to bed," Moshe said, leaving Leah sitting alone in the kitchen.

The next morning Moshe awoke and went into to kitchen to brew himself a pot of coffee. As he scooped the grinds into the percolator basket, he recalled a dream he had just before waking. It was unusual because unlike most dreams, he could remember this one vividly.

He was working in the cobbler shop when Gray walked in.

"Come with me, Moshe," Gray instructed.

"Not now, Gray, I'm busy," he said, pointing to piles of shoes haphazardly scattered on the shop floor.

"You must come now, Moshe."

Moshe followed Gray out the front door of the cobbler's shop and was suddenly in a bar.

"Where are we?" Moshe asked.

"I need to show you something," said Gray.

Gray pointed to another table where an old man was sitting.

"Who is that?" Moshe asked.

"That's Solomon Blass."

Moshe looked at the man. *"Myron's father?"*

"Yes, he is the rasha. You must destroy him," Gray said.

"Destroy him? What do you mean?"

"You will destroy him here— In your dreams."

"I don't understand."

"The power of this rasha is in his dream state. This is where you must take the fight."

"Why are you here, Gray?"

"To show you the way. But you must perform the act."

"What act?"

"To destroy the rasha."

Moshe poured himself a mug of coffee and considered his disturbing dream. Why was Gray telling him to destroy Solomon in his dreams, of all places?

He sat down at the breakfast table, stared out the window, sipped at his coffee and wondered how his life and Solomon's had suddenly became intertwined. First was Solomon's awareness about his trip to Safed and now this dream.

Moshe's hands started to shake, spilling some coffee. He put the mug down, closed his eyes and massaged his forehead. What dark tunnel had he entered? Would there be a flicker of light that he could follow, or was this a cavernous black hole with no way out?

Chapter 32

The taxi ride from City Island to the Grand Concourse took about forty-five minutes. Solomon used his cane to help himself out of the back of the cab and stood before the cobbler shop.

"Wait for me. I won't be long," he instructed the cabbie through the open window.

The cabbie nodded and kept the meter running.

Solomon opened the door and saw a young man with blond hair. "Are you the cobbler?"

"No, sir. I am a helper. Can I help you, sir?"

"Where's the cobbler?"

"Moshe just stepped out for a minute. He should be back soon. Would you like to wait for him?"

Solomon clenched his lips in frustration but resigned himself, sitting in the lone chair by the front window and waiting for the cobbler. He looked across the street at the marquee of the Loew's Paradise Theater. Playing was the Alfred Hitchcock thriller *Psycho*, starring Janet Leigh. Solomon seldom went to the movies, but this one he might actually make an effort to go see, he thought.

Just then, Moshe walked in.

"Moshe, this gentleman has been waiting to see you," Jack said.

Solomon pushed himself up with his cane and stood before Moshe. He was several inches taller than the cobbler.

"How can I be of service?" Moshe asked.

"My name is Solomon Blass."

Moshe said nothing, but gave a frightened stare that pleased Solomon.

"Do you know who I am?" Solomon asked.

"You're Solomon Blass. Why are you here?"

"I want to talk to you about your father, Moshe."

"My father? What about him?"

"Your father, Pincus Potasznik, murdered my friend, Leo Gorpatsch."

Moshe drew back, blinked slowly and said, "Leo Gorpatsch was your friend?"

"We grew up together in Poland. By the time I immigrated to America he was already gunned down by your father."

"Leo Gorpatsch was a gangster and got what he deserved," Moshe said sternly.

Solomon wagged his finger at Moshe and said, "Your father never paid for his crime."

"My father's dead."

"Then the son must pay for his father's misdeeds."

"Is that why your son tried to kill me?"

"Consider that just a warning, Moshe."

"Are you threatening me, Solomon? I have a witness." Moshe said, pointing to Jack who was watching the interaction.

Solomon looked at Jack, and then back at Moshe and said, "Watch yourself, cobbler. I'm not a man to trifle with, and tell your councilman-friend that he needs to back off, or he too will feel my wrath."

"I think it's time for you to leave," Moshe said.

Solomon held his cane out like a sword for a moment, before placing its tip back on the floor, walking out the door, and back into the waiting taxi. "Take me back to City Island," he said.

During the ride Solomon smiled, thinking about the fear expressed in the cobbler's eyes as well as the surprise when he named his father as Leo Gorpatsch's killer.

Solomon knew that his threat of telling Moshe that he must pay for his father's crime was an idle one, but it worked in shaking Moshe up.

Later that evening, after his nightcap at Charlie's and on his short walk back home, Solomon found himself thinking again about Moshe the Cobbler. Despite the fact that he had managed to frighten Moshe, and despite the fact that as a man, Moshe was certainly not a threat, as a *tzaddik* he could be something else entirely. Solomon knew that *tzaddikim* demonstrated their divine ability only through the will of Hashem, so, naturally, Moshe would not have displayed any outward physical or verbal aggression toward Solomon during their encounter. But that didn't mean he wasn't capable of much greater power under other circumstances. Solomon had hoped that his visit would have confirmed that indeed Moshe was one of the thirty-six. But in a way, he already knew, especially after what Myron had told him.

"I don't know what it was, Pops, but just after the rabbi fell to the floor he was in obvious pain. We all saw it. Moshe then knelt down and comforted him. The agony seemed to disappear upon his touch. The rabbi was truly at peace for a few moments, before he passed."

Okay, so he had the power of an empath, Solomon thought. But that was hardly an existential threat to him, and regardless, he was pleased he finally got to meet the man.

The Righteous One 131

Solomon headed straight for his bedroom. Perhaps a dream tonight would enlighten him.

He taught himself when he was in his twenties to keep a journal next to his bed and immediately record his dreams, or they would fade quickly if he waited too long. After a while, he became lucid, where he knew he was dreaming and was able to force himself to wake up in order to write down his dreams.

This worked beautifully for years and made him and his son wealthy men. But something went wrong on the Giant's football game. This never happened before and was most troubling for Solomon.

Results from games didn't come to him like reading a score in the newspaper the next day. A visitor would come to him in his dream and show him something.

The last visitor was a man dressed in all gray. In his dream they were sitting together at the Giant's game, and Solomon saw the scoreboard showing the score of 21-20, with no time left on the clock. He woke himself at that moment and wrote the score down. But it was wrong, and he needed to know why.

That night he dreamt of the gray man standing on his front porch.

"Who are you?" Solomon asked.

"I am Gray," he said, with darkness surrounding the stranger, making it difficult to distinguish the man among the shadows.

"It was you who showed me the wrong score," Solomon said.

"I needed your attention."

"Why are you here?"

"I have been looking for you." His voice blended with the swirling winds.

"Why?" Solomon asked, again.

"To make things right," Gray said. His image vaporized into the shadows.

Solomon woke himself. His hands were shaking as he wrote down the ominous words spoken by the visitor named Gray.

Chapter 33

Myron had not been this excited in years. Tonight he was going to the Stork Club on Fifty-Eighth Street in Manhattan. He had heard the stories of the movie stars, celebrities and the wealthy who frequented the infamous nightclub. Famous couples like Lucille Ball and Desi Arnaz, Marilyn Monroe and Joe DiMaggio, Nancy and Ronald Reagan were frequently seen patronizing the establishment.

But he couldn't care less if he met someone famous tonight. He was going to see Niko. Since their meeting at her father's estate he hadn't been able to stop thinking about her.

He looked at himself in the mirror, wondering if he could keep up with this twentysomething-year-old beauty. He had just turned forty-five, but people said he looked younger. He imagined himself with Niko in a rapturous embrace, tearing off each other's clothes, sweaty bodies intermingled, giving in to their passions.

He instructed his driver Benjamin to open his car door when the black Cadillac Coupe de Ville arrived. As they pulled up, Myron could see people gathering at the entrance to catch a glimpse of a celebrity entering the club.

Of course, no one noticed Myron as he stepped out onto the sidewalk. He shrugged and thought, *Perhaps when I run for mayor, I'll be recognized.*

The entrance to the Stork Club reminded Myron of a foyer of a grand mansion on Fifth Avenue, where he was once a dinner guest. After he dropped his overcoat at the coat check, he walked over to the podium where people were gathered asking the hostess for a table.

Myron waited by the podium for his turn. When the hostess returned, Myron saw to his delight that it was Niko.

When she saw Myron, her eyes sparkled in delight.

"Myron, what a surprise," Niko said with a smile that would melt the coldest heart.

She was wearing a tight fitting black cocktail dress that hugged her curves and ended just above her knees. Myron felt a surge of warmth sweep through his body.

"You're looking elegant," Myron said, trying to tone down his excitement.

"Thank you, Myron. I love your suit," Niko said, stroking the suede of his jacket across his chest.

"What time do you get off work?" Myron leaned in to whisper.

"At eleven. Will you wait for me?"

"Sure, I'll wait."

"Come, I'll give you a table," she said, leading him through the crowded floor of the nightclub. "Here's a nice table. I'll pop over when I can, to see how you're doing."

"Thank you, Niko."

Myron sat down at the small table and watched Niko return to the front. She looked back and gave him a smile that caused Myron to kick the table and knock the candle to the floor. He clumsily picked it up and noticed a clump of wax dripped on to one of his alligator shoes.

"Dammit," he said, just as a cocktail waitress approached.

"Good evening, sir, my name is Gina. Can I get you a drink?"

Myron sat back up, took a breath to compose himself and said, "Yes, please. Scotch on the rocks."

Myron looked at his watch. It was still another hour until Niko was free. She stopped by twice to say hello, and even though each visit lasted only seconds, it was like a fix for a drug addict, keeping his carnal desires in a constant boil.

Then disaster struck. Decked out in a black silk Italian suit, surrounded by an entourage of large, muscular men, was Mickey Coppola. He was strutting his confident attitude down the center of the club when he spotted Myron.

"Myron Blass, is that you?" Mickey bellowed.

"Good evening, Mickey," Myron said, his heart now pounding in fear instead of lust.

"This is a surprise. Come join me at my table," he said, sweeping his arm.

"Of course," he said and as he rose from his chair, he saw Niko waving goodbye. She was putting on her coat and walking out the door. He nodded slightly, not wanting to be caught waving to Mickey's daughter, then he turned and followed the mobster to his table.

Chapter 34

The next morning, Agnes ran into Arnold's office in a near panic announcing, "The mayor's office just called. They say he'll be here in thirty minutes."

"Who will be here, Agnes?" Arnold asked.

"The mayor."

"The mayor is coming here?"

"Yes, the Mayor of New York City, Nathan Douglas, will be walking through that door," Agnes said.

Arnold and Agnes had not moved from their perch since the call. They stood overlooking the Grand Concourse from the majestic window, high above the movie marquis.

"Where is he already?" Agnes said, rubbing her hands together nervously.

"Obviously he's late, Agnes," Arnold said.

"Look," Agnes said pointing. "Is that him?"

A black limousine had pulled up in front of the theater.

"Okay, Agnes, get back to your desk and look busy, and let's not bring up what we found about Solomon's dreams. The mayor would think we're nuts," Arnold said.

Agnes hustled out, while Arnold stepped into his private bathroom to check his appearance in the mirror.

Moments later, the mayor and his assistant, Stanley Bennet, entered.

"Mr. Mayor, what an honor, sir. Please come in and make yourself comfortable," Arnold said, shaking the mayor's hand.

"Arnold, it's good to see you. You remember Stan?" the mayor said.

"Of course. Can we get you coffee or water?"

"No thanks," he said, as he and Stan took a seat on the sofa.

Arnold sat across from them on a wood frame chair, and silently prayed that the sofa would hold the excessive weight of the mayor.

"Tell me, Arnold, any updates on Solomon Blass?"

Arnold shook his head. "I'm afraid not. We searched the records at the forty-fourth, but found nothing unusual."

The Mayor shifted to the front edge of the sofa, leaned forward, elbows on his knees and his belly hanging in between his thighs and said, "We've heard some disturbing news."

"What news?" Arnold asked.

"It's actually more of a rumor. Apparently Mickey Coppola is planning to back a candidate for mayor to run against me next year."

"I've heard that too," Arnold said.

"What did you hear?"

"People are saying it's Myron Blass," said Arnold.

"Dammit. I'm hearing the same thing. You think it's true?"

"Sounds absurd, but we shouldn't be surprised."

"We need to make sure he doesn't win. A stooge of Mickey Coppola's as mayor would be a disaster for the city," said the mayor.

"I agree. So what are you planning?" Arnold asked.

"We came here today to get you on the team," Stan said.

Arnold looked back and forth at the two men sitting on the sofa. "I'm already on the team. Aren't I?"

"We want you to run my campaign up here in the Bronx. You'll make the Paradise Theater the campaign office," Stan said.

Arnold leaned back in his chair and gently rubbed the stubble on his chin. "I appreciate that, but what makes you think I can do this? I ran my city council campaign, but never one for mayor."

The mayor said, "It's not much different. Stan will help get you started, and there's some time before things get going." Raising a finger, he added, "You know, Arnold, this can be a boost to your political career if I get reelected. You may want to run for mayor yourself one day, and I can be very supportive when that time comes."

"Again, I appreciate your trust, sir, but—"

The mayor interrupted and said, "Good. It's settled, then. In the meantime, I want you to find out if this rumor about Myron is true."

Arnold sighed and then relented. "Sure, I'll try to do that."

"Perfect," the mayor said, clapping his hands together and standing up.

After the mayor and Stan left his office, Arnold sat in his chair trying to assemble together the many pieces of his rapidly confusing life.

"Are you all right, Arnold?" Agnes asked, snapping him out of his thoughts.

"I'm sorry, Agnes, I didn't even see you come in. I'm fine, just exhausted trying to keep track of what's happening. Speaking of which, I need to make a call. Can you see if you can get Myron Blass on the phone for me, please?"

"Myron Blass? Why would you want to speak to him?"
Agnes asked.

"There's a rumor he's running for mayor, and I want
to ask him straight up if it's true or not."

Agnes shook her head. "That's the craziest thing I have
ever heard," she said exhaling and walking to her desk.

Chapter 35

Solomon sat in his office gazing out the window onto Southern Boulevard. He rarely came into the office, but he wanted to meet with the rabbi to discuss his disturbing dreams. He hadn't said anything to Myron. He had enough to worry about with Mickey's sudden interest in having him run for mayor.

Solomon opened his dream journal and reviewed the past several days. On Thursday was the dream showing him the football game outcome. Then a few days later, came the visit of the gray man along with his ominous warning *of making things right.*

Solomon's dreams had never felt like they'd been infiltrated by an outsider before. There had been visitors, or more like guides. But no one ever like this gray person. *Who was he, and who sent him? Does this have anything to do with the tzaddik?*

His thoughts were interrupted by a knock at his office door.

"Come on in, Rabbi."

"Solomon, it's good to see you. Are you well? You look tired," Henryk said squinting.

Solomon rubbed the back of his neck. "I haven't slept well the past few days."

"What's troubling you?" Henryk said, and took a seat in front of Solomon's empty desk.

Solomon explained his dreams to Henryk.

"I don't know if the *tzaddik* has powers to penetrate one's dreams, but someone has, and I wouldn't be surprised if he's connected," said Henryk.

"What do you think I should do?" Solomon asked.

"If the gray man returns, ask him who he is, and what he wants."

Solomon just nodded, and ran his open palm across his wooden desk top. It had been years since he did any actual work here. That was why his desk was free of a single sheet of paper or even a pencil. He liked his life and wondered if it was time to stop trying to squeeze every dollar out of each day. "Maybe it's time to stop, Rabbi. I've been at this a long time. It looks like Myron has found a place for himself."

"There's nothing wrong with spending your remaining days just fishing, and hanging out at Charlie's," Henryk said.

In the taxi on his way back home to City Island Solomon had a feeling that perhaps he should listen to the rabbi and retire, and let Myron take full control of their enterprise. After all, it was only a matter of time, maybe a few years, that his body would die. It wouldn't be a bad idea if he took what was left of this life and focused on the passing of his soul into the afterlife. He convinced himself that he wasn't afraid of death. Though when the time came, he wondered if he would feel so brave.

Chapter 36

"I'm going to grab a sandwich at the deli. Can I pick up something for you, Jack?" Moshe asked.

Jack looked up from the worktable where he was cutting into a hide of leather. "I would love a corned beef sandwich," he said reaching into his pocket.

"It's on me, Jack, and I'll get you one of those garlic pickles that you love, too."

"Thank you, Moshe," Jack said with a warm smile.

Moshe walked out of his cobbler shop and crossed the busy Grand Concourse to the delicatessen. As he stepped onto the curb, he saw Arnold walking toward him.

"Hi, Arnold, where you headed?"

"Right here for lunch, care to join me?"

"Absolutely," Moshe said holding the door open for Arnold.

The two men squeezed into a small table by the window, ordered and within a few minutes were served their sandwiches.

"So, Moshe, who is this new guy you hired?" Arnold asked in between bites of his overstuffed pastrami sandwich.

Moshe explained the story of how he stumbled upon Jack sleeping under the bushes in the park and ended not only hiring him, but also renting him out his basement to live in.

Arnold scrunched his forehead and asked, "Do you trust him?"

"Sure I trust him. He's a good man," Moshe said taking a sip of his cream soda.

"You're a better man than I am."

"Nonsense, Arnold. You're a good and generous person. Speaking of employees, what's happening with Gray? I haven't seen him around lately."

"Agnes just said the same thing. He does that at times. He disappears for a few days, then he's back," Arnold said.

Moshe thought of his dream of Gray and asked, "How did you meet him, anyway?"

"He just started hanging around the theater. I really don't remember exactly when. He would help out during showtimes. But he was never actually hired. He just comes and goes. He likes hanging around and doing things for me."

"He came to me in a dream a few weeks ago," Moshe said.

"You had a dream about Gray?"

Moshe leaned over the linoleum table top, and whispered, "He warned me about the *rasha* and said that I must destroy him in my dreams."

Arnold slapped his hands to the table, causing several heads of nearby dinners to turn and look. "This is interesting. Solomon's power comes from his dreams and Gray told you to battle the *rasha* in your dreams."

"Stop it, Arnold. You need to listen to your words."

"No, Moshe, you need to listen to your dreams," Arnold said, wagging a finger at him.

With the sandwich and pickle wrapped up in a paper bag for Jack, Moshe said goodbye to Arnold. Just as Moshe was crossing the large expanse of the Concourse nausea swept over him. His knees buckled, and he almost collapsed in the street.

He barely made it to the other side when he recognized the symptoms. Something terrible was about to happen.

He struggled to his feet and felt a hand helping him up. It was Arnold.

"Moshe, are you okay? I saw you fall from across the street," Arnold said.

"Something bad is happening. Quickly, help me get back."

Arnold helped Moshe stumble his way to the cobbler shop.

Shards of the storefront glass, sparkling in the sunlight, were scattered across the sidewalk. Moshe saw a crop of blond hair before he saw the body. It was Jack. He was on the floor inside the cobbler shop. His head was propped against the counter, his arms dangled alongside his limp body. Blood was seeping through his new white shirt that Moshe bought for him at Alexander's.

Moshe knelt down beside him. "What happened, Jack?"

"He thought I was you," Jack said, and grabbed his belly and cried out in pain.

Moshe gently touched Jack's cheek.

Jack released his grip on where the bullet entered his belly and let go a long exhalation. He looked at Moshe, squeezed his hand, and said, "You've touched my soul."

Arnold leaned over, and asked, "Who shot you, Jack?" But it was too late. Jack was dead.

Chapter 37

Myron was determined to find a romantic place for dinner, one where he wouldn't run into Niko's father. Then he would bring her back to his place, where he knew privacy was assured.

It had been weeks since he had seen her at the Stork Club. Myron knew that Mickey wouldn't think fondly of him dating his daughter. More likely he would insist, in his most persuasive and likely painful way, that Myron not even look at his precious little girl. But Niko was an adult and free to see anyone she desired, Myron convinced himself.

It was late afternoon when he picked up the phone and called the Stork Club. He was hoping to catch Niko preparing for the early dinner crowd.

"Thank you for calling the Stork Club, this is Niko, how may I help you?"

Immediately, Myron felt his face flush. *What luck*, he thought. He exhaled to calm himself and said, "Hello, Niko, this is Myron Blass."

A momentary pause of silence worried him. Then she replied with a smile in her voice, "Myron! It's so good to hear from you! Are you calling to make a reservation?"

"No... Actually, I was calling to ask you out for dinner."

"That would be lovely," she said.

Myron told her he would send a taxi to pick her up from her apartment on East Nighty-Second Street in Manhattan and take her to a small restaurant in Riverdale with only six tables, called Martio's.

Myron had known Martio, the owner, for years, and he promised him complete discretion along with an amazing dining experience. From there, Myron's home was only a short five minute walk, where, he hoped, he and Niko could extend the evening.

When the time arrived Myron paced the sidewalk in front of Martio's like a tiger in a cage. He repeatedly looked at his watch. The taxi should have arrived twenty minutes earlier. Finally, he saw a Checker turn the corner and pull up to the curb.

Niko waved through the window as the taxi came to a stop. Myron waved back and opened the door. She stepped out showing off shiny white boots that ended at her knees. When she stood before him Niko performed a twirl, showing off her outfit. She was wearing the shortest skirt Myron had ever seen.

She grabbed onto Myron's arm and kissed his cheek.

"I'm so hungry. Is this the place?" she said, pointing to the front door.

"This is it. Martio is holding our table," he said.

They entered the restaurant, and the moment they stepped onto the lush carpeting in the candlelit reception area Martio Giovanni appeared to greet them. "Ah, Mr. Blass and Miss Niko, how lovely to see you both," he said in a heavy Italian accent.

"You know my name?" Niko asked, putting her hand over her heart and tilting her head.

Martio bowed slightly at his waist. "My dear, it's all I heard about from Mr. Blass. He described your beauty, but I couldn't imagine such a goddess," he said with a smile.

"Mr. Martio, you are very charming," Niko said, her cheeks a lovely shade of pink.

Dinner was just as Myron had imagined it to be. Niko laughed at his wit and seemed to hang on his every word.

"Tell me, Niko," Myron said, "what's it like being the daughter of the renowned Mickey Coppola?"

She smiled, tilted her head to the side and said with a giggle, "I'm Daddy's little girl."

"So what type of man would Daddy find suitable for his princess?" Myron asked with a smirk.

Niko shrugged. "That's hard to say. Daddy is very moody when it comes to my boyfriends."

Myron nodded and took a sip of his red wine.

"Tell *me*, Myron," she said, leaning in close to him across their table, "have you ever been in love?"

Myron pursed his lip and thought for a moment. "I don't think so."

"Why is that?"

Myron shrugged. "I don't know. I've just never found the right woman—so far. When it happens, I think it will be obvious."

"I like your answer," she said pointing at him with one hand and sipping her red wine with the other.

Myron took a breath and held it a moment while he thought that perhaps he had found the right woman to make a life with—that is, if her father approved.

They finished off two bottles of wine from Montepulciano. They were both drunk, and laughed and stumbled the entire walk back to Myron's home.

"This is it," Myron said, standing before the front door and fumbling with his keys.

"Hurry up, Myron, I need to pee," Niko said.

"Sorry – I got it now."

The door opened, and she ran in. "Where's the bathroom?" she asked, squeezing her legs together.

"Down the hall. Last door on the right."

Niko ran, her boots clonking on the marble tile.

Myron walked into the living room, turned on the light, and walked over to the bar.

"Good evening, Myron," a voice said.

Myron turned quickly and saw sitting in his Queen Anne armchair, Mickey Coppola.

"Mickey, what the hell are you doing here?"

"I see you've been taking care of my daughter," he said stone faced.

"How in the world…" Myron started to say when Niko walked into the room.

"Daddy?"

"Hey, baby girl. Why don't you go wait in the car. I'll be there in a few minutes. I need to speak with your friend," Mickey said.

"Oh, Daddy, why?"

"We'll talk in the car," he said, flicking his hand at her.

Mickey waited for the sound of the front door to close before he spoke.

"Do you really think you can fuck my daughter?"

"We were just having dinner," Myron said.

"Shut the fuck up and sit down."

Myron sat on the sofa as Mickey stood up.

"This is a warning. If I ever catch you even looking at Niko again, I will personally cut your balls off, and shove them down your throat. You understand me?"

Myron nodded.

"You know, Myron, I came here tonight to surprise you, instead you surprised me."

"I'm sorry, Mickey. It won't happen again. What was your surprise?"

Mickey walked over to the window and pulled back the drapes to look outside. He then turned back to Myron. "Tomorrow morning at nine, you will be announcing your run for mayor on the steps of City Hall."

"Tomorrow morning?"

"Look your best and be on time. The press will be there. Big day," Mickey said, walking to the front door.

Myron rubbed his forehead, wishing he was not so drunk.

"Oh, and one more thing. That cobbler who your dad has been obsessed with. The one who you tried killing in Israel."

"Moshe?"

"Yeah, Moshe the Cobbler. He's no longer a problem," Mickey said closing the door behind him.

Myron stumbled out of bed minutes before his alarm clock engaged its annoying ring. He had hardly slept, having woken up every few minutes to check the time. He showered, dressed and finished his coffee before Benjamin pulled the Caddie up front.

"Good morning, sir. Where are we heading?"

"City Hall, Ben. Today's a big day."

"Yes, sir."

Myron gazed out the window. There was so much to sort out from the previous evening. It was apparent that any lustful idea of dating Niko was over. Mickey's threats were not to be taken lightly. At least he was given a second chance. Perhaps Mickey thought he had a real shot of beating Mayor Douglas, and putting up with his bluster was worth the aggravation.

Benjamin interrupted Myron's thoughts. "Hey, boss, did you get a chance to see the Daily News this morning?"

"Not yet, why?"

Benjamin swung his arm over the front seat and handed the folded paper to Myron. "Check out page nine. It's about that cobbler."

Myron reached forward and took the paper. He remembered what Mickey told him about Moshe the Cobbler no longer being a problem.

He turned to page nine and read the headline:

Gangland Style Shooting at Cobbler Shop

Yesterday afternoon, on a busy afternoon on the Grand Concourse in the Bronx, an unknown assailant entered a cobbler shop and shot at close range, Jack McCoy, an employee of the cobbler, Moshe Potasznik.

Mr. Potasznik, who had had fate on his side, stepped out for a few minutes when the incident took place. According to Mr. Potasznik, the assailant thought the victim was him, not his assistant, Jack McCoy. Police detectives are investigating the murder.

"Damn," Myron said.

"That's something, huh, boss?"

"It looks like Moshe the Cobbler has a guardian angel," Myron said, looking out the window as the car sped south on the Major Deegan Highway, toward City Hall.

Chapter 38

Arnold's telephone conversation with Myron the day after the mayor had asked him to look into Myron's intentions had confirmed his and the mayor's fears that Myron was indeed running for mayor.

"Do you seriously think you have a chance against Mayor Douglas?" Arnold had asked.

"It doesn't matter what I think. What matters is that Mickey Coppola believes I can."

"Well good luck to you, Myron," Arnold had said, and then hung up.

Arnold knew that the mayor could outdebate Myron on the issues of the day important to New Yorkers with his eyes closed. But the problem was that voters kept their eyes open, and the outward appearance between the three hundred pound mayor, in contrast to the fit, trim, and good looking contender was dramatic.

"He'll get the female vote for sure," the mayor said, as they watched the news broadcast of Myron Blass' announcement that he was running for mayor.

"Women vote on issues too, Mayor," Arnold reminded him.

"People vote on who they like more, and who wouldn't like him?"

"I know quite a few people who don't. But you're right, we mustn't take anything for granted," Arnold said.

The mayor shrugged, took a puff from his stub of a cigar, blew the smoke up to the towering ceiling of his grand office and said, "What the hell happened yesterday with that shooting? I understand you walked in on it."

"We almost did. Moshe and I missed it by a few minutes."

"Is it true that the gunman thought he was shooting the cobbler?"

"That's what Jack McCoy said right before he died. It was quite upsetting watching the poor man pass," Arnold said, slowly shaking his head.

"I'm sorry you had to see that, Arnold. Any idea who the shooter was?"

"No, but I have no doubt it was one of Coppola's goons."

The mayor pushed his large body out of his sagging and aching chair. He stood by the window and looked out onto the park in front of City Hall. He ran his fingers through his hair and scratched the back of his head.

"It took me thirty years to get here, Arnold. I started out just like you, a councilman. I paid my dues to the political machine here in the city, and this unqualified nobody thinks he could challenge me? And on top of that, how in the world would anyone vote for a murderer?" the mayor brooded.

"Well, he's been acquitted. But I do agree with you, the whole thing is absurd. Even the Republican leadership is nervous about him. But his poll numbers are high. People believe he's a visionary. He's had remarkable business success," Arnold said.

"How does he do it, Arnold? He seems to know things before they happen." The mayor tapped his cigar into an oversized, nearly full ashtray on his desk and continued, "Like that land deal at Locust Point last year. He bought those

The Righteous One 153

properties months before the Throgs Neck Bridge deal was even announced."

Arnold now knew how this was done and wondered if this would be a good time to share his knowledge about Solomon and his dreams. After all, it was the mayor who gave him access to the police archives where he and Agnes discovered the surveillance document. Perhaps the mayor could be convinced of wiretapping the phones, and they could be caught in the act. But in the act of what? After all, it wasn't a crime to have a dream.

Chapter 39

"**M**oshe, all I have to say is thank god you hired that poor homeless man, otherwise it would be your burial we would be going to," Leah said from the passenger seat.

"Leah, please, we are going to Jack's funeral. He's dead because of me," Moshe said, as he turned into the Saint Raymond's Cemetery entrance.

He looked into the rearview mirror and saw Arnold's car following him in. The ceremony would be a small gathering of Moshe, Leah, Arnold and Agnes. Moshe arranged and paid for the burial, as well as for a priest to say a few words.

"It's the least I can do," Moshe added. "Show some respect."

After Jack McCoy was buried, Moshe walked with Arnold back to the cars while Leah and Agnes chatted a few feet behind them.

"I read in the paper about Myron running for mayor. Does he have a shot?" Moshe asked.

"Actually, the polls show him ahead by a few points," Arnold said.

Moshe shook his head. "I don't get it. What do people see in him?"

"You have a biased opinion. He did try to kill you," Arnold said, with a sarcastic smile.

"They've tried twice now, and you know what they say, third time is the charm."

"I've spoken to the mayor about getting you police protection, but he thinks it wouldn't look good politically. You know, since he's running against Myron."

"Seriously, Arnold? Leah is already a nervous wreck as it is," Moshe said.

"I know, Moshe. But it seems that Myron and Solomon have this impenetrable ring of protection around them, and now with Mickey involved, everything becomes more problematic."

"Arnold, when we first met you recruited me to fight a *rasha*. Since then I picked up a few enemies along the way, not to mention the attempts on my life."

"I know, Moshe, and I'm sorry things have gotten out of control. But we must find a way to stop them. With Solomon's foresight and Mickey's muscle in the hands of Myron as mayor, our city is doomed."

"So what do we do, Arnold? Move to Florida? Actually, Leah would like that," Moshe added, with a chuckle.

"I wish it was so easy. But there is no running away from this evil. It will grow larger if we don't find a way to stop it now. Think of your children, Moshe, and your grandchildren."

Moshe nodded. "I understand, but no matter what you say, I have no special powers. I'm a cobbler with a gift of touch that helps people upon their passing."

"Then why are people trying to kill you, Moshe?"

Moshe nodded slowly and said, "Good question, Arnold."

Chapter 40

Myron sat on a long sofa in between two of Mickey's top lieutenants, Sal and Vinnie, watching the humiliating dressing down of Joey Catalano. Myron had just learned that Joey was the idiot who shot Jack McCoy, thinking he was Moshe the Cobbler.

Myron was able to commiserate with Joey's blunder. After all, he too had missed the same target back in Safed, and shot the rabbi by mistake, instead of the cobbler. But Joey's fate was apparently not going to have the same outcome as his.

Joey sat in a wooden chair, his arms bound behind his back, and looked up to Mickey who was pacing the floor around him.

"Tell me again what happened," Mickey barked at Joey.

Beads of sweat rolled off Joey's forehead, even though Myron felt a chill in the room.

"Um, I don't know, boss. I walked into the shop, and there he was, working on shoes in the back. How am I supposed to know he was the wrong cobbler?" Joey said.

"You're a fucking idiot. You ask the man, are you Moshe the Cobbler?" Myron said.

"Oh, yea, right. I-I-I guess I could have," Joey stuttered nervously.

Mickey turned to the men sitting on the sofa. "Sal, you and Vinnie get rid of this fucking moron. I'm done with him."

Sal and Vinnie stood up, grabbed Joey by his arms, his hands still tied, and escorted him out of the office.

"Please, Mickey, have some mercy. I have two small children, and a wife," Joey pleaded.

"Shut him up, I don't want people hearing him barking in the neighborhood," Mickey said, closing the door as they left.

Myron squirmed nervously on the sofa. He gathered enough nerve to ask, "What's going to happen to him?"

"Don't worry about it, Myron. Now let's talk about the campaign. How are things going?"

"Pretty well, but can you tell me why you tried to kill Moshe? You know the police will suspect me."

"They can try. There were no witnesses, no proof. Plus you have an alibi," Mickey said, lighting up a cigar.

Myron tried to remember where he was that afternoon when Joey shot Jack McCoy. Then he pointed at Mickey and said, "I was campaigning in Queens."

"That's right, and there were plenty of the news media covering you."

"Yeah, you're right," Myron said.

"So stop worrying."

"But can you at least tell me why, Mickey?"

"Why do I want Moshe dead?"

Myron nodded.

"I'm trying to tie up your loose ends. If you're going to be mayor we can't have these old problems, whatever they may be, hanging over your head."

"I don't think Moshe the Cobbler is a loose end."

"Then why did you try to kill him in Israel?" Mickey asked.

Myron paused a moment before answering. He certainly couldn't tell him that his father thought Moshe to be this so-called *tzaddik* and a threat to his life. Instead he shrugged his shoulders and said, "I don't know. I guess it was poor judgment."

"Poor judgment? I doubt that. Whatever the reason was, Myron, and you don't have to tell me why you wanted the cobbler dead, just know that you have options," Mickey said with a satisfied smirk.

Myron wondered if Mickey was going to kill Joey, or if it was just a farce in order to intimidate him. Whatever it was, he was finally able to exhale and relax once he was back in his car and heading to his campaign office.

When he walked in his assistant told him that his father was waiting for him inside. Myron opened the door and greeted his father.

"Ah, you're finally here," Solomon said.

"Sorry, Pops, I was with Mickey."

Solomon lifted his body out of the chair and looked out through the glass wall of Myron's office onto the campaign staff milling about. This was the first time Solomon visited his son's new *Myron for Mayor* campaign office in midtown Manhattan.

Myron had been operating out of this location for several weeks and wanted his dad to see the impressive operation. But the news that Myron shared obviously disturbed Solomon. Furrowing his forehead and rubbing the back of his neck, he asked, "Did he say why he tried to kill the cobbler?"

"He said something about tying up my loose ends."

"No, he mustn't touch him," Solomon insisted wagging a finger.

Myron turned to face his dad. "Why, Pops?"

"I've been having this recurring visitor in my dreams lately. He says his name is Gray," Solomon said.

"Who is Gray?" Myron asked, sitting on the front edge of his desk.

"He's a messenger, sent from the *tzaddik*."

"Moshe is sending a messenger called Gray in your dreams?" Myron asked.

Solomon looked up and nodded. Myron noticed his father's hands shaking; he gripped his thighs, trying to control them. Myron had never seen Solomon this frightened before.

"In my dream, I was young, maybe twelve years old and living in the Great Synagogue of Warsaw. I was standing alone in the dark sanctuary where a few flickering candles offered a bit of light in the cavernous space. Then he appeared from nothingness. His shape formed before my eyes. It was Gray, and he was as clear as you are standing before me now. I reached out touched his arm, like I'm touching yours."

Myron clasped his father's hand and said, "Pops, it's okay."

"I looked into his eyes and saw a horizon, miles away. He was drawing me into it and I felt helpless. Do not harm the *tzaddik*," he said.

I asked Gray, "Why do you protect him?"

"He is the hand of Hashem."

"I don't need to listen to you. You can't do anything to me."

"I saw Gray fade into smoke that swirled and evaporated into the cavernous ceiling of the sanctuary. His voice faded with these words, '*You have been warned, Solomon*'."

Solomon broke eye contact with Myron and looked away.

"Pops, are you all right? Let me take you home."

Solomon stood up and grabbed Myron by the shoulders. "Promise that no harm will come to the cobbler, Myron."

Myron pulled his father in and hugged him and whispered into his ear, "I promise, Pops."

"And make sure you tell that ganef, Mickey, not to touch him."

"I will, Pops, I will."

"Good, now take me home."

Myron sat alone in the back seat as Benjamin drove him home after dropping off Solomon. Now that his father was so out of sorts, what if his dreams, which were the most reliable source of information he knew of, were becoming unreliable? This was not what he was hoping for. If he was elected mayor, having his father's foresight would allow him to wield power like never before. Where would he be without it?

In the meantime, he promised his father not to harm the cobbler, but he had no control over Mickey. Maybe with voting only weeks away he could at least convince the mob boss that they should deal with the cobbler after election day.

Chapter 41

Arnold stood at the podium and looked out upon the full house. The only other time his theater had been filled to capacity was during the premiere of *The Ten Commandments* four years earlier when the actor John Derek, who played Joshua in the film, made a live in-person appearance as part of a nationwide promotional campaign.

But tonight's event was not a movie premiere, it was a campaign rally for the reelection bid of Nathan Douglas for Mayor of New York City. Arnold caught the attention of the band leader to bring the music to a close and began his introductions.

As the crowd took their seats Arnold scanned the dignitaries in the first row. Sitting alongside the Police Commissioner was the former mayor, several City Council members from other districts, and Moshe the Cobbler.

Arnold smiled when he made eye contact with the cobbler. Moshe offered a thumbs up, and a warm smile in return.

Arnold's eyes then caught sight of two men sitting directly behind Moshe. It was Myron and Solomon Blass. *I should have known they would be here,* he thought, as a fresh wave of nervousness churned his stomach.

Arnold looked offstage and saw the mayor looking poised while waiting for his introduction.

"Ladies and gentlemen, my name is Arnold Lieberman, City Councilman for the Sixteenth District," Arnold began, to a spattering of polite applause.

After introducing a few of the minor politicians in attendance, Arnold began his speech about the mayor.

"I have known my friend Nathan Douglas for over twenty years. He began his political career as a Councilman in Manhattan's Fourth District. In the past three and a half years as mayor of our city, we have seen a resurgence in the city's economic growth unlike any of his predecessors before him. Under his administration, crime is at an all-time low and he has provided the leadership in raising the educational standards in our public school system.

"Yet, there are still many challenges still facing us. That is why we need to reelect Nathan Douglas for another term. We've heard plenty of bluster and lies from the challenger Myron Blass, who by the way, is sitting in the second row, ladies and gentlemen," Arnold said, pointing.

Myron turned his head around at the audience who were casting hateful glares. Arnold smirked at his spontaneous humiliation of the opponent.

"This man murdered a friend of mine, right before my eyes, yet here he sits a free man, challenging the most honorable man I know, Nathan Douglas. We must make sure that we work hard to reelect the man with more integrity on his little finger then this crook, Myron Blass," Arnold said with an outstretched arm, wagging a pointed finger at Myron.

Myron stood up to a cacophony of boos and hisses. He leaned over and helped his father stand, and they made their way up the center aisle. Solomon, with his cane, followed behind his son.

Arnold continued his taunt over the din of the audience, "We all know that your campaign is being funded by the Coppola crime family. Our city does not want your kind."

This sent the capacity crowd to their feet, cheering wildly.

As Arnold watched from the podium he saw the two men reach the exit doors leading to the lobby. Suddenly, out of nowhere, Gray appeared and blocked the large double swinging doors. It looked like Solomon had stopped dead in his tracks and stared at Gray for a moment. He couldn't tell if words were exchanged, but Gray eventually stepped aside, allowing the men to leave.

Chapter 42

Moshe had a dream that shook him awake. He flipped his legs off the side of the bed and pushed himself up to seating.

Leah was already out of bed. He heard the percolator popping away in the kitchen. He slipped his bare feet into the slippers stationed by his bedside. He needed to gulp down a throatful of coffee before he could absorb his dream. But then he saw the Daily News sitting on the kitchen table and read the large bold block style letters: BRONX COUNCILMAN FIRED!

He ran back to the bedroom, grabbed his eyeglasses from his nightstand, returned to the kitchen sat down and started reading.

Arnold Lieberman lost his job last night as Councilman for the Bronx's 16th District. During the councilman's introduction for Mayor Douglas at his Campaign Rally at the Paradise Movie Theater in the Bronx, several violations of election ethics laws were cited.

The article continued describing the event, and the public takedown of the mayor's opponent Myron Blass.

The mayor sadly said that he had no choice but to relieve Mr. Lieberman of his civic duties.

Moshe put the paper down and put his hand to his mouth. "Oy vey," he said.

"What?" Leah asked.

"The paper... it's about last night. I knew Arnold shouldn't have said those things."

Leah looked over Moshe's shoulder and said, "They fired Arnold? Can they do that?"

"I guess they can. I've got to go and see Arnold before I open up. I'll tell you about it later tonight, Leah," Moshe said, stepping into the bathroom.

"Okay, Moshe, I'll pack your lunch."

"Arnold, what got into you?" Moshe asked as soon as he arrived at Arnold's office.

"I admit it. I let the moment move me, but you know what, Moshe? I don't regret saying it, and if I had a do over I'd say it again," Arnold said, kicking his feet onto his desk top.

"Aren't you the bold one," Moshe said.

"It doesn't matter, Moshe. This councilman's position is starting to annoy me. I told the mayor that I will still help campaign for him. There's no hard feelings."

"But what about Mickey? You're not worried about pissing him off?" Moshe said.

"I said nothing that everyone doesn't already know," Arnold said, taking his feet off his desk.

"Something else happened last night, Arnold," Moshe said, standing up and moving towards the window.

Arnold rose too and touched Moshe's shoulder. "What is it? You look upset."

Moshe scanned the busy concourse and saw his cobbler shop across the street. He looked at his watch, he still had fifteen minutes before he needed to open.

"Last night Gray came to me in my dream," Moshe said, turning his head to face Arnold.

"You had another dream about Gray?"

Moshe nodded and said, "Just like you and I are speaking to each other now. It was that real."

Arnold nodded quickly.

"I was working in my shop," Moshe said, pointing out the window, "and Gray walked in, like he's done before."

"Moshe, come, we need to talk."

"The next moment we are sitting on a bench in St. James Park."

"This is where you met Jack?" Gray said, looking over to the bushes where Jack slept.

Moshe nodded.

"Very unfortunate what happened to him," Gray said.

"The bullet was meant for me," Moshe said.

Gray shook his head and said, "It wasn't your time."

Moshe looked around and felt an unease, then a realization. "Wait a second, this is a dream, right?"

Gray smiled and said, "Yes, Moshe, you're dreaming."

"Oh, for a moment, I thought this was real life."

"Do you think this is not real?" Gray asked, gesturing to the surroundings.

"Dreams are not real," Moshe insisted.

"Why do you say that? Are we not speaking to each other?"

"What does that prove?"

Gray held out his hand, "Touch me. Do you not feel me?"

Moshe squeezed Gray's hand. "I feel you."

"What does that tell you?"

"That you are real?"

"Yes, and if you can become aware that you are dreaming, an entire new world opens up to you. Just imagine

the possibilities of moving around your dream world, with none of the earthly obstructions of your awakened life."

"Sounds entertaining," Moshe said, smiling.

"Entertainment is not the reason for my visits. I am here to show you how to be awake in your dreams for a purpose."

"My purpose? What is my purpose?"

"To destroy the rasha."

Arnold's mouth remained open as he tried to express himself. But no words came out.

"Arnold, are you all right?"

Arnold shook his head, bringing himself out of his stupor. "I could never figure out why Gray started to appear just before I found you. He knows about the *rasha*, Moshe?"

"At least he does in my dreams," Moshe reminded him.

"I have a feeling there's more to it than that."

Moshe scratched his chin and said, "It's starting to look that way."

Chapter 43

The polls were set to open in three hours, and Myron was still in bed with Niko. He wasn't too concerned, because he realized there was only one good outcome - which of course was to win. This way Mickey wouldn't care if he was fucking both his daughter and his wife at the same time. But if he lost, well, he knew that would be worse in so many ways. Not only would Mickey cut off his balls and shove them down his throat for fucking his precious daughter, he would also feed him his fingers and toes, one by one.

He hadn't planned to have Niko in his bed, but he had no choice. She just showed up at his home after midnight. He was practicing his acceptance speech when the doorbell rang and there she was, in her full glory.

"What are you doing here?" he said, looking past her to see if anyone else was there.

"Do you want me to go?" she asked, offering her most alluring smile.

"Come inside, quickly," he said, closing the door, and bolting the lock.

"It's freezing out there," she said.

"I'm surprised to see you after last time."

"I know. Daddy is very protective. But I want to be with you, Myron," she said and dropped her shoulder, allowing her long shearling coat to slip off her.

Myron caught her coat and had to catch his breath as well upon seeing what she was wearing underneath. Her colorful, low cut blouse and short red skirt stirred all his senses. No wonder she was cold.

"Wow, you look great," he said.

"Thank you, Myron. Can you pour me a drink, and help me warm up?"

Myron took two tumblers and poured scotch into each one. He handed the drink to her, pointing to the fireplace. "Would you like to sit by the fire?"

"I have a better idea," she said grabbing his hand. "Show me your bedroom."

In the morning Myron showered, and as he toweled himself off he took a moment to admire himself in the mirror. He was ready for the biggest day of his life, and he felt even better about the woman lying in his bed. But for now, he would have to leave her as he was about to go to the polls at the Riverdale High School to vote for himself for Mayor of New York City.

He leaned over and gave a soft kiss on Niko's cheek. "Wish me luck."

An arm suddenly appeared, wrapped around his neck, and pulled him close.

"Come back to bed," she purred.

"That's a wonderful idea, but you know what today is."

"Oh right, I forgot. Happy birthday," she said, with a laugh.

"Funny girl. If all goes well we will be celebrating at Antonio's tonight. I assume you'll be there."

"Maybe I'll come in a disguise," she said, giving him a kiss on his lips.

"Really? Tell me, what do you have in mind?" he asked, feeling himself getting aroused.

"I always wanted to be a tall, blonde, Scandinavian woman."

"Oh, I like it. What's your name?"

"My name is Ingrid," she said, with a questionable Swedish accent.

"I'll look forward to meeting Ingrid later tonight," Myron said.

With his campaign staff gathered around, Myron fiddled with the rabbit ears on top of the black and white television set. After a few minutes of trying to find a station without the annoying snow or rolling screen images he was finally able to tune to Channel Two News.

The dozen young volunteers who helped Myron with the campaign let out a cheer upon Myron capturing a watchable station. Myron turned, rubbed his hands together and said, "Okay, here we go."

A commercial was finishing for Canada Dry Ginger Ale. Then a graphic appeared on the screen that said *Election Results -1960 New York City Mayoral Race*, which faded to a newsman sitting behind a desk holding a piece of paper in his hands.

"The polls have been closed for two hours and forty-five minutes and we are ready to call a winner for mayor," he said without emotion.

The staff blurted out with conversation that quickly died down when Myron waved his arms, insisting upon silence.

The broadcaster stared into the camera and said, "Based on over ninety-percent of the precincts reporting, CBS News is reporting that the winner for the next Mayor of New York City to be Myron Blass."

Cheers exploded with plenty of back slapping and offers of congratulations. Myron stood up, shook hands and chatted with his staff while they reminisced about the campaign. Then someone asked, "Did you ever think that you could actually win?"

Myron smiled and reflected upon the question. He felt himself breaking out into a cold sweat. He asked the people surrounding him if he could be excused. "I think I need a little time alone to comprehend what just happened."

He walked into his campaign office and closed the door behind him. At the window looking out onto the open area of desks and phones, he pulled the cord and shut tight the slats of the wooden blinds. Except for the continuous buzz of conversation seeping through the thin walls, he was alone.

"I can't believe I won," he said out loud as he sat down in his leather desk chair.

It was one thing running around the city, shaking hands and giving speeches. *But actually winning?* As Myron sat there rolling a pencil back and forth across his desk, he swallowed hard and shouted into his empty office, "What the fuck do I do now?"

The crowd in front of Antonio's filled the sidewalk and spilled onto Arthur Avenue, becoming a nuisance for the long line of black limos dropping off celebrities and politicians. Everyone wanted to be a part of the celebration. Myron Blass was the new Mayor of New York City.

Myron peered out from the window of his caddie at the crowd awaiting his arrival. Television news crews had their cameras positioned. Reporters from all of the city's newspapers were there with photographers poised to capture the moment. He figured that Mickey was behind the big turnout of the press and well-wishers.

Myron wished his dad had decided to go. But he refused. Ever since his dream of the gray man he had sunk into a depression and didn't want to leave the house, except to go to Charlie's.

"This is the biggest day of my life, Pops. I want you there," Myron pleaded, when he called him earlier that day.

"You don't need me anymore, Myron. This is your time, I'm proud of you."

Myron had never heard his dad this way before. He always was upbeat and positive. But the gray man certainly put a scare into him. Maybe his gift of foresight was coming to an end. *This was not great timing*, Myron thought, as this ability would certainly be helpful as mayor. But he had faith in himself that he could do a good job, even without his father's prophetic dreams.

He did worry about how to handle Mickey Coppola. There would be expectations that as mayor he would need to be Mickey's puppet, carrying out his wishes. Unless, Myron thought, he learned how to wield the power of his office effectively. Perhaps he could curb Mickey's influence. After all, he did have the power of the New York City Police Force behind him now.

After waiting in front of the restaurant for a few minutes the crowd started to chant his name. "Myron! Myron! Myron!"

This was the moment to greet his constituents and commence the celebration.

"Okay, Benjamin, let's do this," Myron said to his driver.

Benjamin exited the car, walked around to Myron's passenger door, and opened it. Myron stepped out and the crowd roared. Photographer's flashbulbs exploded, television cameras rolled, and the crowd pressed forward.

The police created a pathway through the well-wishers for Myron as he made his way to the podium set up in front of

Antonio's. Mickey insisted on using his restaurant as the venue for the big event, to which Myron had no objections, and even if he did he knew he didn't want to start disagreeing with Mickey so soon.

After months of campaigning throughout the five boroughs Myron had memorized a handful of stump speeches, written by some political guru Mickey set him up with. He even had Myron take lessons on how to deliver effective speeches. By the end of the campaign he had become a fairly good public speaker.

The speech that he was expected to give was neatly folded up in his breast pocket. He placed it there after reading it on the way to the restaurant, but decided that tonight was his night, and he would, for the first time, speak from his heart, with his own words.

"What the hell was that?" Mickey asked in the private dining room in the back of Antonio's.

"Was it that bad?" Myron asked.

"You're kidding, right?"

"No, I thought I did okay. I spoke from the heart."

"You spoke from your ass. You sounded like a bumbling moron."

Myron gave an awkward smile and said, "I thought it was okay."

"Don't ever go off script again," Mickey said, wagging a finger at Myron.

Myron nodded, but thought that soon this hoodlum would know that he, Mayor Myron Blass, was no one to trifle with.

"Okay," Mickey continued. "Later tonight, after this little shindig, I want to introduce you to some of my business associates. So go out there, Mr. Mayor Elect, and mingle. You're the man of the hour," he said with a sly smile.

"Yes, sir," Myron said, and walked out into the packed restaurant.

Chapter 44

When Henryk showed up at Charlie's Oyster Bar, Solomon raised an eyebrow and said, "Hey Rabbi, what are you doing here?"

"Solomon, you called me this morning and said you wanted to see me. Did you forget?" Henryk said, looking at his watch.

"No Rabbi, I didn't forget." He stroked his forehead and offered a less than reassuring smile.

"Solomon, are you okay? I've never seen you like this before."

"I need to talk to you about my dreams. There's been a visitor."

"A visitor?"

"He calls himself Gray, and he wears only gray color clothing. Even his skin looks gray," Solomon said, and drifted off for a moment.

"Your visitor is a Mr. Gray?"

"No, just Gray," Solomon said, regaining his focus.

"So what does this Gray fellow talk to you about?"

"He told me not to harm the *tzaddik*. I asked, why, do you protect him? He told me that he is the hand of Hashem."

Henryk's eyes widened, and he rubbed the back of his neck. "This is interesting indeed, Solomon."

"Interesting to you. It could be deadly to me."

"Do you feel threatened by the *tzaddik*? After all, he's just a cobbler, what can he do to you?"

Solomon stared at Henryk, thinking of what to say. "He's not just a cobbler in the dream world. There, you can do anything, be anything. A cobbler can even be a warrior."

"Oh come on, Solomon. You've had these dreams all your life. What's different this time?"

"Up until Gray appeared, my dreams just provided me with information of what was yet to come." Solomon lifted his glass, stared at the melting ice cubes, and then looked up to Henryk. "I had a second dream last night, Rabbi."

"Also about Gray?"

"No, this time I was visited by the cobbler himself, Moshe."

"What did he say?" Henryk asked, leaning in.

"He didn't say anything. He just stood there in the corner of my bedroom looking at me, while I was lying in my bed."

"Did you try speaking to him?"

"I asked him why he had come. But he just stared at me and said nothing before he disappeared."

Henryk rubbed his chin, absorbing the details. "What do you think it means?"

"He's learning how to move about in his dreams. Gray is teaching him."

"Are you worried that he can harm you in the dream world?" Henryk asked.

"I don't know, Rabbi. But I need to know how to defend myself, and you need to help me learn how."

Chapter 45

Agnes was reading the Daily News when Arnold walked into the office.

"I can't believe this," she said pointing to the front page headline.

BLASS BEATS DOUGLAS

"I've seen it, Agnes. The whole thing disgusts me. The city is screwed."

"It looks like you would have lost your seat anyway, even without being fired. It's a Republican sweep across the board," Agnes said, pointing to the results.

"It's a disaster."

"What's going to happen?" Agnes asked.

"Looks like the mob bosses will have free rein. Corruption is no longer corrupt."

"What does that mean?"

"Corruption is powerful people doing dishonest things, behind a veil of honesty. If the veil has been lifted, can you still call it corruption?"

"So what do you call it?" Agnes said, staring at the newspaper.

"I wish I knew." Arnold patted Agnes on her shoulder and took a step towards his office.

"What do we do now?"

"I don't know," he said, closing his office door behind him.

Standing by the window overlooking the busy concourse was Gray.

"Gray, when did you get here?" Arnold asked.

Gray turned to face Arnold. He pulled a hanky from his pocket to wipe the sweat off his brow. "Good morning, Arnold. I just arrived a few minutes before you," Gray said.

Arnold took a peek at the thermostat on the wall. It read 68 degrees. Certainly not too warm, yet Gray was perspiring as if it was twenty degrees warmer.

"You're sweating again, Gray. Are you all right?"

"Yes, of course. It's just my constitution."

"Right, that's what you told me. Hey, I've been meaning to ask you. I was speaking with Moshe, and he told me that he had a dream about you," Arnold said.

"Did he?"

"He said something about you warning him about the *rasha*."

"Isn't that interesting. What do you think it means?"

Arnold shrugged. "I was hoping you could tell me."

Gray shook his head. "Sounds like a crazy dream. But the reason I'm here is to ask you what your plans are for dealing with the new mayor?"

Arnold shook his head and said, "What can I do against such a powerful political machine?"

"You organize a resistance, by keeping people informed about the truth. The truth is a powerful weapon."

"How would I do that? I no longer have a platform after losing my councilman seat."

Gray adjusted his gray suit jacket as he stood up. "You have one of the largest venues in all of the Bronx."

"Are you talking about political rallies here, in the theater?" Arnold said.

Gray nodded as he patted the sweat off the back of his neck.

"You want me to back some candidate to run against Myron?"

"No, Arnold. I want you to run against Myron in four years," Gray said.

"Are you kidding? I just got fired as councilman, and I would have lost my seat anyway in the election. I have no credibility, no following. I'm a joke."

"That speech you gave at the rally will prove to be your rebirth."

"What, when I said that we all know that Myron's campaign was being funded by the Coppola crime family?"

"You will provide an alternative for voters in the years to come. But you have work to do."

Arnold listened, and thought about his desire to do something of significance with his life. He tried to stop Myron and Solomon from gaining power by finding the *tzaddik*. But that seemed to have gone nowhere. Perhaps the answer was not in some Kabbalistic fantasy, but from something he could do himself. Maybe he could challenge the new power structure and prove himself as a worthy opponent. But he would need allies with power to take on such corruption.

"Excuse me for a moment, Gray. I need to ask Agnes to make a phone call for me."

Gray nodded, and Arnold opened his door.

"Agnes, see if you can get Mayor Douglas on the phone," he said.

Chapter 46

Myron scanned the crowd from the podium. Seated in the front row were Mickey Coppola and the other Mob bosses. It looked like an FBI most wanted lineup, he thought. This was the second time he had seen all the bosses together. The first time was at his election night celebration at Antonio's when he received their wish lists, which was what he expected: a realignment of trash pickup territories, union contracts for new construction in the city, and of course no interference from the police. Amid all these demands, he wondered if he had the stomach to enable such corruption, not to mention deal with the public backlash that it was sure to invigorate.

Today, he was surprised to see them out in public. The news media were in a frenzy photographing the elite of organized crime in the city. Myron imagined the headlines tomorrow,
MAFIA BOSSES WELCOME NEW MAYOR.

But today was Inauguration Day, and he planned on relishing the attention. He looked down at his speech, took a breath, and began.

"Welcome friends, distinguished guests, and to all the people of New York City who supported our campaign. This has been a tough fight against a strong competitor, and a good man, our outgoing Mayor Nathan Douglas."

Myron paused to allow Nathan to push his hefty body out of his seat at the dais and acknowledge the polite applause from the audience.

"I want to say right here, from day one, that my administration will fight for the good people of our city. There will be law and order. We will fight corruption wherever it rears its ugly head."

Myron caught a glimpse of his father seated a few rows back, who offered a warm smile. This gave him a sudden surge of pride that elevated his tone, and put excitement in his voice.

"I am here, not as a puppet of the powerful, but as a leader for the average man," he said, veering off the written speech in his hands.

"This will be an administration that represents everyone looking to make an honest living, raise a family, and live a rewarding life in this country's greatest city."

A round of applause caused Myron to look up from his speech, and saw Mickey smiling and carrying on with his cronies. Apparently they liked his hollow message, though Myron was feeling an urge of truthfulness in his words.

After the ceremony concluded Myron asked his staff to allow him and his father a few minutes alone in his new office. He stood and looked out through one of the six towering arched windows onto the park. This was a day he would never forget. *How was this possible? Just last year I was a real estate investor, and a small-time bookie in the Bronx. Now I'm the most powerful man in the largest city in the United States.*

Solomon sat in one of the red upholstered chairs looking at his son.

"You've done well, Myron," he said.

"Thanks, Pops."

"I hope you understand, though, that your life is no longer your own."

Myron turned to face his father, who looked tired and old. The past few months had not been kind. He had complained to Myron that he was afraid to sleep, because of what would happen in his dreams. But so far, since the visits from Gray and the cobbler, he hadn't been disturbed in weeks.

"I know, Pops. But I was thinking that I shouldn't just be their puppet. Sure, I'll give them some things to keep them happy, but they will not take total control of this city."

Solomon pushed on his cane to help him up. He walked over to the window and stood by his son.

"Myron, don't think you have any power just because this is your office," he said waving his finger about. "You were put here because of Mickey Coppola, and he won't allow you to do anything he doesn't want done."

"I know, Pops, but let me figure it out. This is my time," Myron said, laying his arm around Solomon's shoulder and giving him a hug.

Solomon looked at his son, shook his head, and said, "Okay, Myron, I wish you luck."

As Benjamin drove up to the front gate he caught a glimpse of Myron in his rearview mirror, and said, "Gracie Mansion, Mr. Mayor. Your new home."

Myron fell silent with reverence as he took in the legendary estate, surrounded by a freshly painted white picket fence and partially hidden by huge oak and tulip trees. With its wrap-around porch and wooden shutters, the two-story mansion looked like it belonged out in the suburbs and not along the river in Manhattan's Upper East Side.

"I still can't believe all of this. It's like a dream."

"You deserve it, sir."

"Thank you, Ben. You've been there with me for the entire ride, and we're not done yet."

"Looks like we're just getting started, boss. I mean, Mr. Mayor," Benjamin said with a laugh.

"You better believe it," said Myron.

After Myron met the house staff, he was served dinner in the mayor's private dining room and then settled down in the master bedroom suite. It was a long day, and he was exhausted. Just as he lay his head upon the feather and down filled pillow, there was a knock at his bedroom door. He got up, put on his robe with word *Mayor* embroidered on it, and opened the door.

"What is it, Frank?" Myron asked the house butler.

"I am sorry to disturb you, sir, but there is a young lady at the gate saying she knows you," Frank said quietly.

"Who is she?"

"She said her name is Ingrid."

"Ingrid?" His heart pounded hard, hearing the name.

"Yes, sir. Should I send her away?"

"No, please show her in, and have her wait for me in the library."

"Yes, sir," Frank said, turning away.

"Oh, and Frank, please be discreet."

"Always, sir."

Chapter 47

Solomon could fight it no longer, and allowed sleep to consume him. Though he was aware he was in the dream world, he was unable to move about like he was accustomed. He felt helpless of his destination, his desires or even an ability to understand what was happening to him.

Smoke swirled in ringlets, as he floated upon silver clouds. Solomon tried to force himself awake, but the dream world would not release him. Like a sauce ready to boil, his fear simmered just below the surface. Solomon knew it could explode at any moment.

Out of the smoke a face formed. It was a face of many shadows, at first unrecognizable, then he understood who it was. Gray was standing before him. Solomon reached out to touch his visitor, but he grasped smoke.

"He is here," said Gray.

Solomon tried, but couldn't speak. Gray vanished, and out of the silver mist stepped a man. There was no denying it, it was Moshe the Cobbler.

Moshe did not smile, but Solomon spotted a light sparkling off a blade in his hand. Moshe suddenly swung his arm back, and then swiftly sliced the blade through the air. A piercing sound of metal cutting through the silver mist rang through Solomon's awareness.

As the blade sliced through Solomon's throat, Moshe said, "I am here to stop you."

Solomon gasped, and clutched his neck. His vision blurred, grayness turned to black.

To Solomon's delight he woke up alive, but not well. He was lying in a bed of sweat. Nausea consumed him. He felt his body sink into the mattress. Even his fingers hurt. He reached for his phone and called his son. Some moronic operator at Gracie Mansion answered.

"I'm sorry, sir, but it's two-thirty in the morning, the mayor is asleep. Would you like for me to take a message?"

"This is his father, you idiot. Wake him up."

He was answered with a click, followed by a dial tone.

Solomon swung his legs off the side of the bed and sat up. His head was pounding. He made his way into the bathroom, where he found an old bottle of aspirin in his medicine cabinet. He swallowed two pills with a gulp of water from the bathroom sink.

He looked in the mirror and ran a finger across his neck to confirm that it was unharmed. His eyes, however, were bloodshot and featured heavy, puffy bags under each one. It looked like his face was slowly melting away.

The nausea soon passed, and his headache faded. He looked out the window and considered a walk, but it was too early. After shuffling around the house for a few minutes, Solomon lay back in his bed, and within minutes fell back asleep and swiftly returned to the dream world.

A black crow perched on Mickey's shoulder. Its beady eyes sparkled back at Solomon. Mickey spoke to a large man whose belly stretched his suit jacket tightly. Antonio placed a large white ceramic bowl of pasta upon the white tablecloth.

"You're going to love this, Carmine," Mickey said.

"What you going to do about that nitwit mayor friend of yours?" asked Carmine, plunging his fork and spoon into the spaghetti.

"I've allowed him some leeway to sow his oats. But that's over, Carmine."

"It better be, Mickey. The other bosses are upset you let him go this far. You know he's pushing for tax legislation on the parking garage contracts."

"I understand, Carmine," he said, taking a sip of his wine.

"I don't think you do, Mickey. I own ten garages downtown. If this law passes, my costs will double."

"Don't worry, Carmine," Mickey said, reaching over and patting Carmine on his beefy shoulder. "I'll get Myron in line."

Carmine spun a load of spaghetti on his fork and shoved it into his mouth. He washed it down with a healthy gulp of red wine and said, "Don't let this fuck get carried away. He needs to be reminded who put him there."

The black crow began to caw and stood behind the table where Mickey and Carmine continued to drink and eat, taking no notice of the bird, or the visitor.

"Solomon," the tzaddik said, and took a step forward.

"What do you want, cobbler?" Solomon asked, standing his ground.

"It's best not to share what you've seen here with your son."

Solomon looked over to the table. The men were gone. But the crow was eating the bread crumbs off the tablecloth.

"I'm not frightened of you, cobbler. You have no power over me."

The tzaddik reached out and grabbed Solomon's forearm. A searing pain shot through him. He pulled his arm out of the tzaddik's grasp. Solomon looked at the burning flesh where he held him. He screamed.

"Pops, wake up," Myron said.

Solomon heard his name as if he was called from deep within a cave. He felt his shoulders shake and he opened his eyes. "Myron?"

"Are you okay, Pops? I've been trying to wake you."

"I'm fine," he said, raising up onto his elbows. "Can you make me coffee, I'll be right there."

"Of course," Myron said, and left his bedside and walked to the kitchen.

Solomon sat up and reached for his journal. Just as he did, he saw a burn mark on his forearm. It was an imprint of four fingers seared into his flesh. He gasped, and gently touched the wound. The pain was severe. He went into his bathroom and found a jar of skin cream in his medicine cabinet, and applied it to the wound. It stung at his touch. He grabbed from under the sink a box of gauze pads and first aid tape. He slipped on his robe and walked into the kitchen.

"Here you go, Pops," Myron said, placing a steaming cup of freshly brewed coffee on the kitchen table.

"Thank you, Myron. Can you help me with this please?" he said handing his son the gauze and tape.

"What did you do, Pops?" Myron asked, staring at the ghastly wound.

"He burned me?" Solomon said, his eyes bulging forward.

"Who burned you?"

"The *tzaddik*, in my dream."

As Myron applied the bandage, Solomon told him his dream.

"I don't understand how something that happens in your dream can result in a real injury," Myron said.

Solomon stood up, grabbed his cane and pointed it at his son. "I need to speak with the rabbi."

"Sure, Pops, I'll have him picked up and brought over right away."

Chapter 48

"**D**ammit, Arnold, what's with the elevator?" Nathan said, stumbling into Arnold's office, drenched in sweat.

"Nathan, I'm so sorry. It broke down a few days ago. We're still waiting for a part to fix it. Come sit down, let me get you some water," Arnold said.

Nathan lumbered himself over to the chair and squeezed himself into the wood frame. "Those stairs nearly killed me," he said, patting the sweat off his forehead with a hankie.

"Here you go," Arnold said, handing him a glass of water.

Arnold watched the former mayor guzzle down the water.

"Thank you, Arnold," Nathan said, looking at his watch.

"You said on the phone that you were coming with the commissioner."

Nathan looked at his watch and said, "He should be here in a few minutes. I'm sure he won't like walking up all those steps. Though he is in much better shape than me."

"Commissioner Aldrich will be fine. I hear he's a runner."

"Better him than me." Nathan chuckled.

Police Commissioner Frank Aldrich had led the New York City Police Department for over eight years. He had a reputation for unwavering integrity and brutal honesty. In his thirty years on the force the word was that he never accepted a bribe and had no tolerance for those who did. Under his watch, the department cleaned house and was known as the least corrupt police force in the country.

But with the election of Myron Blass and his gangster backers, the commissioner's real test was about to begin.

When Frank entered Arnold's office Nathan lifted his heavy body out of the straining chair and said, "Good to see you, Frank. Let me introduce Arnold Lieberman."

"Mr. Lieberman," the commissioner said, extending his right hand.

Arnold gripped his hand, and both men shook hard.

The commissioner smiled, showing off the whitest teeth Arnold had ever seen. But that was only where it started. Obviously, he was interested in making a good impression with his appearance, though Arnold thought it unusual for someone in his position to wear such expensive clothing. But the navy blue silk suit was beautiful, and the commissioner's slim physique only added to its elegance.

"It's a pleasure to meet you, Arnold. Nathan has told me very encouraging things about you," said Frank.

"It's an honor to meet you as well, sir. Your fine reputation precedes you," Arnold said.

"Gentlemen, I wanted us to get together to discuss strategy. We can't wait for the '64 campaign to do something. The city will be too far gone by then," the former mayor said.

Frank stood up and walked over to the window, looking out upon the Grand Concourse. "This is a wonderful building," he said.

"Thank you," Arnold said.

Frank continued, "I like the idea of Arnold running against Myron in '64. We have time to build upon his credentials. I'll hook you up with the right people in the city. Many of the same people Nathan knows, plus a few he doesn't." He turned and winked at Nathan.

Nathan laughed, and said, "No doubt."

"This sounds good," Arnold said, joining Frank by the window. "But what about the meantime? We need to stop Myron from wielding his power now."

As Nathan was speaking, Arnold thought about the battle between the *tzaddik* and the *rasha,* and how the result could affect Myron's ability to govern. The reason Myron got elected was because of his father's prowess of foreseeing events and moving upon them for financial advantage. If that weapon was destroyed the dynamic would certainly change.

This idea of positioning Arnold for mayor involved many moving parts in order to succeed, including keeping Frank Aldrich as the Police Commissioner for as long as possible. Myron could fire Frank at any time and put someone in his place as his puppet.

"You need to show Myron that you're willing to play his game. Give him some wins. Let him think you're with him. This will give us time," Arnold said.

Frank turned from looking out the window to facing Arnold, and asked, "Time for what?"

Arnold took a breath, and considered telling them about the tzaddik, but lost his nerve, and said, "Time to organize our campaign."

Chapter 49

Moshe had been a cobbler for forty-five years. He learned the craft from his father, who in turn, learned it from his father. This legacy of carrying on the family business was well into its third generation, lasting nearly one hundred years.

This thought would occasionally pop into Moshe's head during his daily tasks at work, and cause him to smile. His father would have been proud knowing that after all these years, through good times and bad, the cobbler shop was still there to serve its customers.

Just as he was walking to the front door to unlock it for the day he saw Gray standing and staring at him through the glass.

Moshe unlocked the door.

"Hello, Moshe," he said, the usual beads of sweat glistening on his forehead.

"Gray, what are you doing here?"

"I've come to talk," he said, walking in.

Moshe locked the front door, and said, "Let's go to the back room."

Gray and Moshe sat across from one another at his worktable.

"You know, Gray, I've been dreaming about you," Moshe said.

"That's because I've been visiting you in the dream world."

Moshe jerked his head back a quick inch, and said, "What do you mean?"

"Just what I said. I can enter your dreams."

"How can you visit a place that exists in our minds?"

"If it exists in your mind, then it exists."

"I don't understand."

Gray smiled, and a bead of sweat rolled down his cheek and landed on Moshe's table. Gray wiped it off with a finger. "Sorry."

"That's okay," Moshe said, looking at the salt stain already forming on the canvas table cover.

"Moshe, I have been with you in both the dream world and the awakened world. Am I not real," he said, pointing to the sweat stain.

"This is true. But dreams feel different."

"That's because you're just learning how to awaken within them. As you improve your skills, you will find them just as real."

"But what about you? How do you come from the dream world?"

Gray shook his head. "No one comes from the dream world, Moshe. But if one can awaken while dreaming, then it's possible to move about there."

Moshe paused, trying to comprehend the complexity of Gray's words. "Are you saying that you can live a life while you're asleep?"

Gray smiled and said, "Indeed. I live in both worlds, Moshe."

"Last night, in my dream, I saw Solomon and grasped his arm. My touch burned him. I felt his flesh melt," Moshe said.

"That should shake him up."

"How is that possible?

"It's not possible for me, but apparently you can."

"I can inflict physical harm in the dream world?"

"Looks that way, Moshe. But you'll need to go further than just a burn."

Moshe rubbed his fingers across his lips and asked, "Can the *rasha* do the same?"

"Probably," Gray said shrugging his shoulders with a tilt of his head.

Moshe exhaled and asked, "What will happen if Solomon retaliates?"

"If he can harm you in the dream world, you need to be ready. I am sure his rabbi friend will be offering wisdom from the dark side to battle you."

"When I'm dreaming, I don't feel at all in control. How can I defend myself?"

"It will take time, and practice," Gray said, patting the sweat off his forehead and neck with his hankie.

Moshe stood up and looked past Gray and onto the busy concourse, reflecting for a moment before he said, "I need to destroy Solomon in the dream world, before he harms me. Is that what you're saying?"

Gray nodded. "That's what I'm saying."

Moshe sat back in his chair, contemplating the words Gray spoke. Then he leaned forward and asked, "How do you know these things, Gray? You appear in my dreams, in my life, and you have this knowledge. Who are you? Why are you here?"

Gray smiled, and looked at Moshe. "I was born in Amsterdam in 1915. My father was Frederick van Eeden, a famous Dutch writer and psychiatrist. He liked to write poetry and people described him as a Bohemian, which I gather to mean that he lived an unconventional lifestyle. He hung out with artists and intellectuals."

Gray continued, "Anyway, it was Father who coined the term *lucid dreaming*. He was strongly influenced by Hindu practices, and their belief of being awake in the dream world."

As Gray spoke, Moshe got up, filled a glass with cold water and handed it to Gray.

"Thank you, Moshe," Gray said, taking a gulp.

"Please continue, I'm fascinated," said Moshe.

"Father used me as his lab assistant. I was eight years old when we started. He would watch me sleep, and after a while, he could tell when I was dreaming. When he thought there was a break in my dreams, he would wake me up and I would describe them. That was the first step. Next he started a way to send me a signal that would tell me that I was in a dream without waking me."

"What was the signal?" Moshe asked, with his hand was on his chin, expressing his interest.

Gray grabbed Moshe's hand. "Open your palm," he said.

Moshe did so, and Gray ran a gentle finger across it.

"That was it, and it worked. The light brushing of his finger was just enough for my conscious self to become aware that I was dreaming. Soon, I was able to become lucid without the stimulation, and I have been that way ever since."

"What happened to your father?"

Gray offered a strained smile and said, "He passed away when I turned twenty. But he gave me a gift that few people have."

"But why are you here, helping me?" Moshe asked.

"When you are living in the dream world, you're able to see disturbances. I have been observing Solomon in the dream world for years. His manipulations create an imbalance and I have been trying to find a way to stop him, but without success. That is, until I met you."

"What do you mean he creates an imbalance?"

"The dream world, not unlike the awakened world, requires certain rules or laws. When someone crosses the line at the expense of others, people like me take notice and try to restore order, like a police force."

Moshe turned his palms up and said, "But what's your connection with Arnold? When I first met you, you were working for him."

"That is where Solomon's dreams have led me. This imbalance is not only in the dream world, but it has its reach into the awakened world as well, as you can see with his son Myron, who has no qualms about breaking the law."

Moshe slowly nodded. "This is not easy to understand. But perhaps you can explain your name, and everything else," Moshe said, gesturing to his grayness.

"I call myself Gray because it's my way of moving between the two worlds without notice. I'm visible to those I choose to be—in either world."

Moshe shook his head. "I've never met anyone like you before, Gray."

Gray patted Moshe on his back and said with a smile. "I'm uniquely Gray."

Chapter 50

When Myron finally arrived back at the mansion it was nearly midnight. His workday had begun at six in the morning and concluded with dinner with the Police Commissioner. All he wanted to do was to go to bed.

After his shower, Myron wrapped a towel around his waist and made his way out of the bathroom into his bedroom, when he saw Niko. She was lying under a thin bedsheet on the king size bed, waiting for him.

"What took you so long?"

Myron spread his arms and said, "Niko, when did you get here?"

"Just now, when you were in the shower," she said, offering a sultry smile.

"I'm exhausted. I need to sleep."

"Of course, Myron, you'll sleep. Just not yet," she said, tugging and releasing the knot in his towel.

Like an ember in a hot fire, it didn't take but a moment for Myron to ignite. He lifted the bedsheet, crawled in, and embraced Niko. As they kissed, his heart started to race. Of all his previous girlfriends—and there had been many—he had never felt quite the same way as he did with this one.

He heard the alarm bell ring first in his dream, and it kept ringing until he woke up and reached to turn it off. Myron opened his eyes and saw it was six am. He was scheduled to leave the mansion in thirty minutes and head downtown for more meetings with Police Commissioner Frank Aldrich. Last night was less of a business meeting, and more of a getting to know you dinner.

Myron liked that Frank was interested in what he had to say. He even surprised Myron by offering to implement a few of his ideas. This was more respect than he ever got from Mickey and his lineup of mobsters. *What if I could dial back the criminal influence a bit and become a mayor that people can actually be proud of?* he wondered. *Wouldn't that be something?*

He imagined himself being praised by the news media as the savior of the city. The mayor who punished the mob and regained the city for the people. This made him smile as he looked at himself in the mirror.

Niko was still asleep and would be for several more hours. He gently kissed her cheek, and thought he heard a soft moan.

When Myron reached the garage his car was waiting for him, but Benjamin wasn't there. Someone else was sitting in the driver seat. As Myron walked over to the driver-side window, it rolled down and a man with slicked back black hair and matching black eyes told him to get in.

Myron took a step back and was met with a hard object jamming him in the kidney.

"Get in," the voice said.

The back door was opened, and Myron climbed in.

"Slide over," the voice said.

Myron was sitting in between one of Mickey's goons and Mickey himself.

"Good morning, Mr. Mayor," Mickey said.

"How did you get in the garage? Where the hell is my driver?"

Mickey rolled his head to the side and said, "He woke up with a headache this morning. Not to worry, he'll be fine."

"What the hell are you doing, Mickey? I'm the goddam mayor. You can't kidnap me."

"Stop worrying, Myron. I'm not kidnapping you. We have a meeting to go to."

"And so do I, with the commissioner in fact."

"Well, isn't that a coincidence, Myron. That's exactly where we're going, too."

The car sped down FDR Drive with two police motorcycle escorts opening a pathway through the morning rush-hour traffic. Twenty minutes later, they pulled into the underground garage of One Police Plaza.

"Here we are," Mickey said.

The men exited the car and took the elevator to the tenth floor where the commissioner's suites of offices were located.

"We're here to see the Commish," said Mickey to the receptionist.

An older woman with black rimmed eyeglasses looked up at Mickey and offered a look that said, *who the hell are you?* But when she saw Myron she sat up tall and said, "Ah, Mr. Mayor, the commissioner is waiting for you. Let me tell him you're here."

Just as she was about to press the intercom button on her phone Mickey reached over and grabbed her hand. "Let's surprise Frank, why don't we?"

The receptionist pulled her hand away as if she was being touched by someone with a communicable disease.

Mickey gave her an awkward smile and approached the office door. He turned the knob and entered with Myron following behind him.

"Mr. Commissioner, so good to see you," Mickey said.

Frank was sitting at his desk. He quickly rose and put his hands on his hips, obviously annoyed at the sudden intrusion. "Mr. Coppola, this is a surprise. Tell me, what's this about?" Frank said.

"Call me Mickey. May I call you Frank?"

Frank nodded.

"I would like for the three of us to have an understanding," Mickey said, gesturing to Frank and Myron.

"What kind of understanding?" Frank asked, shooting an inquisitive look at Myron.

"Let's stop pretending. I'm expecting a certain level of cooperation from your people."

"My people?"

"Do I need to spell it out for you? I put this man in office for a reason. He's your boss now, and I'm his. Capiche?"

Frank pointed a finger at Mickey and said, "How dare you threaten the Mayor and Police Commissioner of New York City? We won't be intimidated by a two-bit gangster. Get the fuck out of my office before I have you arrested for threatening government officials."

Mickey stood up and walked over to the door, then turned to face Myron and Frank.

"Careful, Commish, your words may come back to haunt you. Myron, we will talk later," he said, and slammed the door behind him.

Chapter 51

*M*oshe was playing in the woods just north of the village when he heard men coming. He ducked behind a fallen tree to hide. As they approached, Moshe peeked out and saw Solomon and his son Myron pushing a blindfolded man with his hands bound behind his back.

They pressed the man against the tree and removed the blindfold. It was Moshe as an old man.

Moshe stood up, exposing himself to the men and pointed, "Is that me?"

Solomon turned to Moshe the younger and said, "You think only you have the power of inflicting harm in the dream world?"

Moshe stood still for a moment, staring at Solomon. Then he turned and ran toward the village, and just as he reached his home the front door opened and his mother, Clara, appeared.

"Mama, I'm in danger. The rasha is coming."

"Moshe, quick, come inside," Clara said.

He dashed for the door, and just as he did, Solomon grabbed his arm and pulled him back.

"Mama!" Moshe screamed.

But she was gone, and so was the village. He was his elder self again, standing inside his cobbler shop. It was nighttime, the street outside was desolate. He heard the front door squeak open, and in walked Solomon.

Solomon's face was washed in shadows. Only his eyes reflected the small amount of light in the room. He approached holding his cane like a baseball bat, ready to swing. Moshe backed up in fear.

Solomon swung his cane, connecting on Moshe's thigh, just below his right hip.

"Moshe, wake up, you'll be late for work," Leah said, gently shaking her husband.

Moshe opened his eyes. "I'm getting up," he said, and swung his legs off the bed and sat up. He reached for his glasses on the nightstand and slid his feet into the slippers by his bed. When he stood, a sudden pain shot through his right leg, forcing him back onto the mattress.

He pulled down his pajama pants and saw a large purple bruise on his right thigh. "Dammit! How in the world?"

"What's wrong, Moshe?" Leah asked.

"Oh, nothing," he said, gently touching the contusion. He stood up and limped to the bathroom to further examine his leg. He looked at himself in the mirror, and upon seeing his reflection, he recalled his dream.

"Solomon," he said aloud. *But how is this possible?*

Moshe's heart started to beat faster. His bowels churned, forcing him to sit on the toilet to relieve himself. The last time he had been this frightened had been when he was a young boy during the war, when Captain Berbecki and his Russian soldiers dragged the wounded Jewish fighters from the synagogue, lined them up against the wall, and assassinated them by firing squad.

Moshe got dressed. He winced in pain when he pulled up his pants and limped his way through the kitchen, giving Leah a kiss on her cheek as he passed her by. "I need to run, Leah."

"Looks like you're not running anywhere," she said, watching him hobble out the front door.

Moshe greeted Agnes and pointed to Arnold's door. "Is he in?"

"Moshe, why are you limping? Did you hurt yourself?"

Moshe held up his hand and shook his head. "You wouldn't believe it, Agnes."

"What I have heard lately, Moshe, nothing would surprise me."

"You and me both," he said, knocking and opening the door simultaneously.

"Good morning, Arnold," Moshe said to Arnold sitting at his desk.

"Good morning, Moshe. What's with the limp?"

"Solomon did this to me," Moshe snarled.

"What do you mean?"

"He came to me in my dream and smacked me with his cane."

"And you woke up with the injury?"

"Yeah, and you should see the bruise. It's purple," Moshe said unbuckling his belt and pulling his pants down to show Arnold.

"Wow, that's serious," Arnold said, looking at Moshe's beefy, black and blue thigh.

"He did this to me in my dream, Arnold."

"It's time you learn how to fight back, Moshe," said a voice from behind him.

Moshe turned, and saw Gray.

"Gray, I didn't see you," Moshe said.

"It's time to see Noa," Gray said taking a step toward the door and gesturing for Moshe to follow.

"Who?" Moshe asked.

"Come, I'll tell you on the way. Arnold, is it all right if we borrow your car?" Gray asked.

"Um, sure, no problem," Arnold said, throwing up his hands.

At the traffic light, Gray stopped the car. Moshe looked over to Gray, who had his window open even though the weather was hovering around forty degrees.

"I'm freezing, Gray. Can you close your window a bit?"

"Of course, sorry, Moshe," he said rolling the window shut.

"Now can you tell me where we are going?"

"To see Noa."

"Who is that?" Asked Moshe.

"Noa will show you how to live in both worlds."

"I thought you were teaching me."

"I can only show you the very basics. Noa will open your mind to moving about in the dream world."

"How do you know this person?"

"She taught me what I couldn't learn on my own."

"Who is she?"

Gray glanced over to Moshe and said, "She's a descendant of the Jewish mystic Francesa Sarah of Safed, from the sixteenth century. Every eldest daughter since, in this long line of women, were teachers of how to live in the dream world."

Moshe paused for a moment, and then said, "Gray, why do you sweat all the time?"

"Ah, finally, you've asked." Gray smiled.

"You're always sweating, even when I'm freezing."

"The sweats happen when you spend more time in the dream world than in the awakened world."

"Lately I think this *is* the dream world," Moshe said, finishing with a sigh.

"Excellent, Moshe! Once you understand that the two worlds are not much different, then you can travel between both with ease, just like me."

"You speak of this so casually, yet you seem to travel between the awakened world and the dream world effortlessly, except for the sweating," Moshe said with a smile.

"All of us dream every night, Moshe, so there's plenty of time to practice," Gray said, as he pulled into a parking spot on Queens Boulevard.

The elevated train rumbled above as Moshe lifted his aching body out of the car. Gray walked up to a glass door that was obscured with aged white paint. He pressed the bell on the wall and the door's lock buzzed open.

"Come, Moshe, it's time to meet Noa."

Chapter 52

As Niko sipped her coffee, Myron thought how lovely she looked in her blue silk nightgown embroidered with colorful butterflies, that he bought for her at Bergdorf's. They were sitting by a large window, overlooking the freshly fallen snow blanketing the gardens of Gracie Mansion.

"I love how the snow makes everything look so perfect," she said, cradling her cup between her hands, like an eggshell.

"I like it too," Myron said, looking at himself in the mirror and adjusting the knot of his tie.

"Tell me, Myron, what's it like being mayor?"

Myron walked over and took a seat at the front edge of the chair facing Niko. He exhaled a long breath before he said, "I don't know, Niko, I think I may be in over my head."

Niko placed the teacup down and asked, "Why do you say that?"

"You know your father's the one who put me in office."

Niko shook her head. "That's not true, Myron. He may have supported you and financed your campaign, but you were the person people voted for. You were the one who gave campaign speeches to hundreds of groups, day after day. You were the one who debated the former mayor and gave countless interviews to the press. It is you, Myron, who the people of this city believe in, not my father."

Myron sat back in his chair, allowing his stiff posture to relax into the upholstery. "I suppose that's true," he said.

"Of course it's true and I am proud to be here with you as you begin your journey. You're going to be a great mayor. So stop worrying so much and don't let my father rattle you. Show him the respect he deserves and you'll be fine," she said reaching for his hand and squeezing it.

A knock at the door interrupted them.

"Excuse me, sir, you have a call. It's your father."

"Okay. Thank you, Edward," Myron said. He stood up and walked over to the phone on the nightstand.

"Hello, Pops, is everything all right?"

"Listen, Myron, I had a dream last night."

"What was it?" Myron asked quietly and turned his head away from Niko.

"You're not alone, are you?"

"No, but that's okay, just tell me."

"Are you with the gangster's daughter?"

"That's right, Pops."

"Well, you best just listen. There's going to be a hit on Mickey Coppola."

"Are you kidding me?"

"Don't act alarmed. It's going to be tonight at Antonio's."

Myron glanced over to Niko, who seemed preoccupied with a magazine.

"Do you know by whom?" Myron asked, quietly.

"Have you heard of Carmine Rizzo?"

Myron knew this name. He was one of the mob bosses he met at Antonio's the night of his mayoral win celebration. "Yes, I know who he is. Is that it?"

"That's all I saw. Are you going to warn Mickey?"

Myron looked over to Niko and said, "Not sure. I need to think about it."

"Think about what, Myron? You must warn him. Getting rid of Mickey won't make your life easier, don't fool yourself. The other bosses will step in once Mickey's gone."

"I understand, Pops," he interrupted his father. "Let me go. I'll speak with you later," he said, and hung up.

Myron sat in his office at City Hall staring at the phone. He churned over in his mind the benefits of not telling Mickey. If Mickey was gone, then he would have no one to answer to. He was certain that the commissioner would support him and help keep the other bosses from infiltrating influence into his office.

On the other hand, he didn't want to hurt Niko, especially after she demonstrated that she could provide him with the emotional support and practical guidance he craved, not to mention assuming the role as a mediator between Mickey and himself. She deserved to be protected from the heart wrenching grief of losing a father. Myron picked up the phone and dialed Mickey's number.

Later that evening, Myron walked into Antonio's.

"Mr. Mayor, what an honor to have you joining us tonight. Please follow me," Antonio said.

"Good evening, Antonio. I'm assuming I will find Mr. Coppola in the back."

"Yes, please, this way," Antonio said, as he led the way through the crowded restaurant.

Myron was recognized by the patrons who greeted him enthusiastically as he followed Antonio past the tables, and through the door marked PRIVATE.

"Mr. Mayor, I am thrilled you can join us," Mickey said, as he entered the smoke filled room.

"Good evening, Mickey," he said, shaking hands as the gangster rose from his chair.

Still seated at the table, waiting to greet the mayor, was Carmine Rizzo.

"Carmine, it's nice to see you," Myron said, reaching over to shake Carmine's hand.

"What's this, Mickey? I thought we were having a private meeting?" Carmine asked, his face turning red.

"Come on now, Carmine, don't be upset. You know we need the support of our mayor for our businesses to prosper," Mickey said.

Carmine slid his chair back and pushed his hand against the table to lift his fat body to his feet and said, "I'll go use the john."

"Of course, Carmine," Mickey said.

The door closed, and Mickey patted Myron on the shoulder. "It's obvious something was planned. How did you know about the hit?" Mickey whispered.

"Let's just say, I have a good team," Myron said with a smile.

"Indeed you do."

"Are you out of danger?" Myron asked.

"Oh, did you think he would try to kill me here?" Mickey said.

Myron shrugged. "I don't know."

"It would happen outside, after dinner. Probably as I was getting into my car."

"Did Carmine leave to call off the hit?" Myron asked, nodding toward the door.

"Maybe. My men are watching him now."

Myron felt his stomach loosen at Mickey's assurance that there would be no violence tonight. Just as that thought was ruminating in his head, he heard multiple gunshots and screams.

Myron quickly rose and started for the door. Mickey grabbed his forearm.

"It's best to wait here for a minute," Mickey said.

"What the fuck is going on, Mickey?"

"Carmine should know better," Mickey said.

"People saw me coming in here, Mickey. This is fucked up," Myron said, rubbing the back of his neck.

"You worry too much, Mr. Mayor. Those people are my people," he said pointing, "and no one saw you walk in here tonight, as long as I say it's so."

Myron stared at Mickey, then said, "Is this the thanks I get for saving your life?"

Myron stood up and opened the door. To his right, he saw Carmine's legs. He stepped closer and saw the rest of his hefty body sprawled between the bathroom and the hallway. Blood was seeping out of bullet holes and spreading onto the floor.

Myron looked down and saw he was standing in Carmine's blood with his alligator shoes. "Are you fucking kidding me?"

He turned, walked to the first table, grabbed a white cloth napkin, and attempted to wipe the blood off the bottom of his precious shoes. None of the patrons had moved from their tables, and no one dared speak as they watched the mayor finally give up the cleaning, drop the blood soaked napkin, and march out of the restaurant, leaving a trail of bloody footprints along the wooden floor behind him.

Chapter 53

There was a frenzy of activity as Arnold walked into One Police Plaza. Mob hits typically caused an uproar, especially since the commissioner proclaimed that his department was committed to putting an end to the mob's influence, and violence.

When Arnold called to ask if the meeting was still on, he was told that there was a mob hit and he should get downtown as soon as possible. An hour later he was climbing the wooden staircase to the top floor and walking down the double wide hallway to the commissioner's suite of offices. As he reached the end of the corridor the door opened and Frank appeared.

"Arnold, you're here. Quickly, come in," Frank said, holding the door open.

"What's going on, Frank?" Arnold asked.

"Come, let's sit," Frank said, pointing to the two chairs arranged by the window with a spectacular view of the Brooklyn Bridge.

"What's this I hear about a mob hit?" Arnold asked.

"We found Carmine Rizzo's body floating in the East River this morning."

"No shit?"

"Well, that's where he ended up, but the deed was done at Antonio's Restaurant up in the Bronx."

"How do you know that?"

"The mayor told me."

"Wait a second, doesn't Mickey own that place?"

"That's right," Frank said putting his hands behind his head.

"Did he do it?"

"Looks that way."

"Are you bringing him in for questioning?" Arnold asked.

"The mayor told us not to."

"Why the hell not?"

"Myron told me, 'Hands off Mickey Coppola.'"

"Did he say why?"

Frank stood up and leaned against the window, watching the morning traffic over the bridge. He turned to Arnold and said, "He was there when it happened."

"He was where?" Arnold asked.

"The mayor was at Antonio's last night when the hit went down," Frank said, sitting back down.

"Are you serious?"

Frank nodded.

"Does the press know about this?"

"Not yet. According to Myron, Mickey has promised to keep his presence a secret."

Arnold shook his head. "This certainly complicates things. This will make Myron more inclined to protect Mickey."

"We need to change course if you're going to have any chance of beating Myron in the next election. We need a way to slow him down."

"What are you thinking?" Arnold asked.

"We need someone we can trust in the mayor's office."

Arnold nodded, "Do you have someone in mind?"

Frank smiled, and said, "Actually I do, Arnold."

"Who?"

"Your secretary, Agnes."

Arnold laughed. "You're joking."

"No, she's perfect. I know that Myron has been unhappy with his personal secretary. He's been asking me if I know of someone. I recommended Agnes, and he seemed interested."

"Why would I let Agnes go work for him. Plus, she would never agree. We've been together for twenty years."

"She's been unhappy after you lost your City Councilman seat and has been looking for a new job," Frank said.

"That's not true, Frank. Where did you hear that?"

"I know it's not true, Arnold, but we need a reason for her wanting to leave you," Frank said.

Arnold let out a big sigh. "All right, Frank, let me ask Agnes what she thinks about it."

"Why don't you ask her right now?"

"Now?" he asked, shrugging.

Frank got up, and walked over to his desk, and pressed the intercom button. "Hi Millie, can you please send Agnes in."

Arnold stood up as the door opened and Agnes entered.

"Agnes, what are you doing here?"

"I'm about to cross the street and go into City Hall for an interview with the mayor. Wish me luck, Arnold," she said with a huge smile.

Arnold looked at Frank, and then back to Agnes, and said meekly, "Good luck, Agnes."

Chapter 54

It had been nearly ten years since Solomon had seen her. Now she was sitting a few feet away from him at a table at Charlie's with a young man, probably a boyfriend. Solomon swirled the ice around in his nearly empty glass of scotch and replayed in his mind his first dream about Rebecca.

He walked down the hallway of the New York Public Library and into the main reading room. A librarian was pushing a cart stacked with many books. She picked one up, looked at the label on the binding and slid it onto the shelf.

She was young and pretty and Solomon approached her. He tapped her on her shoulder. She turned around and smiled. "How can I help you?"

"Where can we be alone?"

She took his hand and said, "This way."

Solomon followed her to a spot along the end of a long row of bookshelves, where a sofa sat against the wall. They sat down and Solomon said, "Kiss me."

She wrapped her arms around his neck and brought her lips to his.

Solomon gently kissed and caressed her, until he was lost in their lovemaking.

The moment he awoke from the dream, he decided when morning came he would go pay a visit to the New York Public Library on 5th Avenue in Manhattan.

With a burst of energy he hadn't felt in a while, but still with the aid of his cane, he bounded up the stairs, in between the two majestic lion sculptures holding guard. He found his way to the main reading room and that was when Solomon saw the librarian from his dream.

He recognized her instantly by her auburn hair and large green eyes. She was helping a young male college student with a project. He patiently waited for her to finish, before he approached her desk.

"I was wondering if you could help me?" Solomon said.

"That's what I do," she said looking up with a smile.

Solomon looked at her name plate on her desk. "Rebecca, that's a pretty name."

She tilted her head and said, "Thank you."

"Rebecca, I am here to do some research on a book I am writing on a new concept called lucid dreaming."

"I've read about that," she said wagging a finger at him. "That's being aware you're dreaming, isn't it?"

"That's right. You know about it?"

"I am a librarian, sir."

"I didn't mean to insult you, Rebecca. It's just that not many people have heard of it."

"Can you really be lucid in your dreams?" she asked.

Solomon couldn't resist her charm, and he shared a few things he knew about the dream world.

"Are you awake in your dreams, Solomon?" she asked.

"I am."

"What's it like?"

"You can do anything you want, once you've become aware."

"Can you fly?" she asked, with her bright eyes sparkling in wonderment.

"You can fly into the clouds, and even up to the stars, if that's what you want."

That was his first visit to the library, which he continued to make every few days. These frequent visits fueled his love making dreams with Rebecca, while Rebecca had no clue what Solomon was experiencing. All she saw was a nice old man coming to spend time at the library and who was becoming a good friend.

Solomon was never happier until after a few months of his erotic dreams a visitor appeared to him in the dream world.

Solomon was watching his uncle supervise the stone masons as they lay giant slabs of granite for a retaining wall at The Great Synagogue of Warsaw. Solomon was his younger self, maybe ten years old.

"Solomon, what are you doing here? I told you not to show up on the work site. You can get hurt," his uncle said.

"I'm sorry, Uncle," Solomon said, and ran out through the gate and back onto the street.

Sounds of children playing caught his ear, and he ran to the park to see if his friends were there. As he entered the park a woman stood before him, blocking his way.

"Hello, Solomon," said the woman.

Solomon had never seen a woman this beautiful before. Her long wavy locks of red hair framed out a delicate face with a pale complexion, and her bright blue eyes froze Solomon in place.

"My name is Francesa Sarah," she said.

"Do I know you?" Solomon asked.

"I have been watching you."

Solomon tried, but was unable to speak.

"You have violated Rebecca," she said, her voice echoing in Solomon's mind.

"The librarian?" Solomon said, trying to sound innocent.

"You cannot violate Rebecca," she repeated.

"I do not know what you mean."

"Solomon, you are the thoroughly wicked son, and destined to spend eternity in Gehenna, where the eternal fires burn," Francesa Sarah said.

When Solomon awoke his bed was damp from sweat. He sat up, put on his glasses and reached for a glass of water that he kept on the nightstand. He guzzled it down and pulled the library card out from his wallet. Solomon got up, walked into the kitchen, pulled out a drawer where he kept the scissors and cut the card into pieces.

In the intervening years he had not thought about Rebecca. Certainly the visit, and the warning by the mysterious Francesa Sarah, had frightened him enough for his decision not to go back to the library. Though Rebecca did appear in a few dreams from time to time, he never acted on his urges to pursue her.

But there she was, sitting at a table at Charlie's. It took a few minutes for Rebecca to notice Solomon. During this time, he couldn't help staring at her. A familiar warmth coasted through his veins, surprising himself that he could still have sexual urges.

"Solomon Blass, is that you," she said, interrupting his erotic thoughts.

"Rebecca, how nice to see you. What are you doing here?"

Rebecca stood up and walked over to Solomon's table, leaving her boyfriend behind. He noticed that her auburn hair was longer than he remembered.

"Chris and I," she said pointing back to him, "heard about Charlie's Crab House, and decided to check it out. City Island is such a cool place. Do you live here?"

"Yes, I live a few blocks away. Is Chris your boyfriend?" Solomon asked.

"We just started dating."

"That's nice," he said, trying to sound convincing.

"Well, I saw you, and just wanted to say hello. By the way, how is your book coming along?" Rebecca asked.

"My book?" Solomon hesitated, and then remembered his story he told her when they first met at the library. "Oh, that's still a work in progress. How's the library?"

"It's good. I've been there over ten years," she said.

"That's wonderful, Rebecca."

"Well, Solomon it's nice to see you again. Take care of yourself."

"It's nice to see you too," he said, but was thinking that he would be seeing her again, very soon in the dream world.

Chapter 55

The building reminded Moshe of the tenement on the Lower East Side where his family first lived when they arrived in America. But instead of people claiming portions of the public hallway as a makeshift home due to overcrowded conditions, they were all tucked away behind closed doors, in the privacy of their apartments.

Gray took out his hankie and patted his forehead and the back of his neck when they reached the fifth floor walkup.

"Here we are," Gray said, knocking on apartment 5G.

"This is it?" Moshe whispered.

"She lives simply," Gray said, as the sounds of several deadbolts on the front door clicked open.

"Come in, Gray," the voice said, as the door opened.

Gray walked in, followed by Moshe.

"Is this him?" asked the old woman.

Gray nodded enthusiastically, and said, "Moshe, this is Noa."

He hesitated for a moment, unsure if offering a handshake was appropriate. Noa helped him out by sticking out her right hand and giving a Moshe a healthy squeeze. "It's an honor to meet you, Moshe. Gray has told me your story. Come, let's sit, and talk."

Moshe smiled, taking in the thin woman with piercing blue eyes who seemed to have maintained a youthful sparkle, despite her elderly years.

The first thing he noticed as he entered the apartment, besides the piles of aged, yellowed newspapers and books stacked along the narrow hallway, was the chill in the air.

The old woman gestured to a tiny kitchen table and three chairs set under an opened window. "Can I make you tea or coffee, Moshe?"

"Coffee sounds good," Moshe said, seeking something warm.

"Can I have a cold glass of water?" asked Gray.

"Of course," Noa said, with a smile.

Moshe watched Noa tuck a strand of her long, stringy, silver hair behind her ears. "Here you go, Moshe," she said, placing his coffee, along with a glass jar of sugar and a ceramic cup filled with milk, on the table.

"Thank you, Noa," Moshe said.

"I have cake, would you like a piece?" she said, unwrapping a piece of sponge cake and placing it on the table.

"Come, sit, Noa. We need to talk," Gray said.

Noa lifted the glasses hanging around her neck and placed them on her face. Moshe noticed a glow of perspiration clinging to her olive-colored complexion.

"You sweat like Gray?" Moshe said.

Noa nodded, and said, "That's why I keep the window open. I love winter, it's my favorite season."

"Moshe, Noa is going to teach you how to live in the dream world. She's quite good at it," Gray said, taking a sip of his water.

"There's no doubt that life is better in the dream world, Moshe," Noa gloated.

Moshe took a sip of the hot coffee. "You make this sound like some sort of an amusement. I was physically attacked in my dream that left me with this bruise," he said pointing to his leg.

"My apologies, Moshe. Gray and I were just having some fun. But you're right, this is serious."

Moshe nodded. "I would say so."

"I want to be honest with you, Moshe. In all my years of guiding people in the dream world, I have learned what we try to achieve can sometimes result in some form of unintended consequences."

"What sorts of consequences?" Moshe asked.

Noa shook her head. "Hard to say. The dream world, as you probably know by now, is unpredictable."

"What do you mean?" Moshe asked, and looked at Gray to express his confusion.

"Like that bruise," she said pointing to his leg. "Physical injuries in the dream world rarely manifest themselves in the awakened world."

Gray lifted a finger in the air. "I forgot to tell you that Moshe burned his handprint onto Solomon's arm."

"Isn't that interesting," she said rubbing her chin. "Perhaps you and Solomon have been destined for this confrontation."

Moshe's eyes grew large as he looked over to Gray and said, "Are you sure this is a good idea?"

"Don't worry, Moshe, Noa has a great deal of expertise," Gray said.

Noa patted Moshe on the knee. "I'm a descendant of Francesa Sarah of Safed. I understand you were there recently."

Moshe nodded.

"I love Safed," she said taking a sip of water. "Anyway, Francesa Sarah is the protector of the dream world. When a disturbance arises, like the activities from Solomon Blass, the dream world is put out of balance and must be corrected. My purpose is to keep the equilibrium in the dream world with whatever means possible. That is why you are here, so I can teach you how to travel in the dream world and take care of this problem."

Moshe rubbed the back of his neck as Noa continued.

"My lineage goes back to the seventeenth century. The women who have come before me have passed on this knowledge. I am the last in the line, what I know will die with me, because I have no daughters. In the meantime, let's see how I can help you. Do you have any questions?"

"What happens if we're working together and I don't dream?" Moshe asked.

"You may not remember every dream, but that doesn't mean you're not dreaming at all. In fact, humans dream every ninety minutes. Our first few dreams may last only a few minutes, but just before we awaken in the morning, our dreams can last as long as an hour," Noa explained.

"Then how does that explain what you told me, Gray?" Moshe asked.

"That I spend more time in the dream world than the awakened world?" Gray said.

Moshe nodded.

"Good question, Moshe," Noa said. "That's because each minute in the dream world is about an hour in the awakened world."

"Will I start to sweat too?" Moshe asked.

Noa nodded. "You will, if you're lucid for more than ten or so minutes in the dream world, then your mind will adjust your nervous system, resulting in the sweats. But it's not so bad, and you'll get used to it."

Moshe looked at Noa and Gray, who looked comfortable in the freezing apartment, and wondered if this would soon be his life too.

"Wait a second, what about Solomon. I've never seen him sweat, and I'm sure he's lucid for at least ten minutes," Moshe said, with some exuberance at asking a good question.

Noa took Moshe's cup from his hand, stood up, and walked over to the stove, where she poured some more coffee. "There's a reason for that, Moshe."

Moshe looked at Noa and asked, "Is it because he is *rasha*?"

"Indeed," said Noa.

Chapter 56

"It's her," Arnold said, as the front doorbell rang.

"Finally," Frank said, looking again at his watch.

Arnold walked from his kitchen, where he and Frank had been drinking coffee for the past hour and a half, waiting for Agnes to arrive.

"Hi, Arnold," Agnes said as she entered, while Arnold stood in the doorway for a moment, looking out into the darkness. "It's fine, no one followed me."

"Good, come in the kitchen, Frank is here."

Agnes greeted Frank and took a seat at the round kitchen table.

"How's it going?" Frank asked.

Agnes shook her head. "It's a complete disaster. Myron has no idea of what he's doing."

"I'm not surprised. What's happening with Mickey?" Arnold asked.

"It's pretty much what you expected. Last week the Commissioner of the Department of Consumer Affairs was in the office with applications from Mickey Coppola for parking garage licenses. The mayor told him, after ten minutes of arguing, that he should approve them," she said.

Frank nodded. "I heard about that."

"There's more," said Agnes, as she reached for the sugar bowl on the table. She scooped out a teaspoon and sprinkled some into her tea. "It's the same with the contracts for garbage collection, and the awarding of major building contracts to mob controlled unions."

"So much for our mayor pushing back against Mickey," Arnold said, looking over to Frank.

"Disappointing, but not surprising," said Frank with a smirk.

"With Carmine Rizzo gone, Mickey Coppola now controls all of Manhattan and the Bronx," Arnold said.

"Jesus," Frank said, shaking his head.

"Now boys, don't be so distraught. I also learned some things that might be useful."

Arnold looked at Frank and said, "Like what?"

"Mayor Myron Blass is having an affair with Mickey Coppola's daughter, Niko."

Arnold leaned forward in his chair. "How do you know this?"

"He told me," she said.

"Why would he do that?" Frank asked.

"He asked for my advice," Agnes said, with a hint of smugness in her smile.

"Advice about banging Mickey's daughter?" Arnold said.

"Nice language, Arnold," Agnes said, shaking her head.

"What did he tell you?" Frank said.

"Yesterday morning he came into the office looking like hell. He was still drunk from the night before. His eyes were bloodshot, and he hadn't shaved. I told him he looked like crap, and he should try to clean himself up for the press conference that was scheduled for later on that morning. He walked over to my desk and sat down on the chair next to it. He looked at me with his tired and baggy eyes and said that he was in love."

"In love?" Arnold interrupted.

"More like lust, I'm guessing. He confessed that he didn't know what to do. If Mickey found out he was secretly seeing his daughter, he would have him killed," Agnes said.

"Where are they having these rendezvous?" Frank asked.

"At Gracie Mansion. The butler sneaks her in and out through the service entrance."

Frank clapped his hands together. "We have our leverage back."

"Just hold on, Frank, there's more," Agnes said holding up her index finger. "Myron also told me in his drunken stupor that he warned Mickey that Carmine Rizzo was planning to murder him at Antonio's later that evening,"

"But instead, Mickey took the initiative and shot Carmine," Frank interrupted.

Agnes nodded.

Frank held out his palms. "But how would Myron possibly know what Rizzo was planning?"

Agnes shared a private look with Arnold who rolled his eyes.

Frank said, "Well, it seems our mayor is at least guilty of obstruction in a murder investigation. Perhaps we can use this, along with our knowledge of his romance with Mickey's daughter to our advantage."

"Who is going to talk to him?" Agnes asked.

"It has to be Frank," Arnold said.

"I agree. It should come from me. The sooner I do this, the faster we will get some control back," Frank said.

"When will you do it?" Arnold asked.

Frank thought for a moment, then said, "Tomorrow at our weekly lunch meeting."

"Wait a second, isn't he going to suspect Agnes?" Arnold asked with concern.

Agnes laughed and flipped her hand at Arnold. "There's not a chance in hell he remembers our conversation. As I said, when he spoke to me he was still drunk from his nighttime frolic with Niko. After we spoke, he lay down on the sofa and passed out. I couldn't even wake him for the press conference, which we needed to cancel."

Arnold rose from the kitchen table, spread his arms like he was addressing an audience, and said, "Our drunken, corrupt, playboy mayor is about to get a wakeup call."

Chapter 57

*S*olomon watched the snow fall upon the shoreline of the *City Island Harbor. He thought of Rebecca, and her soft, young body lying in his bed. She was exhausted after making love many times that night.*

Solomon refocused his vision onto his reflection in the window. He saw himself as a young man. His shirtless, muscular torso was impressive. He touched his chest and felt its hardness. Even his abdomen was displaying rows of muscle. A sight unseen for nearly seventy years. He was a god, and loved his life in the dream world.

Then she appeared. It was a mist traveling across the frozen waters of the bay. Standing before him was a woman dressed in a long white dress, with a red sash wrapped around her waist.

"I warned you, Solomon," she said, without speaking, the words appearing in Solomon's mind.

Solomon recognized the image of Francesa Sarah of Safed from his previous dream all those years ago. He reached out to touch her, but she vanished into smoke.

The voice spoke to him. "You have violated her after I warned you of the consequences. Do you mock my resolve, Solomon?"

He felt his body being pulled through the wall and swept out above the bay. Solomon found himself rapidly crossing a great ocean until he was looking down upon a land between two mountains.

The voice returned. "Solomon, this is the Valley of Gehenna. Your destiny, your soul lies before you."

Solomon looked out onto the valley from high above.

"See what awaits you," the voice said, and pulled him down.

Solomon glided a few feet above a river of burning sewage. The stench seeped into the deepest parts of his lungs. Along the shoreline, naked men and women were screaming in agony. Their flesh burned and singed. Maggots and worms crawled among the mountainous landscape of human waste.

"Why am I here?" he screamed.

The voice said, "Your journey of evil ends here, Solomon. Among the dead, you will endlessly walk, your soul vanquished."

"Show yourself," Solomon demanded.

The white mist turned gray, then black. It swirled before him into the shape of a woman. Long, straight white hair hung down to her lower back. Her eyes were colorless, almost transparent like glass. Long thin arms were outstretched with palms cupped as if she was capturing the air. She floated before him until her image evaporated into nothingness.

Henryk sat in Solomon's kitchen watching the snow fall upon the shoreline of City Island Harbor.

"Here you go, Rabbi," Solomon said, placing down a hot cup of coffee in front of him.

"Thank you," Henryk said, wrapping his palms around the steaming mug.

Solomon sat down, rubbed his forehead, and said, "She brought me to hell."

"Ah, you mean Gehenna."

Solomon flicked his hand and said, "Whatever you call it."

"I read about Francesa Sarah when I studied in Safed. She was a spiritual leader, with skills of living and teaching others how to live in the dream world. Actually, her skills were similar to yours."

"She's nothing like me, Rabbi," Solomon said.

"Of course not," Henryk obediently agreed.

"I don't know why I am still here. It sounded like I was destined to remain in Gehanna and walk among the dead, with my flesh burning in perpetuity."

"She must have allowed you to return for a reason, Solomon."

"What do you think it is?"

"There's no way of knowing, but if I had to guess, I would say that maybe she doesn't actually have the power to send you to Gehanna. Maybe it was just a warning. If you want my advice, I would stop pulling this young lady librarian into your dreams."

"I haven't felt this good in a long time, Rabbi. You have no idea how amazing it is to be with Rebecca."

Henryk shook his head. "Solomon, apparently there are boundaries you cannot violate in dream world, and this must be one of them."

"How does that make sense? The cobbler burns my arm, and I hear that he is walking with a noticeable limp from when I smacked him with my cane. We can hurt each other in the dream world, but love making with Rebecca is off limits?"

Henryk took a sip of his coffee, and said, "The difference is that you and the cobbler are both awake in the dream world. Whereas in your exploits with Rebecca, she is unaware."

"If what you're saying is true," Solomon paused for a moment, then added, "what if I can teach Rebecca how to be awake in the dream world?"

"I am no expert, Solomon. But it's better than spending an eternity in Gehenna."

Chapter 58

Myron walked into Delmonico's Steak House on Beaver Street, twenty minutes late.

"Good day, Mr. Mayor. The commissioner is already at your table. Right this way, sir," said the maître 'd, gesturing to the private dining room in the back of the restaurant.

"Sorry I'm late, Frank," Myron said, shaking hands.

"It's fine, sir, I'm sure you're overwhelmed."

"My life is not my own any longer."

"I can relate to that," Frank said, taking a sip of water.

"So let's get to business, I have to be back for a meeting in forty-five minutes. What have you got for me?"

Frank got up and closed the door to the private dining room. "What I have to say is sensitive."

"You piqued my curiosity."

Frank took a breath and exhaled before he spoke. "Let me get right to it." He leaned in, and whispered, "I know about you and Niko."

Myron stared at Frank for a long moment before speaking. "Who told you?"

"I'm impressed you're not denying it."

"What's this is all about?" Myron said leaning back in his chair, his arms folded upon his chest.

"There's more," Frank said leaning forward before adding, "I also know you had advance knowledge of the murder of Carmine Rizzo."

Myron scratched his chin. "How would you know that?"

Frank tilted his head and said, "Come on, Mr. Mayor, I'm the Police Commissioner."

Myron pinched the bridge of his nose and said, "Okay, Frank, I knew that Carmine was planning to murder Mickey. So I warned him. But I had no idea that Mickey was going to kill Carmine. You need to believe me on that."

Frank nodded. "I do believe you and I want you to know that I will protect you. But we need to start working together."

Myron got out of his chair and walked over to the window. He pulled the red gingham curtain back and looked out to the empty alleyway in the back of the restaurant. "You know, Frank, I was thinking that keeping Mickey in check would be good for my businesses after this mayor thing is over. I'm afraid if I don't stop his expansion plans I'll have nothing left for myself."

"Of course. Let's work together. You help me now, and I'll help you later."

Myron stared at Frank. "How do I know I can trust you?"

Frank stood up, walked over to the window next to Myron and placed his hand on his shoulder. "Mr. Mayor, we don't need to worry about trust, since we're in this together. It's a mutually beneficial arrangement. Our success, even our survival, depends on both of us staying in power."

Myron nodded, and extended his hand. "You're right, Frank, we need to work together."

Chapter 59

It had been a week since Moshe had begun his training with Noa. During this time, while the city had been in a deep freeze, Moshe had been sweating like it was the middle of July.

It didn't take long for Leah to notice. "I'm freezing cold, and you're schvitzing. What's happening?" she asked, wrapping her arms around herself.

"I'm fine," he said, filling his second glass of water at the kitchen sink.

"Maybe you should go see Dr. Wagner."

Moshe guzzled down the water, and said, "I'll do that."

"Today, you should go today," she said.

Moshe grabbed his coat, more for Leah's sake than his own, and walked out the front door into the frigid winter morning.

As he closed the door behind him, he heard the scraping of a windshield. He looked over to his car parked in his driveway and saw Gray removing snow and ice from his car windows. He had even shoveled the few inches of snow that fell overnight from the driveway, and sidewalk.

"Gray, what are you doing?" Moshe asked.

"Giving a friend a hand," he said, smiling.

"I appreciate that. But why are you here?"

"I thought you would fill me in on your sessions with Noa. Come, we can talk on the way to the cobbler shop," he said.

Moshe unlocked his door and reached over to pull up the knob to unlock the passenger side. Gray opened the door, and got in.

"What's that on your hand?" Gray asked, noticing a large dot drawn on Moshe's hand.

"Noa had me do this," he said, holding his hand up.

"Is that your reality check?"

Moshe looked at the dot he drew on with a fountain pen and explained. "I look at the dot throughout the day, and ask myself if I'm awake, or if I'm dreaming. She said that eventually this question would start to pop up in my dreams too, and become a sign that I was dreaming."

"Has it happened?"

"It did, a few nights ago," Moshe said, his eyes widening with excitement. "I looked at my hand, and I saw the dot, and realized I was dreaming."

"Tell me about it," Gray asked.

"I was in the shop cutting a leather sole, and the blade slipped and sliced into my left hand. When I looked at my cut I saw the bone, but there was no blood. I covered the cut together with my right hand, and that's when I saw the dot, and realized that I was dreaming."

"That's wonderful, Moshe."

"I said to myself, this is a dream. I squeezed the gash together, and the cut healed."

"That's it, Moshe, you're doing it. Soon you'll be able to move about at will and do things that are unimaginable in the awakened world."

"I've had more dreams since then. Two nights ago I found myself swimming great distances underwater, without a need to breathe," Moshe said nodding. "And the craziest thing is that I don't even know how to swim."

"Marvelous!"

"Last night, though, was the most interesting. I was a young boy, back in Krzywcza. Mother and I were walking to the market, when the local village police captain jumped out in front of us and grabbed me. Mother yelled for him to release me, but he ignored her, and dragged me through the market, announcing that I was under arrest. I looked at my hand and saw the dot, and I knew was dreaming. A blade from the shop appeared in my hand and I cut into the captain's forearm. He screamed, and released his grip."

"Incredible, Moshe. Soon enough, you'll be ready to learn how to move about in the dream world."

"That's what Noa said."

"You're sweating too," Gray noticed.

"It started a few days ago," Moshe said, wiping his brow with the back of his hand.

"You'll get used to it."

"My wife thinks I'm sick."

Moshe pulled up to a spot on the concourse in front of the cobbler shop. He turned off the engine and turned to look at Gray. "I assume you drove in with me for a reason?"

"I did, Moshe. Sorry, I almost forgot, after hearing about your wonderful dreams."

Gray looked out the window, and said, "Tonight, after you close the shop, you'll need to go to Noa's."

"Tonight? For how long?"

"Until morning, and again for the next three nights."

"What are you saying, Gray?"

"You'll need to sleep at Noa's."

"And why would I do that?"

"It will be like a crash course. You can't expect to be able to battle the *rasha* without being properly trained."

Moshe shook his head. "But sleep there for three nights? What will Leah think?"

"I don't know, tell her you're going to a conference for cobblers, or something."

"A cobbler conference? You can't be serious?"

"Come on, Moshe, you'll think of something."

Moshe sat in his car, staring out the front window. "What have I gotten myself into?"

"Stop worrying, Moshe. I'll be back at six and drive over to Noa's with you. In the meantime, call your wife."

Chapter 60

"He's such a moron, Arnold. I can't stand him anymore."

"I know, Agnes. But it's important. You're providing with us with critical information," Arnold said.

"Yeah, yeah, that's what Frank says. But if you could just hear what goes on in that office, you wouldn't believe it," Agnes said, shaking her head.

"Is it true that Mickey was there the other day?"

Agnes nodded, her red coiffed curls bobbing along, and said, "I thought he was going to kill him. He charged right by me, without even a glance over, and nearly knocked Myron's door off its hinges."

"Why was he so angry?" Arnold asked, sipping at his steaming coffee.

Agnes looked at a couple sitting a few booths away from them, and asked, "Are you sure it's okay to talk here in the diner?"

"It's fine. No one can hear us."

Regardless, Agnes leaned in to the table and lowered her voice, "I don't think he realizes, but I can hear every word that comes from his office. Those walls are paper thin."

"What did they say?" Arnold asked enthusiastically.

"Looks like the contract for the new convention center on Columbus Circle was awarded to a Brooklyn firm."

"He didn't give it to Mickey's construction company in Manhattan?"

Agnes shook her head. "Nope, and you know what else?"

"What?"

"This Brooklyn construction company that's got the job, it's legit."

"No mob ties?" Arnold said.

"Not only that, it's also a non-union shop. Mickey was fuming. I'm sure his shouts were heard all the way down to the basement of City Hall."

"That was a huge contract."

"It's the biggest public project in the city for the past five years."

"I wouldn't worry too much about Mickey. He'll still have his hand in the pockets of the subcontractors. After all, you can't build anything in this city without the carpenters, steelworkers or the electrical unions," Arnold said.

"But the real money is running the job, and Mickey is not used to getting the scraps."

"That's true, Agnes. Looks like the commissioner was persuasive with the mayor. Apparently, the threat of exposing him with the obstruction charge, along with his affair with Niko, was enough to put pressure on Myron."

"Myron is infatuated with Niko. The way he speaks with her on the phone, it makes me blush, Arnold."

Arnold smiled and said, "What does he say?"

"Enough. I'm not going to sit here in the diner and talk about Myron's phone sex with you. Anyway, I have to go to work. Thanks for the coffee," she said and she stood up, grabbed her coat and left.

"Thanks, Agnes. I'll call you," Arnold said as she left the Fordham Diner, and went out into the fresh inch of snow covering the sidewalk.

Arnold worried that awarding the convention center contract to the Brooklyn firm was going to be a mistake. But this was typical of Myron, who always took things to the extreme. Frank's intention was to encourage Myron to push back in small doses against Mickey, and not to award the city's largest building contract to someone else. This was certainly not going to end well.

Chapter 61

The next morning after Solomon's conversation with Henryk he was anxious to test his theory by seducing Rebecca into becoming a willing partner in their lovemaking, and hopefully cease his disturbing visits from the spirit of Francesa Sarah. To do so, he would need to guide Rebecca on becoming lucid in her dreams, before he could lure her into his dream world. He mulled over his plan. When he heard a car horn beep outside, Solomon grabbed his cane and headed out the front door for his cab ride to the library.

When Solomon arrived, he found Rebecca helping a young man, probably doing research for a college paper. As she was leaning over the large wood table her blouse opened slightly. She quickly corrected the mishap by fastening another button and looked up to see if anyone noticed. That was when she saw Solomon staring at her.

"Oh, Solomon. What are you doing here?" she said, blushing.

"Hi, Rebecca. Sorry to startle you."

"That's okay," she said, still fussing with her blouse.

"I've come to talk to you. Is there a quiet place we can sit, and chat?"

She looked at her watch and said, "I'm due for a break in thirty minutes. Would you mind waiting for me? We can talk in the reading room on the lower level?"

"Perfect, I'll be there."

While Solomon waited, he pulled a few textbooks off the shelves on dream interpretation and on lucid dreaming. When Rebecca found him, he had the books placed as props on the table, in full view.

"Thank you for waiting, Solomon," she said, as she sat down across from him, and took notice of the books he laid out.

"I thought I would stop by and get a few books for my research," he said gesturing to them.

"*The Interpretation of Dreams*, by Sigmund Freud. I've read that. He writes about the theory of the unconscious as it relates to the interpretation of dreams."

Solomon nodded, not knowing how to respond.

"Oh, and this one is on lucid dreaming. I've been looking into this lately."

"Have you?" Solomon asked. He glanced around the reading room before he said, "This is what I wanted to talk to you about." He paused, and looked at the books before him and continued, "How to be awake in your dreams. That is, if you're still interested."

"I've been reading about it. But actually working with someone, I haven't given much thought. Are you offering to teach me?"

Solomon felt himself blush unexpectedly. "I am. I've been lucid dreaming for many years and can provide insights that you can't find in here," he said patting one of the books sitting on the table.

"What did you have in mind?"

"I thought we could set up a time each week to talk about your dreams, and techniques on how to become lucid in them."

"You know, Solomon, I can't believe that you're asking me this now," she said, picking up the book on lucid dreaming. She leaned over the table slightly, and said in a low voice, "Can I confess something to you?"

Solomon shrugged, and said, "Of course."

Rebecca gave a quick glance around her, to make sure no one was listening.

"I've been having these, um, dreams lately," she paused, and then continued, "I'm embarrassed to tell you."

"What is it, Rebecca?"

"Well Solomon, they've been sexual, and they have been with you."

"With me?" Solomon, said as a chill ran through him.

"But you're much younger. Probably my age."

Solomon felt himself breaking out into a cold sweat. He placed his palms on the table to steady himself."

"Are you okay?"

"Are you sure it's me you were dreaming about?" he said, feeling dizzy.

"Without a doubt, it's you. It feels so real."

Solomon tried to compose himself, and said, "Do you mind if I go use the men's room. I'll be right back."

"Of course, Solomon. I didn't mean to shock you. Are you all right?" Rebecca said, rising from her chair, and touching Solomon's elbow.

Solomon couldn't face Rebecca after her ground shaking confession. After washing his face in the men's room, he took the stairwell back to the main level and snuck out of the library without saying goodbye to her.

On the cab ride home, he tried to make sense of what Rebecca said. She was aware of him in her dreams, but at least she didn't know that he was the instigator of these dreams.

A frightening image appeared in his mind of Francesa Sarah warning him of the dire consequences of spending an eternity in the bowels of Gehenna if he continued to engage sexually with Rebecca in the dream world. *On the other hand, what if this spirit of Francesa Sarah was nothing more than a trick perpetrated by Gray? Perhaps there was nothing to worry about.*

With that thought, Solomon felt his tension evaporate, replaced with a pleasurable warmth that coasted through his veins. Rebecca's confession stirred a desire within him that was joyful. He would disregard his fears and visit her tonight in the dream world.

Chapter 62

"Hymie's complaining about sharp pains in his stomach," Moshe told his wife.

"But why you, and not your sister?" Leah asked.

"Because he asked for me. I'll be back Sunday. You'll be fine at Barbara's. Candy will be happy to see you."

"Okay, let me pack up what I need, and don't rush me, Moshe," Leah said.

"Take your time. We'll leave after dinner."

Moshe dropped off Leah at their daughter's home on Long Island. Thank goodness she was happy for an excuse to spend a few days with their two-year-old granddaughter, Candy. But Moshe was not thrilled that he had to lie to her.

The city streets were a mess with the two-day-old snow. Cars that got plowed under appeared like statues carved into soot colored ice that he thought would never melt. Moshe circled the block a few times before he found a spot on Queens Boulevard.

He grabbed his valise and looked up and down the sidewalk to make sure no one was watching. Though he knew this was not what it seemed, he still didn't want to explain why he was sneaking into the apartment of a woman who wasn't his wife.

I can't believe I'm doing this, he thought as he climbed the stairwell. As he reached the fifth floor landing the door to apartment 5G opened, and Noa's head popped out.

"Come in, Moshe. I've been waiting for you," Noa said.

Moshe stepped in.

"Hang up your coat on the hook," Noa said, pointing.

The invigorating climb up the five floors turned up his sweat into a full-out drenching of his undergarments and shirt.

Anticipating his condition, Noa appeared with a glass of water. "Here you go."

"Thank you," Moshe said, as he gulped down the water.

"Come, put your valise here," she said, pointing to a spot next to the sofa.

"Is this where I'm sleeping?" Moshe asked, gesturing to the three-cushion sofa.

"No, you'll take my bed."

"And where will you sleep?" Moshe asked, nervously.

"I'm not sleeping. I'll be observing you."

Moshe looked around Noa's shoulder to the doorway to the bedroom.

"Come, I'll show you."

While he waited for Noa to return with groceries, Moshe looked out the window onto the frozen world, soaking up the cold drafts from the open window. From this fifth floor walkup, he was level with the elevated Queens Boulevard train station where he could watch people climbing the metal staircase, bundled up against the frigid winds.

As a train rumbled into the station the glass in the window vibrated. He wondered how he would sleep that night with the continuous noise of the neighborhood and reverberations of the trains.

He thought of Leah and wondered how she was doing. *What if she calls Hymie, looking for me? Hymie won't know what she's talking about. Shit, I should have told him.*

Moshe heard keys engaging the apartment door locks. He hurried to the door to offer Noa a hand with the groceries. Moshe turned the door knob and opened the door.

Standing there, with a key pointing at him, was a young man wearing a lightweight jacket, and no hat. A trickle of sweat ran down the side of his face, and his blue eyes expressed surprise.

"Who are you?" asked the stranger.

"I'm Moshe."

"Where's Noa?" he said, looking past Moshe into the empty apartment behind him.

"She went to get groceries. She'll be back soon," Moshe said, stepping aside to allow the man in.

"I'm Sammy, a friend of Noa's. I thought she was out of town."

"No, she's here," Moshe said, feeling awkward.

"Why are you here?" Sammy said, taking a seat by the open window.

"I'm a friend," Moshe said, unsure if he should discuss the real reason with this stranger.

Besides the familiar sign of sweat dripping down his forehead, Sammy looked to be about thirty years old, and a handsome man, with short curly auburn hair.

"Are you friends with Noa?"

"Oh, we are more than friends," Sammy said, with a mischievous lifting of his eyebrows.

Moshe didn't know how to respond, except with a nod. Just then, the door opened and in walked Noa, clutching two bags of groceries.

"Sammy, what are you doing here?"

"You told me I could stay here, don't you remember?"

Noa placed the groceries down on the counter top in the kitchen and said, "Oh my god, I completely forgot. I changed my plans because of... well, I guess you met Moshe."

"We just met. So what am I supposed to do? I need to stay here a few days."

"That's fine, you can sleep on the couch. I'm going to be working with Moshe at night, so we'll be in the bedroom."

"Can you tell me what's going on?" Moshe asked.

Noa walked over and patted Moshe on his cheek. "Sammy and I are lovers."

Moshe blushed, and sweated even more.

"I know what you're thinking, that I'm too old for that stuff now. But not in the dream world," Noa added.

"Oh, you should see her, Moshe. She's a young, beautiful woman, full of sensuality," Sammy said, squeezing Noa around her shoulders.

"Stop it, Sammy. You're embarrassing Moshe."

"I don't think I need to know any of this," Moshe said, sitting down at the kitchen table.

"It's what's beautiful about the dream world, Moshe. Sammy and I are happy together, but I'm forty-five years older, and we can't have a sexual relationship that would be pleasing for either of us."

"But we can in the dream world," Sammy interrupted with a grin.

"All right, let me make dinner. I have plenty. After dinner, I'll take Moshe into the bedroom and we'll get to work," Noa said.

Moshe rubbed the back of his neck and wondered if he had made a mistake in coming. Certainly, if he was able to learn how to move about in the dream world he wouldn't waste it on sexual encounters, unless Leah wanted to learn, which he doubted. But he did imagine dreaming about being with his parents, Pincus and Clara, who passed many years ago. Now that would be exciting.

Chapter 63

Myron sat at his table near the front of the ballroom. As mayor of the country's largest city, he was a featured attendee at the 1961 Conference for American Mayors, held in Miami. The organizers of the event had even asked if Myron would provide one of the keynote speeches to the group. But he declined. His interest was just to show up, and get out of there as quickly as possible, in order to spend time with Niko.

Niko had told her father that she was going away with friends for a few days, which wasn't unusual. But Myron wasn't as calm as Niko. He prayed that no one would recognize her during the conference.

While he sat there through another dull address, this time by the Mayor of Los Angeles, he doodled mindless geometric shapes on a note pad that featured a line drawing of the Fontainebleau Hotel.

The speech was about the usual things mayors needed to deal with, like crime, trash pickup, snow removal, and education. But the only thing that Myron thought about was Niko, and the men who were, most likely at this very moment, gawking at her as she pranced about the pool in her tiny bikini.

Myron hurried out of the convention hall and up to his room in the adjacent hotel. He smiled at the DO NOT DISTURB sign hanging off the doorknob to his room. He took out the large brass key and unlocked the door.

"Hey, I'm back," he shouted.

There was no reply in the large penthouse suite. Myron stepped onto the patio that offered a sweeping view of the Atlantic Ocean and saw Niko relaxing on a cushioned lounge chair.

"There you are," he said.

"How did it go? Did you learn anything new and exciting?" she said, standing up, wearing a white bathrobe with the Fontainebleau logo embroidered upon it.

"Oh, I was mostly bored, to tell you the truth."

Niko lifted her hand and said, "I would think that hanging around with other big-time mayors would be a good opportunity to learn how they do things."

Myron nodded. "That's true. Actually, there were a few ideas I liked."

"Tell me, Myron?" Niko asked.

Myron thought for a moment before he said, "The mayor from Philadelphia spoke about smaller class sizes in elementary school."

"That's an excellent idea," Niko said wagging a finger. "I always thought that there were too many children in my classes when I went to school. Education reform is one of the biggest responsibilities you have as mayor."

Myron nodded. "There was also an idea from a roundtable discussion about the police getting out of their patrol cars and walking their beats, like they used to do years ago."

Niko opened her palms out wide and said, "Myron, that's obvious. When the police are among the citizens they make a better connection to the people they are serving, instead of isolating themselves inside a vehicle."

"Wow, Niko, maybe *you* should run for mayor."

Niko smiled, shrugged and turned to walk into the bedroom.

"Tonight we're having dinner with the Mayor of Chicago, Richard Daley, and his wife Eleanor," he called after her.

Shouting from the bedroom, Niko said, "I've heard good things about him. He has that city under his control. Father says he is one of the most powerful men in the country."

Myron followed Niko into the bedroom. "We have a half-hour to get ready."

Of course Niko wasn't ready in thirty minutes, so Myron waited for her on the patio smoking a Cuban cigar, his favorite. There were rumors circulating at the convention that President Kennedy was considering an embargo of products from Cuba, which would include Myron's precious cigars.

Myron slipped two extra cigars into his jacket pocket for the evening. Perhaps if he shared a smoke with Mayor Daley he might convince the mayor's good friend, President Kennedy, not to include the cigars in the ban.

Agnes, who had also accompanied Myron to the conference, had become his right-hand woman. She educated Myron about the warm relationship between the Chicago mayor and the President of the United States.

"The rumor is that the mayor helped steal the 1960 presidential election by stuffing the ballot boxes in Chicago," Agnes said earlier that day during a break in their meetings.

She also told him about numerous scandals plaguing his administration.

"This mayor is notorious. He's been accused of ticket fixing, inflating government construction projects, and accepting bribes for influence," Agnes told Myron.

"Sounds like my kind of guy," Myron quipped.

Myron loved watching the waves as they crashed upon the white-sand shoreline of Miami Beach. Getting out of the city, especially in the dead of winter, was a great idea. Even if he had to endure hours of mind-numbing presentations.

"I'm ready," Niko said, emerging from the bedroom.

Myron turned and needed to grab onto the back of the chair to steady himself.

"Wow, you look amazing."

"You like?" she asked spinning around, showing off a long, yet shapely black gown.

Myron nodded, and said, "You should be quite a sight next to Daley's wife, Eleanor. I hear she's rather, um, plain-looking."

"Stop it. I'm sure she's very nice."

When they arrived in the lobby of the hotel Myron saw a crowd of photographers surrounding Mayor Daley and his wife. "There he is," Myron said. He grabbed Niko's hand and ushered her behind a series of columns and planters that camouflaged them as they sneaked by without being noticed.

"What are you doing?" Niko asked.

"Discretion, my dear. Let's just find our table. I'm sure the mayor and his wife will join us shortly."

When Mayor Daley and his wife Eleanor made their way over to the dinner table, Myron and Niko rose and greeted them. Myron noticed how the expression on Richard Daley's face changed from a jovial smile to a momentary frown when he introduced Niko. But he dismissed it as nothing important.

After dinner, with the ladies chatting away in the bar, Myron shared his Cuban cigars with the Chicago mayor in the men's smoking lounge.

"I was in Cuba right before the revolution," Richard said and blew a cloud of smoke up into the wood beams stretching across the ceiling.

"I hear it used to be amazing," Myron said.

"I prefer Miami. It has that Latin charm, but it's still in America," he said with a wink.

Myron nodded and looked at his watch.

"You're in a hurry to get back to that hot little package?"

"Mr. Mayor, I didn't think you noticed."

"I may be old, but I'm not dead."

Myron laughed, and slapped Richard on the back. "That's a good one."

Richard's demeanor suddenly shifted. He leaned into the table and grabbed Myron's wrist hard. Myron was surprised at the sudden move and tried to jerk his arm back. But Richard wouldn't release his grip.

"What the hell?" Myron protested.

"Now you listen to me, Mr. Mayor. You're fucking the wrong man's daughter. I know what Mickey Coppola is capable of, and it's not pleasant."

With a burst of anger, Myron ripped his wrist free for Richard's grasp, and said, "What's it to you?"

Mayor Daley stood up, picked up his hat, and with one slick move, placed it on his head, pointed at Myron, and said, "That scumbag also does business in Chicago."

Myron watched him leave. He picked up his whiskey, swirled the ice around in the glass, put it to his lips, and downed it.

Chapter 64

Arnold gulped down his coffee and peeked out the window to see how much snow had fallen overnight. From what he could make out, there was a fresh coating of about an inch or two. *Not so bad*, he thought. He took his coat and hat from the stand and was about to walk out the front door when the phone rang.

He reached for the receiver on the wall and answered, "Hello?"

"Hi, Arnold."

"Agnes?"

"Listen, I just heard from Myron. There was a huge altercation at the Colosseum site."

"What happened?"

"Not sure. Apparently the local carpenters union took offense to the subs brought in."

"I'm going to head over now. Thanks for the heads up, Agnes," Arnold said and hung up the phone.

By the time Arnold arrived the site was swarming with police trying to keep the curious gawkers back behind the barricades. Several ambulances were pushing their way through the clogged traffic to get to the injured. The media had already descended upon the scene with reporters and cameras.

Arnold tried to enter the crime scene but was stopped.

"You need to stay behind the barricades," ordered a tall police officer.

"Is the commissioner here?" Arnold asked, looking toward a group of men in suits.

The officer turned. "That's him over there."

Arnold thanked the officer, stepped around the barricade and approached the commissioner. "What the hell happened here?" asked Arnold.

"The local carpenters union sent over some of their enforcers. They confronted the subs with baseball bats," Frank said. "Some were beaten up pretty badly. They're being taken to New York Presbyterian," he said, gesturing to the ambulances.

Arnold scanned the construction site. It looked like a war zone.

"Let me guess, Mickey Coppola."

"No doubt," Frank said.

"Have you made any arrests?"

Frank nodded. "We've already taken a dozen or so down to the station for booking."

Suddenly there was a commotion of activity causing the flock of reporters and onlookers to run to the curbside.

"What the hell is it now?" Frank said.

A black Caddie pulled up, and out stepped Mickey Coppola.

Arnold shook his head, and said, "I can't believe he has the balls to show his face."

Mickey walked from his car over to where a recent lumber delivery was spread out on the sidewalk. He stepped upon a foot-high stack of plywood. From his elevated position he was able to be seen by the crowd, as well as by Frank and Arnold.

He held out his hands over his head to quiet the buzz. Frank and Arnold moved closer to hear what he was about to say.

The Righteous One 257

"What happened here this morning is a disgrace," he announced, gesturing to the crime scene. "And the worst part about it, is that all of this could have been prevented. The building of the largest public construction project in our city should be built by our proud New York City unions. Not by some scabs brought in from Brooklyn."

Flashbulbs popped away as the reporters wrote frantically in their notepads.

Mickey pointed a finger into the air and continued, "There is only one person to blame for today's violence." He paused, and let the accusation hang there for a moment before he continued.

A voice from the crowd yelled, "It's those fuckin' carpenters. They came here swingin' bats and bashin' heads."

"Who said that?" Mickey said, looking out onto the crowd.

The crowd went silent.

"That's what I thought. Cowards, you're all cowards. These men," he paused to gesture to the dozen or so men being handcuffed by the police, "have dedicated their lives to their union in order to support their families and would do anything to protect them. Tell me, if you lived from paycheck to paycheck, and suddenly your livelihood was threatened, what would you do?"

The people stirred, but no one dared to bring attention to themselves.

"Do not fret my friends, I'm not here to blame you." Mickey smiled.

He scanned the crowd and saw Arnold and Frank, standing side-by-side. "But there is someone to blame for today's violence, and that is Mayor Myron Blass."

Frank leaned in to Arnold and said, "He can't be serious?"

Mickey held out his palms again and spoke. "I have a message for our mayor. Today you heard from the carpenters. If union workers are not permitted on this jobsite, tomorrow you may hear from the electricians, the next day from the plumbers, and then the steelworkers and the painters."

Mickey Coppola had just backed Myron into a corner. He would either have to back down or take a stand.

"You think Myron will give in?" Arnold asked Frank.

"He better not. Listen, Arnold, I have to go," Frank said, patting Arnold on the shoulder.

"Where are you going?"

"City Hall. It's time to put an end to Mickey Coppola's reign of terror."

Chapter 65

"**A**re you willing to risk your eternal soul for some momentary sexual pleasure?" Henryk asked, sitting across from Solomon at his table at Charlie's.

"Come on, how do I know it's really this ancient spirit, this Francesca Sarah of Safed and not Gray in disguise? In the dream world you never know," Solomon said, leaning back in his chair, his arms folded over his belly.

"I don't know, Solomon. But my advice is to stay away from the temptation."

"Understood, Rabbi," Solomon said, and took a sip of his whiskey.

Henryk slid forward on his chair, and said, "I have some interesting news to tell you."

Solomon flicked two fingers on his right hand to summon him to continue.

"You told me about this visitor in your dreams that comes to you wearing all gray."

Solomon nodded.

"I was in Queens last week, seeing an old friend from rabbinical school. As I was crossing the street, who do I see? The cobbler, and he was walking with a man dressed in all gray. I thought to myself, didn't Solomon tell me about this gray man? So I ran after them to get a better look."

"What did you see?" Solomon asked, with heightened interest.

"As I reached the sidewalk they turned toward me. First I saw the cobbler. Then I looked at the man next to him," Henryk said.

"Was it him?" Solomon asked.

Henryk leaned in over the table, and whispered, "He was just like you described him in your dream. And there was one more thing that was unusual. Both the cobbler and the gray man were sweating, and it was below freezing."

"They were sweating, so what?"

"This triggered a memory that I completely forgot. Years ago, before we met, I went to a lecture about dreaming from a famous kabbalist. So when I got home later that night after seeing Moshe and Gray, I spent hours going through my old journals, and I found my notes," Henryk said, nodding and pulled out of his old case a note pad.

"What does it say?"

Henryk opened the cover and flipped a few pages. "Here it is," he said pointing.

"Read it to me."

"Dreams are the portholes into our souls, and in order to reach our full potential, it is important to make our dreams a significant part of our lives and not just something that occupies our minds and are forgotten or dismissed when we wake up."

"This is nothing new, Rabbi," Solomon said impatiently.

"I can't believe I forgot about this, but it was so long ago. Anyway, it says that people who developed the practice of being awake in the dream world had this unusual side effect," Henryk looked up, allowing Solomon to respond.

"Which is?"

"They sweat when they're awake."

"They sweat?"

"The body somehow adjusts itself when you spend a period of time awake in the dream world, and that's why you sweat. When I saw the cobbler and the gray man, it was freezing. Why were they sweating?"

"Because they are living in both worlds. Just like me. Except I don't sweat."

"Right, that's because you're *rasha,* and *rasha* can live comfortably in both worlds without the sweats. At least, that's what my notes say."

Solomon touched the scar on his forearm left by the cobbler and looked out the window at the snow swirling on the frozen ground. "This is most enlightening, Rabbi."

"I thought so too. But there's even more," Henryk said, tapping a finger on the note pad.

"Tell me," Solomon said.

"Kabbalists believe that the *rashas* source of their power comes from the dream world. Apparently your foresight is not as unusual as you thought, at least among previous *rasha.*"

Solomon shook his head. "Why are you just telling me this now? You've known about my abilities for years."

"I don't know why I didn't remember this. I'm sorry, Solomon. But when I saw them sweating, something triggered my memory," Henryk said.

"Okay, was there anything else."

Henryk nodded. "There were stories of clashes between *rasha* and *tzaddik* from centuries ago. All of these battles took place in the dream world. Because, it was said, that the only way to destroy the eternal soul of a *rasha* was for the *tzaddik* to enter the dream world and deliver him to the valley of Gehenna."

"That's why the cobbler is visiting me," Solomon whispered.

Henryk nodded.

"What does this have to do with the gray man?" Solomon asked.

"Could he be coaching the cobbler on how to enter the dream world and confront you?" Henryk said.

Solomon nodded and said, "So it would seem. Perhaps this gray man is the instigator."

Henryk said, "What are you going to do about it?"

"The gray man will need to understand that I am no one to trifle with."

Chapter 66

When Moshe pulled up to his daughter's home he saw Leah waiting for him by the front door, along with her valise.

"Why are you standing outside?" Moshe said, walking down the driveway.

"You're late, and I want to go home," Leah said with her hands on her hips.

"I'm sorry, the traffic was terrible," he said, leaning in and giving her a kiss on the cheek.

Leah pulled back and reached out to touch Moshe's face. "You're still sweating. Didn't you go to the doctor?"

"I'm perfectly fine," he said and took a step toward the front door. "Can I at least say hello to my granddaughter?"

"No one's here. Barbara took Candy shopping for new shoes."

"All right then, let's get you home," Moshe said, taking hold of her hand and leading her to the car.

During the ride home, Moshe had to skillfully defend against Leah's probing questions about his supposed visit to his sick brother Hymie, and her concerns with his sweats. When he finally reached the house and brought her inside, he exhaled.

All he wanted to do was get back to his normal routine. But after the past three nights with Noa and her *meshuga* boyfriend Sammy, that seemed unlikely.

He told Leah that he was exhausted since he didn't sleep well at his brother's and was going to bed early. It didn't take but a few minutes for Moshe to doze off.

When he awoke the next morning he felt surprisingly refreshed. Moshe realized that he hadn't dreamed, or at least none that he could recall, and certainly he was not awake during them. Perhaps, he thought, he was too exhausted from the activity of the previous three nights.

That first night was something Moshe could have never imagined. According to Noa, her initial plan was to observe his dreaming behaviors while he slept.

"When you're lucid in your dreams, your physical body exhibits physiological changes. I'll be taking notes of how your breathing pattern changes, as well as your body temperature," she said holding up a thermometer.

"You're going to take my temperature while I'm asleep?"

Noa nodded. "You won't even know I'm doing it. When you're in the dream world, Moshe, your mind is in a deep lockdown, allowing me to do almost anything to you without you awakening."

But after Sammy showed up, these plans changed.

Noa was busy preparing a chicken for their dinner when Sammy announced that he had an idea.

"I was thinking, instead of you observing Moshe, why don't we all meet tonight in the dream world and give him more of a guided tour?" Sammy said, looking over to Moshe sitting on the blue and red plaid sofa.

Noa had just placed the chicken in the oven. She wiped her hands on her apron and turned to look at Sammy and Moshe. "You know, that's not a bad idea. There's no reason to waste time."

"Excellent," Sammy said, clapping his hands together. Moshe said nothing.

Sammy came over and sat next to him, slapping his hand on Moshe's knee. "Don't worry, Moshe. You've been awake in the dream world already. I can tell by the sweats."

Noa pointed at Moshe with a wooden spoon she was using to stir the vegetables and said, "I'll need to brew the tea."

Moshe looked up and said, "Tea?"

Noa reached for an old tin sitting on a shelf above the stove. She unscrewed the lid and lifted it to her nose and inhaled. "There's nothing like Mugwort."

She handed the tin to Moshe, who plucked one of the greenish-looking buds and took a sniff.

He jerked his head back and said, "Is it rotten?"

"No, that's just how it smells," Noa said, taking the tin back from Moshe.

With the water coming to a boil she dropped the tea strainer in, turned the stove off, and covered the pot. "We'll let it steep for a while before we drink it."

"What does it do?" Moshe asked, rubbing the tops of his thighs nervously.

"Many cultures use Mugwort for prophetic dreaming and astral traveling. There was a Native American tribe in northern California called the Paiute that called Mugwort the dream plant," said Noa.

"Stop worrying," Sammy said, and took three mugs from the cupboard. He lifted the lid off the pot and carefully filled the mugs. He handed the first one to Moshe. "Here you go, Moshe. Drink up and we will see you in the dream world."

Later that evening, after a decent chicken dinner, Noa and Sammy retired to the bedroom while Moshe stretched out on the sofa. The Mugwort tea had left his eyes feeling heavy throughout dinner. Moments after he lay down, he was asleep.

Moshe left Leah standing on the boardwalk while he went to set up their beach chairs. As he unfolded the frames he heard voices and looked over and saw a young couple lying on a large beach towel. They were clutching each other and passionately kissing.

Moshe shook his head and said, "I don't need this," and moved his chairs further away from the two lovers.

"Moshe, it's me, Noa."

Moshe turned around and looked at the woman. It was Noa, but younger. "Noa, is that really you?"

"It is me. Aren't I beautiful?"

Moshe nodded. "You are, and so young."

"Hey, Moshe, you're here. You're in the dream world!" Sammy said.

Moshe looked at Sammy. He looked the same, but more muscular.

"Bring your wife over?" Noa said.

"Let me get her," Moshe said, and as he turned, Leah was standing in front of him.

Moshe looked at her. She too had transformed into an image of her younger self.

"Leah, you look so young," he said, touching her cheek.

"Are you aware, Moshe?" Noa asked.

"I'm dreaming, aren't I?"

"We all are, except Leah. She's from your mind," said Noa.

Moshe watched Leah smile before she vanished and was gone from the dream.

"You can stay here a while, Moshe, and do what you like," Noa said.

"How will I stop the rasha?" Moshe asked impatiently.

"No time to play?" asked Sammy with a devilish smirk.

"This looks like fun, but I need to get this done and return to my normal boring life as a cobbler."

"I understand, Moshe," Noa said. *"Come with me, I'll show you what you need to do."*

Chapter 67

"We need to take a stand. If we don't he'll take this as a sign of weakness and ramp up these intimidation tactics to other non-union sites," Frank said.

Myron stood by the window and looked out onto the freezing rain coating the trees in City Hall Park. "The entire jobsite is shut down. The trades are scared to send in their work crews."

"It's our job to make it safe. I'll put a protection detail around the project."

"I don't know, Frank. They can always get to them off-site."

"That's right, Myron. That's why we need to put an end to Mickey Coppola's reign of terror."

Myron turned from the window and sat back down at his desk. "What's your plan?"

"Do you mind?" Frank asked leaning over Myron's desk, and pointing to the intercom button.

Myron gestured to proceed.

Frank pressed the button and said, "Agnes, please send in Officer Malone."

The office door opened, and in walked a tall, lanky man wearing a black suit. He had a black hat in one hand, and a black coat draped over his forearm.

Frank said, "Thanks for waiting, Michael."

"Anything for you, Frank," he said, shaking hands.

Frank turned to face Myron, who was now standing beside his desk. "Mr. Mayor, this is Agent Michael Malone. He is the Assistant Director in charge of the New York Field Office for the FBI."

"FBI?" Myron said.

"It's an honor to meet you, Mr. Mayor," Malone said, offering a firm handshake.

"Please, let's sit," Myron said, gesturing to the chairs.

"Agent Malone has been brought up to speed, and he has a few ideas on how to deal with our number one headache," Frank said.

Malone sat with perfect posture at the edge of his seat. Myron thought he had never seen someone with such a straight spine.

"What do you think, Malone?" Myron asked.

"First, I must tell you that Mickey Coppola has been under surveillance by the Bureau for the past year, Mr. Mayor," Malone said.

Myron rubbed his chin and looked over to Frank who shrugged and said, "News to me."

"We know what went down at Antonio's when Carmine Rizzo was murdered," Malone said.

"You do?" Myron said cautiously, not sure if he was implicating him, or just probing.

Malone nodded and said, "And you were there when he was gunned down."

Myron slammed both palms on the desk. "What's this all about, Frank? You brought this G-man in to accuse me of murder?"

"I had no idea about any of this, Myron," Frank said.

Malone inched forward on his chair and said, "No one is accusing you of anything, Mr. Mayor. I only want you to know that the bureau has eyes everywhere. This helps us gather information that may or may not be useful."

"Excuse me, Agent Malone," Myron said, holding his palm out toward the agent. "I'm not sure I understand why you're here. What is it you want from me?"

"The bureau wants what you want."

"Which is?" Myron said impatiently.

"To put Mickey Coppola behind bars for good," Malone said.

Myron looked over to Frank who offered a quick nod of support, and said, "I'm all ears."

Later that night Myron fussed with his suit jacket, trying to smooth out any bumps the recording device that was taped to his chest may have caused. The last thing he wanted was to get caught with a wire by Mickey or one of his goons during dinner at the Stork Club.

When he was satisfied, he walked down the steps and out through a side door of Gracie Mansion where Benjamin was waiting for him.

"Are you ready, sir?" Benjamin asked, holding the car door open.

"Ready as I'll ever be," Myron said stepping into the Caddie.

Myron looked out through the window as Benjamin drove down the East Side Drive toward the Stork Club on East Fifty-third Street. A sudden flash of warmth washed through him, causing him to break out into the sweats. He worried that the perspiration may short-circuit the recording device strapped to him. "Is it warm in here?" he asked Benjamin.

Benjamin looked at Myron through the rear-view mirror and said, "I don't think so, sir. Would you like for me to turn down the temperature?"

"I'm sweating like a pig back here. I'm going to open the window a bit."

"Of course, sir."

Myron closed his eyes as the frigid air rushed in. He loosened his tie, allowing the coolness to seep under his shirt, but the sensation did nothing to quell his anxiety. The visit from Agent Malone had disabled Myron's entire position of power as the Mayor of New York City. How had he allowed himself to become this pawn between the FBI and the Mafia? He had seen his once glorious life whittled down to an anxiety-ridden mess. Now he was going to try to trap Mickey into incriminating himself by recording their conversation. Just as he was thinking this, Benjamin drove into a dark tunnel and Myron feared that his entire future had just done the same.

He hoped he could be ushered quickly past the front door staff in order to avoid any awkward encounter with Niko. She had no idea he was coming, and he didn't want to raise anyone's suspicions that they were still involved with each other.

Before Agent Malone's visit, Myron hoped that if his relationship with Niko did become public that Mickey would be forgiving since he had saved his life. But now with the FBI running surveillance for months and apparently knowing everything about him, he wished that their secret affair was all he had to worry about.

As Benjamin pulled up to the curb in front of the Stork Club, Myron knew that things were not going to go as he planned, because Mickey was standing outside speaking to his daughter alongside a long line of patrons waiting to gain admission to the club.

"Fuck, Benjamin," Myron said.

"Do you want me to keep driving? I can take a loop around the block," Benjamin said.

"It's too late, now," Myron said, spotting Mickey pointing to his car.

Benjamin got out of the car and hustled to the rear passenger side and opened Myron's door.

"Mr. Mayor, how nice to see you," Mickey said, sticking his arm and outstretched hand out.

Myron clutched his hand and gave him a firm shake. "Same to you, Mickey."

Mickey turned and said, "Of course you remember my daughter, Niko."

"I do," was all Myron could muster.

Niko was wearing her full length shearling coat, with her hair lying softly over the thick fur collar. She gave a subdued smile, and said, "Good evening, Mr. Mayor. Please follow me."

Niko led the men past the people waiting in the cold, to get inside the club. Once inside, they removed their coats and handed them to the coat check girl.

"Damn it," Mickey said suddenly. "I forgot something. Wait for me here, Myron, I'll be back in two minutes."

With Mickey gone, Myron and Niko stood alone in the lobby of the club.

Myron leaned in and whispered, "You look amazing, baby."

"You like it? I just bought it," Niko said, offering a provocative pose showing off the tight fitting and short outfit.

"Very much," Myron said, feeling the warmth reignite inside him.

Niko gently put a hand on his chest and touched the recording device.

"What's that?" she asked, moving her hand around the bulk taped to his chest.

"Nothing, stop it. Here comes your father," he said.

Mickey walked back in, slapped his hands together, and said, "All set, let's find our table."

Myron turned away from Niko and walked toward the double doors that led inside to the dining tables. As he reached the doors, he looked about and saw that he was walking alone. He turned back, and saw Niko whispering something into her father's ear. Mickey listened, nodded, and gave his daughter a kiss on her cheek. He then walked over to Myron, slapped him on his back and rubbed his shoulder.

"Let's go have a few drinks and talk, Mr. Mayor," Mickey said, as the two men entered the Stork Club's dining hall. Myron glanced nervously over his shoulder and caught a glimpse of Niko welcoming guests.

"Sure, that would be great," Myron said following Mickey through the cluster of tables already filled with patrons drinking, smoking and chatting away.

Mickey gestured to the semi-circle booth with a reserved sign placed upon the table. "Order yourself a drink, Mr. Mayor. I'll be back in a few minutes."

Myron nodded.

When the waitress came over Myron ordered a whiskey and lit up a cigar. While he waited for Mickey to return, his mind replayed the moment Niko touched the recording device. He casually ran his fingertips across his shirt and felt the outline of the machine strapped to his chest. There was no doubt that Niko knew what it was, and she must have warned her father.

It occurred to him that his recent thoughts of marriage were now just some ridiculous fantasy. He looked into his nearly empty glass and frowned. How could he have been so wrong about Niko? Beside her beauty and alluring charm, she had proven herself to be a woman with formidable intelligence, as well as a resource of valuable political insights that had impressed him—so much so that he had been ready to offer her his unconditional allegiance. Apparently, she was not willing to do the same. Better that he learned about this now, than to discover her misguided loyalty after they were married.

Myron shook his head, deciding that this was the end. He would have nothing to do with her any longer. He slammed his drink down, slid out from the booth and walked toward the front door, ignoring Niko as he passed by her. Once out onto the sidewalk, he saw Benjamin standing by the car a few feet down the street. He marched toward him and said, "Let's go, Ben, we're done here."

Chapter 68

It had been a week since the disturbing Coliseum fiasco. Along with his concerns about Moshe, that was all Arnold could handle. He decided to take a break from the stress and enjoy a coffee and a piece of almond cake at the diner.

He took a seat in a booth and Rosie the waitress poured him his coffee. As he was reaching for the sugar, Gray walked in.

"Good morning, Arnold," Gray said with a wave. "Would you mind if I join you?"

"Please," Arnold said, gesturing to the empty side of the booth.

"Just water, please Rosie," Gray said.

"It always amazes me that you show up just when I'm thinking about you."

"I do my best," Gray said, smiling and taking a sip of water.

"Have you heard from Moshe lately? I haven't seen him in a while," Arnold asked.

"Moshe has been working with my mentor, Noa."

Arnold shook his head. "Who is Noa?"

Gray took a deep breath and nodded. "I think it's time I fill you in on a few things," Gray said, as he patted away the perspiration from his forehead with the cloth napkin Rosie handed to him.

Arnold sat mesmerized in the booth at the Fordham Diner as Gray told his story. He began when he first met Noa at a friend's dinner party in Queens about ten years earlier.

"When she walked in, I knew right away there was something different about her. There was this sense of wisdom that I recognized, even before we said a word to each other. During dinner there was a lively discussion among the guests. Afterwards, Noa and I sat side-by-side on the couch and talked. She told me that she was a dream therapist. When I told her about my father's research into lucid dreaming and how I became proficient at moving about in the dream world, she stood up and took me into the other room so we could speak without anyone overhearing us."

Arnold put down his cup of coffee and said, "What do you mean, moving about in the dream world?"

"That's how I live, in two worlds: the dream world, and the awakened world. That's what Noa is teaching Moshe. It's what he needs to know in order to deal with the *rasha*, Solomon."

"And that's where Moshe is now?" Arnold asked.

"It is."

"I'm assuming your sweats have to do with all of this two-worlds stuff," Arnold said.

"It does, you're right," Gray said with a smile.

"Please tell me more about your connection with Noa."

"In my training with her, she taught me that she was a direct descendant of Francesa Sarah of Safed, a spiritual guide of living in the dream world."

"What does that mean?" Arnold said shaking his head.

"It means that her life's purpose is keeping balance in the dream world. That was how she became aware of Solomon. She saw that he was using his prophetic dreams to make himself rich, even if it meant hurting others in the process. This, Noa understood, had to be corrected. But unlike other disturbances which she was able to rectify herself, this one was caused by a *rasha,* and the only way to stop a *rasha* was through the power of a *tzaddik.* After she explained to me what a *tzaddik* and a *rasha* were, I asked how does one find this mysterious *tzaddik?*"

Arnold felt his jaw hang open as Gray continued, "She told me that since you can't find the *tzaddik* in the dream world, she hoped she could find him by following the trail of the *rasha.* But after years of searching, she had no luck. Noa then grabbed my hands and asked me if I would use my skills in the dream world and see if I could locate the *tzaddik.*

"I enthusiastically agreed to try, as this would be the first time I had something worthy of my skills. I told her I would stay in touch with her and let her know my progress. So I searched the dream world. Finding Solomon was easy. Once I did that, it wasn't hard to find his life in the awakened world."

"And you found me through Solomon?" Arnold asked.

Gray nodded and said, "Solomon had many dreams that included his son Myron. Especially the ones that foresaw events that they could capitalize upon. Once I was able to find Myron in the awakened world, I stumbled upon you, Arnold, as you were running your sports book through Myron at that time. I figured that perhaps you could be a way into the Blass organization."

Arnold rocked his body back and forth, like an adding machine tabulating the information Gray just shared with him. He looked briefly out the diner window and at the parked cars on Fordham Road, then turned back to Gray, and said, "What does Moshe have to do?"

"He needs to take the *rasha* to Gehenna," Gray whispered.

"Gehenna?" Arnold repeated, swallowed hard and asked, "Do you mean hell?"

Gray looked at Arnold with his gray eyes twinkling from the morning sunlight shining through the diner windows, and said, "Yes, I mean hell."

When questioned later by the police, Arnold barely remembered leaving the diner and walking back to the Paradise Theater with Gray. All he could recall was hearing Gray's name being called out. He told the police officer that he turned and saw Henryk Appel pointing a pistol at Gray, and firing.

"Gray's body slammed into the brass doors of the theater and collapsed to the sidewalk. I looked at the rabbi, who stared at me with his disturbed eyes that I can still feel. He then calmly turned and walked away. I tended to Gray, who had been shot in his chest. His gray suit turned blood red and the life drained out of him as I held him in my arms."

Chapter 69

Solomon heard the phone ringing in his dream, before realizing that he needed to wake up and answer it. "Hello?" he choked out through his usual morning congestion.

"Solomon, it's me, Henryk. I've been arrested."

"Arrested? For what, Rabbi?"

"I shot Gray. I'm being held at the Forty-sixth Precinct on Ryder Avenue. Please come," he said before Solomon heard a dial tone.

When Solomon arrived he was escorted to a holding cell where Henryk was awaiting arraignment. He looked at his longtime friend, mentor and confidant, and said, "Why did you shoot him, Rabbi?"

Henryk looked up from the metal bench in his cell, his tired eyes darkened with circles and said, "I did it for you, Solomon. I did it for the *rasha*."

Solomon hired a criminal attorney he used in the past, but it did little good. With Arnold Lieberman as an eyewitness, Henryk was convicted of murder and given a death sentence by the electric chair. He would be held at the Attica Correctional Facility, a high security prison, until his execution.

Solomon felt himself choke up each time he thought of his friend. This emotion was new to him. Not even when he heard about the death of his childhood friend Leo Gorpatsch did he feel this distraught.

While sitting alone at Charlie's, he found himself trying to hold back tears. He had no memory of ever crying in his adult life, as he caught a tear escaping and rolling down his cheek.

This sudden melancholy was accompanied by a wave of guilt. *It was because of me that he felt compelled to shoot Gray,* Solomon thought.

He lifted his glass in the air and rattled the cubes settled at the bottom to attract Ralph's attention for another whiskey.

While waiting for his drink, he looked out the window. The first buds of the spring were exposing themselves on the trees. Another season, after so many in his life. The moment passed when a car pulled up to Charlies' and a young woman stepped out. It was Rebecca. *Why was she here?*

The door opened and Rebecca stepped in. She turned and looked at Solomon and said, "I thought I would find you here."

"Rebecca?" Solomon asked, trying to compose himself from his emotional episode just moments before.

She took off her coat and slid it over the back of the bar chair and sat down. "You disappeared the last time I saw you at the library. Did I scare you away?"

Solomon exhaled. "I guess you did."

Rebecca reached across the old, stained wooden table and put her hand on top of Solomon's. "I need to talk to you," she said, giving his hand a gentle squeeze.

Solomon felt a return of the sweats, though milder than his previous episode at the library.

Rebecca didn't wait for Solomon to respond. She said, "When I didn't see you again at the library after our last conversation, I started teaching myself how to be awake in my dreams. When it happens, I mean when I'm aware that I'm dreaming, I think of you."

Solomon swallowed, and said, "You think of me?"

"Yes, and you come. But you're much younger," she said with a gentle smile, before continuing. "And so handsome, Solomon."

Solomon took a sip of his whiskey.

"We make love, Solomon. It's a spiritual experience. I feel happy, blissful and content as if we were one entity, floating high above the earth. It's wonderful."

"That sounds amazing," Solomon managed to say.

"I'm sorry, Solomon, this is selfish. I know it's only a one-way relationship."

Solomon regained his composure, and his posture. He sat tall in his chair, looked at her, and smiled. "Not necessarily, Rebecca."

"What are you saying?"

"I can show you how we can be together in the dream world."

Rebecca narrowed her eyes as she pondered Solomon's words. "I figured that when I dream about you, it comes from my mind. You're not real. But you're telling me that you can be real, we both can, at the same time."

"This is possible, Rebecca."

"Will you be young or old?"

"I'll be whatever I want to be. I'm assuming you will want the younger version of Solomon," he said.

"Not too young," she said, offering an alluring smile. "I think it's your wisdom that attracts me the most."

Chapter 70

"When is the funeral?" Moshe asked.

"I'm trying to arrange something for tomorrow," Arnold said.

"Another senseless death because of me," Moshe said softly as he looked out the window onto the Grand Concourse.

"There's no point in blaming yourself, Moshe," Arnold said, sitting at his desk.

"Gray was a kind and caring man. Did he have any family?"

"He never mentioned anyone. I don't even know his real name," Arnold said.

"Why would Solomon's rabbi want to kill Gray?"

"I don't know if it means anything, but the morning of his murder Gray told me about your involvement with a woman called Noa, and the dream world."

"There's a lot more than that," Moshe said, rubbing the back of his neck.

"What else?" Arnold asked.

Moshe leaned forward, looked directly into Arnold's anxious eyes, and said, "I've been shaken to my soul."

Arnold nodded slowly and took a deep breath.

Moshe swallowed hard, and continued, "Hell exists, Arnold, and it's where I need to take Solomon."

"The day he was gunned down, Gray spoke to me about it."

Moshe nodded and said, "From what I was told, the only way to eliminate the soul of the *rasha* is to bring the *rasha* to Gehenna, to hell."

"And how do you do this?" Arnold asked.

"It's done in the dream world. I travel with him through the blackness, to the bowels of Gehenna," Moshe said, then stopped. He put a hand to his lips, took a breath, and whispered, "She took me there, Arnold."

Arnold's eyes widened. "What did you see?"

Moshe's face reddened, he dug his fingernails into the chair's arms, and said, "A sea of fire, where the flesh of the damned burns, then regrows, to be burned again. Screams of pain, and cries of sadness fill the air fouled by the burning flesh. There's no escape, once the soul is thrown into it."

Arnold leaned back in his chair, ran his fingers through his hair, and asked, "I don't understand, Moshe. How do you bring the *rasha* to Gehanna without yourself being in danger?"

Moshe held his hands together to keep them from shaking. "I don't know, Arnold. I suppose I too can lose my soul to the fires of Gehenna. Perhaps I should ask Noa?"

Arnold furrowed his brow, trying to make sense of Moshe's words. "Gray told me that Noa traces her lineage back to this Jewish mystic, Francesa Sarah of Safed, from the seventeenth century."

Moshe leaned in to whisper, "She took me to see her."

"She did?" Arnold asked, rubbing the unshaven stubble on his chin.

"After I left her and Sammy on the beach…"

"Sammy? Who is Sammy?" Arnold interrupted.

"Oh that's Noa's boyfriend," he said and noticed Arnold's furrowed forehead. "Don't ask," Moshe said waving his hand. "Anyway, I met Noa in the dream world on some beach. She took me by my hand and suddenly we were in

Safed. But not the same Safed we visited, Arnold. This was of three hundred years ago, when the most illustrious and studied scholars migrated to Safed after their expulsion from Spain.

"We were in a large underground cave-like room, built with bricks of limestone. Women were busy milling about. We remained unnoticed until Noa spoke. She called out, *I have brought the tzaddik for your blessing, Francesa Sarah.*

"I stood alongside Noa, afraid to speak. No one turned to look at us. I wondered if Noa's words were heard. Then suddenly we were in a space of total darkness. I couldn't even see my hands inches from face. Believe me, I tried," Moshe said, holding his two hands up.

Arnold nodded.

"Then she appeared, out of the darkness. She spoke to me, Arnold, as clearly and life-like as you are speaking to me now."

"What did she say?" Arnold asked.

"'You are the righteous one.' I looked around for Noa, but I was alone. I stood there unsure of what to do or say. She reached out and grasped both of my hands. I felt a charge, like an electric shock, coursing through my body. I jerked back quickly, releasing her grip. Then she said, 'The power of the almighty flows through you, *tzaddik*. You cannot elude your purpose.'"

Arnold stared at Moshe, unable to speak for a moment. He rubbed his eyes and leaned forward, resting his elbows on his desk. "What are you going to do, Moshe?"

Moshe shrugged. "I don't know. It seems my life is not my own anymore. I feel like I'm part of some story from Greek mythology where the gods manipulate the humans for their amusement."

"You mean like Hercules?" Arnold said with a grin.

Moshe tried to manage a smile. "If only I had one tenth of his strength."

Chapter 71

"The damn thing was too big," Myron complained, sliding the recorder across his desk.

"The bureau is working on some smaller prototypes, but that's the best technology we have for the time being," said Agent Michael Malone.

"There's nothing on it that we can use, Malone?" Frank asked.

"I'm afraid not," said Malone.

"Once Niko gave him the heads up, he barely spoke to me," Myron said.

"I guess we know where her loyalties lie," Frank said looking at Myron with a shrug.

Myron stood up from behind his desk and stepped toward the window with the view of the Brooklyn Bridge. He pulled on the cord and lifted up the wood venetian blind, providing an unobstructed view of the traffic, which was backed up in both directions. He turned and pointed a finger at Malone and said, "Is this the best you can do?"

"Mickey Coppola is a clever son of a bitch," Malone said.

"Come on now, are you saying you have no other plans to nail him on something?" Frank asked.

"Our wire taps on his phone have come up with some interesting conversations with the Teamsters," Malone said.

"What's that about?" Myron asked, and moved back to his desk and sat down.

Malone looked over to Frank and then to Myron. "They've been talking about the Columbus Circle Coliseum project."

Myron leaned in, his elbows resting on his desk and asked, "What are they saying?"

Malone shrugged slightly and said, "They are going to start with the project managers for each trade and pressure them."

"What are we going to do?" asked Myron.

"We need to play dirty too," Frank said with a mischievous grin.

"Now you're talking. What do you have in mind?" said Myron, rubbing his hands together.

"Go ahead and tell him," Frank said to Malone.

Malone leaned in. He glanced over to Frank and back to Myron and said, "We're going to set up a surveillance."

Myron shook his head. "We just tried that, Malone."

Malone ignored the comment, pointed to Myron, and said, "You're going to need to convince Mickey that you made a mistake by awarding the Coliseum contract to a non-union shop. He's going to say that you can change your mind and find some reason to make the contract null and void, which in itself may be illegal. But that wouldn't be enough to convict Mickey for any serious time."

"So what do you have in mind?" Frank asked.

"First you need to gain his confidence by giving him what he wants, which is the Coliseum contract. Then, in a casual conversation, you're going to need him to confess to organizing the thugs that beat up those subcontractors," Malone said.

Myron nodded. "That sounds doable."

"That's just the first part."

"What do you mean, Malone?" asked Myron.

"You're going to complain about your Police Commissioner," Malone said, cocking his head over to Frank.

"Complain about what?"

"That he has been making things difficult for you to do certain things that Mickey and his friends want."

"He's just going to tell me to fire him and replace him with someone who will listen," Myron said.

"You're right. But you'll say that he's been holding some leverage over you, that prevents you from dismissing him."

"Which is?"

Malone smiled, leaned back in his chair and crossed his arms on his chest and said, "He knows about your affair with Niko, Mickey's daughter."

"Are you fucking kidding me?" Myron blurted out.

Malone shook his head, and said, "I'm sure Mickey already knows you're fucking his daughter, so I wouldn't be too worried. But he will want to do something about Frank."

"Yes, like kill me," Frank said.

"Exactly!" Malone said, pointing his finger at Frank. "At least that's what we are counting on. What we need is for him to say the words, so we can record them."

"So are you going to tape that thing to me again?" Myron said pointing to the recorder sitting in his desk.

Malone shook his head. "Not on you, but in a room. We need to record him in a space he feels comfortable in. Where he will speak freely without worry. Do you have an idea of where such a place would be, Mr. Mayor?"

Myron scratched the back of his head for a minute, and then smiled. "Antonio's in the Bronx is the perfect place. He'll never suspect anything there. Except, how will you plant a bug without being noticed. He owns the damn place."

"Leave that to the FBI. That's what we do best."

Chapter 72

*S*olomon found Rebecca walking on a beach alone. She was wearing something soft, allowing the breeze to flutter it behind her. Her hair was loose and mimicked the motion of her dress.

"Rebecca," Solomon called out.

The waves were softly lapping at her bare feet. She reached down to pick up a shell, and as she stood up, she turned and saw Solomon.

"Is it you?" she asked.

Solomon ran over. His body was young and strong and in no need of the cane he had become dependent on. "It's me, Solomon."

She ran into his arms and they kissed.

"This feels so real," she said.

"You're lovely," Solomon said, gently stroking her face.

"How did you find me?"

"I can find anyone in the dream world. Now that you're lucid, we can experience our lovemaking together."

"Solomon," she said running her hands across his bare chest, "you're so fit and so young.

"And you're incredibly beautiful, Rebecca."

They embraced and their bodies intertwined and floated high above the beach and soared across the vast ocean.

The next morning when Solomon awoke, he did his best to get his aching body out of bed. The first thing he wanted to do was to go to the library and see Rebecca. It took the better part of an hour to get himself ready. Finally he grabbed his cane and he sat himself on his front porch waiting for the cab.

Planting his cane firmly on each step, he ascended in between the two powerful lion sculptures and into the grand entrance of the New York City Public Library. The moment he entered he needed to maneuver himself around crowds filling the large gallery. He pushed people out of his way with his cane as he cut a path toward the main reading room where he would find Rebecca.

The second he saw her eyes without their usual sparkle, he knew something was wrong. Solomon offered a brief wave but she ignored him. He made his way around the rows of large wooden tables where people were sitting, whispering and reading. When he finally got to her desk, she looked up and stretched out her right arm and pointed behind him. "Go wait for me downstairs. I'll be there soon."

Solomon squinted and cocked his head and said, "Sure, take your time."

Two hours he waited. Every time someone entered through the large wooden doors, Solomon looked up. He thought about finding something to read while he sat there, but he figured what was the point, she could show up any minute.

The next thing he remembered he was being shaken awake by Rebecca.

"Solomon, wake up."

He opened his eyes and rubbed his forehead. "Where am I?"

"It's me, Rebecca. You're at the library. I'm sorry to have you wait so long. It's been one of those days. I think every school district in the city sent a class or two."

Solomon pushed himself up from the deep slouch he ended up in after dozing off.

"Okay, I'm glad you're finally here," he said.

"Come, let's sit over here where it's more private," Rebecca said, pointing to a cluster of chairs in a small alcove, partially hidden by a bookshelf.

Solomon groaned a bit as he pushed himself out of the chair.

Rebecca grabbed onto his elbow and helped him stand.

"Thank you. I'm not as young as I am in my dreams," he said with a smirk.

Rebecca nodded.

"Is something wrong, Rebecca? Are you upset by me coming here?"

She shrugged, "No, not really. But there is something I want to discuss with you about last night."

The words *last night*, send a chill through Solomon. He smiled and asked, "What would you like to talk about?"

"It was something you said, and by the way, I remember everything that happened."

"As do I," Solomon quickly replied with a smile.

"When I asked you, how did you find me? You said, 'I can find anyone in the dream world. Now that you're lucid, we can experience our lovemaking together.'"

Solomon nodded slowly. "I remember," he said.

"I thought about those words and realized that it was you coming to me in my dreams before I learned how to be lucid. Were you making love to me, without my consent?"

Solomon straightened his spine, trying to sit tall in the wooden chair. He glanced to either side of him and rubbed his chin. "You're right, Rebecca. It was without your permission."

The words hung there for a while, allowing Solomon to think of the warning he was given by Francesa Sarah to not violate Rebecca in her dreams. He was now regretting not obeying her command.

Rebecca looked at Solomon and shook her head, then said, "I should be angry with you, but for some strange reason I'm not."

Solomon let out a long exhalation. He wasn't even aware he was holding his breath.

"You're not mad?"

"No. Maybe it was your way to get to know me," she continued. "In a strange, weird way, it's kind of romantic. Not that I'm going to ever tell anyone about this," she said with a wide smile, showing off her two dimples.

Solomon reached out and grabbed her hands resting on the table. "You make me happy, Rebecca."

"Thank you, Solomon. You make me happy too."

Chapter 73

"Who is on the phone, Betsy?" Arnold asked his secretary over the intercom.

"She says her name is Noa. N-O-A."

"That's Gray's friend who Moshe told me about. What does she want?"

"She wants to come talk to you about Gray. She can be here in two minutes. She's calling from a pay phone across the street."

Arnold got up and looked out his window. "There she is," he said.

"What do I tell her?"

"Tell her to come up."

A few minutes later Noa walked into Arnold's office.

"Hello, Noa. Moshe told me about you," Arnold said, as he rose from his chair and stepped around his desk with an outstretched hand.

Noa gripped it firmly and shook. "Nice to meet you. Gray was a close friend. I understand you were with him when he was murdered."

"I was. A very tragic end for a good man."

"He was a good man, thank you, Arnold. Moshe told me that Gray worked for you."

"He did, well sort of," Arnold said, and look closely at Noa. "You sweat too, just like Gray, and now Moshe."

"Yes, all dreamers sweat."

"Dreamers? Is that what you're calling yourselves? It makes sense. Gray with his grayness, seemed like a dream. He was a wonderful man, and a good friend. I will miss him."

"Gray told me many things about you. It's because of you we found Moshe the *tzaddik*."

"Tell me, why are you here?"

Noa gripped the arms of the chair and took a breath, and said, "This is hard to say, and I didn't want to come and ask. But Sammy, that's my boyfriend, said I should. We want to give Gray a proper Jewish burial, but we have very little money. So I was hoping…"

"Don't say another word. I've got it covered. It would be an honor."

Noa's shoulder's relaxed, she exhaled and said, "Thank you, Arnold. A Jewish burial is important for the passing of Gray's soul into his next incarnation."

"I agree."

"Tell me, if you don't mind me asking, why did you seek out the *tzaddik*?"

"My rabbi, Rabbi Shapira, may peace be upon him, was my mentor in Kabbalah. He was also the son of Moshe's childhood rabbi, back in Krzywcza. Some coincidence, huh?"

Noa nodded.

"Anyway, he ran into Solomon Blass at a course on the dark side of Kabbalah, many years ago. According to Rabbi Shapira, Solomon had some disturbing comments and observations during the course.

"After a few classes, the rabbi asked Solomon to have coffee with him at the diner. The conversation started with the basic Kabbalah affirmations. You know what I mean, understanding Desire, finding the Light. Then when it got to Opposition, things got interesting. The rabbi's interpretation of the Opposition was not the same as Solomon's, or any Kabbalist."

Noa wagged her finger at him. "That's true, that's where the *rasha* strays from the intended meaning."

"That's what the rabbi thought. He said if Solomon was indeed *rasha*, that people in his path would suffer, while he prospered. This we discovered was true. Solomon had this uncanny ability of foresight that made him, and his son Myron, our mayor, wealthy and powerful men.

"This began ten years ago, and just one and a half years ago I found Moshe the Cobbler, right across the street. And, of course, Gray magically showed up a few weeks before I found the *tzaddik*."

Noa lifted herself out of her chair a bit, re-crossed her legs, and said, "Gray and I have been aware of the *rasha* for many years. His behavior caused a disturbance in the dream world."

"What does that mean?" Arnold asked.

Noa smiled and tilted her head. "When evil appears, the dreamers become agitated and seek to correct the imbalance. But if a *rasha* causes the disturbance, there is little that can be done without the power of a *tzaddik*. That is why when Gray found you, and then you discovered Moshe, we knew we had our chance to extinguish the soul of the *rasha*."

Arnold stood up and walked over to the sink. He filled a glass with water and handed it to Noa. "Gray was always thirsty."

"Thank you, Arnold."

"What do you think about Moshe's chances of seeing this through?" Arnold said.

Noa took a sip of the water and placed the glass down on Arnold's desk and said, "After his encounter with the spirit Francesa Sarah, I would say better. But I'm not sure. Moshe is a kind man and what he needs to do is hard. Even to someone as evil as Solomon Blass."

"But it must be done," Arnold said.

Noa nodded, and said solemnly, "It must be done."

After speaking a while longer, Arnold walked Noa down the stairs and into a taxi. He handed the driver ten dollars and told him to keep the change.

"Don't worry about the funeral expenses. You arrange what you want and send me all of the bills. I'll take care of them," he said to Noa, and closed the car door.

Noa put her palm against the window and mouthed the words, *thank you.*

Every Wednesday, Arnold and Agnes met at the diner to discuss Myron, and the assortment of issues that came up regularly. By the time he arrived on this day, Agnes was there drinking a cup of coffee.

"Sorry, I'm late. I just had Gray's friend Noa in the office."

"I don't know her."

"Yes, she's the same woman who has been teaching Moshe how to be awake in his dreams."

Agnes took a sip of her coffee as Arnold took off his jacket and slid into the booth across from her.

"Before we discuss Myron, I want to hear more about Gray."

Arnold picked up the menu and handed it to the waitress, "I'll have the usual, Ruth, thank you."

"You got it, sweetie," she said, filling his coffee cup.

"What's his real name?" Agnes asked.

Arnold shrugged. "Nothing mysterious, it's Gary. When he was a teenager, he read a book about a Jewish spy who infiltrated Russian headquarters. The character was called the Gray Man. His secret was to blend in with the surroundings, as if he was invisible. He wore only gray clothing and had gray hair.

"After reading the book, all he had to do was flip two letters in his name, and he became Gray instead of Gary. Just like the heroic character, he started wearing only gray clothing. His eyes, at first a pale shade of blue, according to what Noa said, soon faded to gray. Even his hair turned prematurely gray by the time he was twenty years old."

"Here you go, Arnold," Ruth said, and placed an egg sandwich in front of him.

"Thank you, Ruth," Arnold said, twisting the top off the ketchup bottle.

"But what's with the dreaming?" Agnes said.

"It starts with Noa. When she was seven years old she started having recurring dreams about this mystic from the seventeenth century, called Francesa Sarah of Safed. When she told her mother about them, her mother was thrilled. She sat Noa down and explained the lineage of the women in their family, which they could trace back to the seventeenth century in the ancient city of Safed.

"She told Noa about Francesa Sarah's power to live in the dream world, and how she had handed down this knowledge to her daughter, who had passed it on to her own daughter, and so on, through the ages, all the way to Noa's mother, who now said, 'I will teach you what my mother taught me, and if you have a daughter, you will teach her. This is our purpose, Noa.'"

Agnes put her coffee cup down, and asked, "Does Noa have any daughters?"

Arnold shook his head. "She was unable to have children, so it looks like the lineage ends with her when she dies. But she taught Gray."

"Ah, that's how Gray knows how to live in the dream world."

"Precisely," Arnold said. He then leaned forward and whispered, "It falls upon Noa and Moshe to put an end to the *rasha*, Agnes. A tall task for a cobbler and a dreamer."

Chapter 74

Myron sat at the bar at Antonio's sipping his second whiskey.

"I'm sure he will be here soon," said Antonio, wiping the bar top with a wet dishcloth.

He looked at his watch. Mickey was now twenty minutes late for their two o'clock meeting. He wanted to get up and leave, but the FBI had set up their surveillance and were now sitting in a van on Arthur Avenue, hopeful to listen to the potentially incriminating conversation. At least that was the plan.

Myron had never heard a word from Niko about the recording device. Maybe she didn't know what it was when she ran her fingers across his chest. Perhaps he just imagined she was telling her father about the recorder, when he saw her whispering in Mickey's ear at the Stork Club. But regardless, his anger prevented him from reaching out to her and she made no attempts to contact him either. *Perhaps that was the end of it*, he thought.

He looked at the ice cubes swimming in his glass and swirled them round and round. The warmth of drinking the two glasses so quickly caused him to sweat, or maybe it was the anxiety of waiting for Mickey. He stood up and walked toward the back of the restaurant to the bathrooms.

He washed his hands and splashed cool water on his face. Myron looked at himself in the mirror. He ran his hand over his bald head and felt stubble. *Dammit, I should have shaved,* he thought.

Myron stepped out of the men's room and nearly walked into Mickey.

"Jesus, Mickey, I didn't see you."

"I gotta piss," he said, pushing his way past Myron.

Myron returned to his seat and glanced over to a man sitting at the other end of the bar, nursing a beer.

"Mr. Mayor," the grizzled stranger said, lifting his bottle as a salute.

Myron nodded and felt a hand patting his back. He turned to see Mickey taking the barstool next to him.

"How's it going, Mr. Mayor?" Mickey said.

"Fine," he said, looking at his watch.

"Sorry I'm late, Myron, I had an issue I had to deal with."

"All right. Let's get to it. I have a city to run."

"Sure thing, Myron," Mickey said and lifted his arm to get Antonio's attention. "Antonio, a whiskey please."

Both men clinked glasses, and Mickey said, "What do you Jews say? Chaim?"

Myron shook his head and said, "L'chaim."

"L'chaim," Mickey said, clinking glasses with Myron.

"Okay, Mickey, let's get to the reason while I asked you here."

"You have my attention," he said, sipping his drink.

Myron looked at the man at the other end of the bar and said, "Maybe we can talk in the back room?"

Mickey glanced down the bar and pushed back and stood up. "Hey Antonio, we'll be in the back."

"Sure thing, Mickey," Antonio said.

Myron followed Mickey towards the back of the restaurant. He pulled on his shirt collar, releasing the heat from under his layers of clothing. *Here we go*, he thought.

The first thing Myron noticed as he walked into the private dining room was the white table cloth. He ran his hand across the surface as he sat down and wondered how Antonio was able to keep the cloths so perfectly white.

Mickey took the seat across from Myron and folded his hands on the table and said, "Okay, tell me why we're here?"

"I made a decision," Myron said, and let the words hang there for a moment.

Mickey opened his palms, gesturing for him to continue.

"I want to give you the Coliseum contract."

Mickey slammed both palms on the white cloth and shouted, "Myron, you've come through."

"Not so fast, Mickey. I said I want to, but there are a few obstacles standing in the way."

"Tell me what's the problem. I'm sure we can figure out a solution."

Myron held back a smile, not wanting to give away any clues to raise Mickey's suspicions. "I'm getting pushback from Frank."

Mickey leaned back against his chair, shook his head and said, "You're the fucking mayor. Tell him to take a flying fuck."

"I wish I could. But he's holding a bit of leverage on me."

Mickey nodded and frowned. "And what would this leverage be, Mr. Mayor?"

Mickey rubbed the back of his neck, cocked his neck, and said, "I don't know how to say this, but um…"

Mickey held up his hand, gesturing for Myron to stop talking, and said, "Let me guess. You're fucking my daughter."

"You know?"

"Of course I know. Even Niko knows I know. She came to me and begged me to let her see you. For some reason she likes you. Actually, I think it's more than like. So I thought, why not. My daughter could do worse than dating the Mayor of New York City."

Myron shook his head and said, "I'm shocked. After what you said to me…"

"That I would cut off your balls and shove them down your throat."

"Yeah. that."

"If you hurt my daughter, Myron," Mickey said, wagging a finger at him.

Myron smiled and said, "This is easier than I thought it would be."

"Go tell the commissioner to fuck off and get me that contract. And don't worry, Myron, there will be a nice piece put aside for you."

Suddenly gunshots rang out.

Myron nearly jumped out of his chair. He opened the door and stepped into the doorway, where he heard two more shots.

"What the fuck?" Mickey said, appearing just behind Myron.

"Are you in there, boss?" a voice shouted.

"I'm here. What is it, Tony?" Said Mickey.

"I shot this guy in the bar. He's dead."

"I'm coming out. Put your gun down," Mickey said.

Both Mickey and Myron stepped into the main dining area of Antonio's and there lying in a pool of blood was the man who toasted Myron with his beer bottle.

Myron bent down to look at the man's face and looked up to Tony and asked, "Why did you shoot him?"

"I looked in the window from the street and I saw this guy listening to your conversation by the door. I thought I should check it out. When I approached him, he pulled a gun and told me to back off. As I reached for my firearm he shot at me but missed. So I put two into his chest."

Mickey bent over to get a better look and pointed. "Is that a badge?" He knelt down, pulled the dead man's jacket back, and exposed an FBI badge clipped to his belt.

"Maybe you should tell me, Mr. Mayor, why an FBI agent was here?" Mickey said.

Myron's heart pounded hard against his ribcage.

Mickey reached over and took Tony's gun and pointed it at Myron and said, "You're clever, Myron, but not clever enough."

Myron took a step back, but Mickey closed the gap. He jammed the gun hard into his stomach. "I should kill you now."

A commotion was heard at the front doors and in barged Agent Malone with his gun drawn and aiming at Mickey. "Put the gun down," he ordered.

"Fuck you," Mickey shouted and fired at Malone.

Malone simultaneously fired back. Myron watched Mickey spin around and nearly get knocked off his feet. He was shot and stumbled toward the back of the restaurant. Agent Malone was not hit, and advanced on Mickey with his gun positioned to fire again.

"Put your weapon down," instructed Malone.

Mickey was bleeding. He held the gun in one hand and held onto the wall with the other. Somehow he managed to stumble toward the back of the restaurant, and into the private dining room. Agent Malone followed.

Another gunshot rang out and a heavy thud was heard. Myron slowly walked back and cautiously peeked into the room. There was Agent Malone standing over the dead body of Mickey Coppola. Blood was splattered across the table, down the walls and was pooling on the floor next to Mickey's dead body. A bizarre thought caused Myron to wonder, *how was Antonio going to remove the blood stains from the white table cloth?*

Chapter 75

"**A**re we paying for this?" whispered Leah.

Moshe shook his head and said, "Arnold has agreed to pay for the entire funeral, the least we can do is take out a few friends who came to pay their respects to Gray."

"Who is that sitting next to Agnes?" Leah asked, pointing to Noa, sitting at the other end of the table at the Fordham Diner.

"That's Noa and sitting next to her is her boyfriend, Sammy."

"Her boyfriend? She looks old enough to be his grandmother," Leah said.

"Quiet, Leah, don't be rude."

After everyone placed their order Arnold picked up his water glass and said, "It's a little too early for a real drink, but I would like to say something about the man we all came to know as Gray."

A round of approving nods, and hands reached for the glass tumblers.

"I came to know Gray as someone who one day just showed up at my office. He said he wanted to help me out with *things*. I told him I didn't have a budget to pay someone for *things*. But he said he didn't want to be paid. *Try me for a few days. If you don't want me around, just tell me and I'll be gone.* That was two years ago, and during this time he helped me with repairs at the theater, picking up supplies and giving

Agnes extra help when needed," Arnold said with a smile and looked over to Agnes who nodded.

Arnold paused for a moment before he said softly, "It wasn't until the day he was shot that I learned of the true purpose of Gray's mysterious presence, which was not just to do *things*."

Moshe shook his head, trying to signal Arnold not to continue the story. The only person at the table who had no knowledge of what he was about to say was Leah, and the last thing he wanted was to have to explain the craziness to her.

Arnold got the message, and quickly changed his toast. "Apparently Gray came to show all of us how we can be better people and help each other. He was a real mensch."

Moshe stood up, raised his glass and said, "Here's to Gray, a wonderful man. We will miss him."

As he took his seat, Leah lifted her hand and started pointing. First to Noa, then Sammy and finally to Moshe. "You two have the sweats, just like Moshe."

Moshe shook his head. "Not now, Leah. Ruth is bringing our food," he said, trying to change the subject.

"Stop it, Moshe, we just ordered," she said, and turned her attention to Noa and Sammy.

Leah wagged her finger at Noa and Sammy and asked, "I've been asking my husband for weeks now, what's with the sweats? Are you sick? Is this some contagious disease that we're all going to get, and start sweating in the middle of winter?"

"That's funny," Sammy said, pointing back at Leah.

Noa pushed Sammy's hand down and shook her head.

"There's nothing wrong with your husband, Leah, or with me, or Sammy. We've been practicing being awake in our dreams, which has the effect of making us sweat when we're awake. It's nothing to be alarmed about. I've been sweating nearly my entire life," she said and took a healthy gulp from her water glass.

Moshe exhaled, hoping Leah wasn't going to ask any more questions. Then she turned to him, gave him a big smile, and asked, "So Moshe, what have you been dreaming about?"

Moshe looked at Leah and said, "Nothing important. Just trying to save the city from evil."

She put her arm around Moshe and leaned over and gave him a kiss on his cheek and said, "That's a good one. Moshe the Cobbler is saving the city from evil."

There was a moment of silence at the table, with all eyes collectively staring at Leah and then the laughter came. First Leah, then Agnes, and soon everyone was nearly doubled over.

"That's the funniest thing I ever heard," Leah said, trying to catch her breath.

Toward the end of the meal, when coffee and dessert were being served, the conversation turned to the recent killing of the gangster Mickey Coppola.

"It must be a frenzy down at city hall, Agnes," said Arnold.

"Myron's been a nervous wreck. You would think that he would be basking in the glow of taking down the city's most wanted criminal," Agnes said.

"What's he worried about? I hear his popularity has reached over sixty percent," said Arnold.

"I think he's upset about his breakup with Niko, Mickey's daughter," Agnes said.

"Who cares if he's depressed. The city is a better place without that gangster," said Noa.

Agnes nodded. "That's true. But he'll need to figure things out if he wants a second term."

"Oh, he'll be a shoo-in for reelection," Arnold said.

"You're right. I'll vote for him," Sammy said.

Noa elbowed him hard.

"Hey, what was that for?"

Noa shook her head and gestured to Arnold. "Mr. Lieberman is running against him," Noa said.

"Oh, I didn't know. My apologies. I will vote for you," Sammy said, as his sweating face turned beet red.

"That's fine, Sammy. I appreciate your vote, if I can get that far," Arnold said.

As people shared their farewells, Noa leaned into Moshe and whispered into his ear, "Tonight's the night."

Moshe jerked his head back and looked at Noa. "For what?"

Noa glanced around, and saw Leah saying goodbye to Agnes and answered, "Tonight is the night you take the *rasha* to Gehenna."

Moshe stood there and stared at Noa, unable to speak. Leah pulled on his sleeve, trying to get his attention, and said, "Moshe, take me home. I'm tired."

During the ride home, Leah rambled on and on about Sammy and Noa. "I don't understand how they're a couple. She's so much older…"

But Moshe tuned her out, obsessed instead with what Noa had told him, that tonight in the dream world he would forcibly take Solomon and extinguish his eternal soul into the fiery pit of Gehenna.

When they pulled into their driveway Moshe realized that he had no memory of how he drove home, and he couldn't repeat one word of what Leah had said. All he knew was that he was about to risk his life in order to remove a disturbance in the dream world, and in turn eliminate a ninety-year-old gangster in the awakened world. He shook his head and thought, *my life is not my own.*

Chapter 76

Solomon awoke, and pushed his tired, aching body out of bed. He grabbed his cane, sitting in the corner a few steps away, hobbled to the bathroom, and splashed cool water on his sleep-encrusted eyes. He dried his face, slipped on his bathrobe, and made his way into the kitchen.

While the coffee was percolating he retrieved his morning newspaper from outside. He was just tucking the folded Daily News into the deep pocket of his robe and turning back toward the front porch when he saw Myron, sitting in a rocking chair.

"Myron, what are you doing?"

"I've been waiting for you to wake up, Pops," he said, standing up.

Solomon stepped onto the porch, opened the front door and said, "Come inside, it's freezing. The coffee should be ready."

In the kitchen, Solomon filled two mugs and handed one to his son, who was already seated at the table, then asked, "To what do I owe the pleasure of a visit by the mayor of this illustrious city?"

Myron reached over for the sugar bowl and sprinkled a spoonful in the steaming coffee.

"I haven't seen you since Mickey was killed. I thought we should talk."

Solomon shrugged. "He got what he deserved."

Myron sighed, and said, "That I know. So far, under my watch, the city has lost two of its most notorious bosses: Mickey Coppola and Carmine Rizzo."

"You're cleaning up the city. You should have no trouble getting reelected."

"Thanks, Pops, but that's not what I came to talk to you about," Myron said, and stood up and walked over to the window and looked out onto the bay. He turned and looked at his dad and said, "I was thinking that the other bosses will try to take advantage of the power vacuum in the city."

"That's probably true," Solomon said.

Myron rubbed his thumb across his lips and added, "We should fill the void before someone else does."

Solomon looked up, tilted his head, and asked, "You're the mayor. You also want to be a mob boss?"

Myron shrugged. "This mayor gig won't last forever."

Solomon nodded slowly and started to wag his finger. "To do this, you're going to have to set up shell companies so nothing can be traced back to you. After all, you can't be seen awarding lucrative contracts to yourself. First they'll impeach you, and then you'll get twenty years in Attica."

"That's what I want to talk to you about," Myron said, now wagging his finger back at his father. "What if we were able to get someone to partner with? You know, to oversee our interests in construction, garbage collection, parking lots, things like that. We'll advise as silent partners, with an understanding that when I'm done with being mayor, we take back control of the operations. In the meantime, I can direct some hefty contracts this person's way."

Solomon smiled. "I'm impressed, Myron. I like it. But you would need someone with serious business skills, as well as someone you can trust."

"I was hoping you had someone in mind," Myron said.

"Still coming to me for answers, Myron?"

Myron smiled. "Always, Pops. You are my guiding light. Where would I be without you?"

Solomon squeezed Myron's shoulder and said, "Let me think about it. I'll call you later."

Solomon spent most of the afternoon at Charlie's Oyster Bar. It was a good place for him to ruminate about what Myron had told him. With both Mickey and Carmine gone, there was the opportunity of growing an empire that could stretch across all five boroughs. If only he was ten years younger, the joy such power would bring to him. His consolation was that at least Myron could reap the rewards.

Solomon considered the particular qualities a partner would need in order to run a city-wide syndicate. Such a candidate must be a seasoned professional in both the business and political worlds, and not easily intimidated by the other bosses trying to push in on the territory.

Then a name popped into Solomon's mind that caused him to smile. He got to his feet and walked over to the end of the bar.

"Ralph, I need to make a call," he said, reaching for the phone nestled in between piles of old telephone books, newspapers and magazines. He lifted the receiver and dialed the number for City Hall. An operator at the switchboard connected him to the mayor's office.

"Hello Agnes, it's Solomon. Can you put my son on the phone?"

"Sure thing. Just give me a minute. He's saying goodbye to the commissioner."

"Okay," he said.

A few minutes later, Agnes said, "I'm putting you through now."

"Hey, Pops."

"Myron, listen. I've been thinking about our discussion this morning and I have someone in mind. He will need some convincing, but I don't see how anyone would turn down such an opportunity."

"Who is it?"

"Arnold Lieberman, the guy who owns the Paradise on the Grand Concourse."

"Arnold Lieberman? He's the one who mocked us at that fund raiser. Plus, I hear he's planning to run against me for mayor, and he hates us. "

"That's perfect. We know how to deal with hate," Solomon said.

"That we do. So how do you propose we convince him to partner up?"

"The same way we always do. We offer money and power."

"I don't know, Pops, he was a councilman."

"That's why he's perfect. No one would expect anything illegitimate from him. He has a pristine reputation."

"He's very close with the cobbler."

"Don't worry about the cobbler. I'll be dealing with him soon."

"You really think he'll agree?"

"I think so. It's not hard luring a politician with the bait of money and power."

"Sounds good, Pops. Let me know how it goes."

After Solomon said goodbye to his son, he called for a taxi. The excitement had given him a burst of adrenaline that he hadn't felt in a long time. As he slipped into the backseat, the cabbie asked, "Where to?"

"The New York City Public Library on Fifth Avenue," Solomon said.

Solomon took the steps to the entrance of the library with renewed vigor. His body felt, for a brief moment, pain free. His bones didn't ache and his back wasn't sore. Arnold had agreed to meet with him and the prospect made him feel twenty years younger. What a way to put a cherry on top of a lifetime of achievements. But in the meantime, he was going to see Rebecca.

Their sexual encounters in his dreams had been the best of his life. She had brought him to spectacular climaxes he hadn't thought possible. He looked forward to discussing them with her in their private hideout, downstairs in the research room.

Solomon saw her walking across the large reading room as he entered. She was patting her forehead with a handkerchief. *Maybe she isn't feeling well,* he thought.

As he approached her, Solomon noticed that she was sweating. Then he realized what was happening. She wasn't sick, she was sweating because of her time in the dream world. Solomon wondered if she was aware of the condition.

He waved his hand and caught her attention. She waved back. Solomon pointed to the floor, indicating that he would be going downstairs and wait for her. She acknowledged with a quick nod of her head.

Solomon didn't wait long. Rebecca appeared only a few minutes later and she was still sweating.

"I see you have the sweats," he said.

"It started last week." She leaned in closer and said, "I'm glad you finally came. I was worried about it."

Solomon nodded. "That's normal. There's nothing to be alarmed about. When you're awake in the dream world for a period of time, your nervous system adjusts and you get the sweats when you're awake."

She wiped her brow and the back of her neck with her hanky, and reached out and touched Solomon's forehead. "Why don't you sweat?" she asked.

"For some reason, I don't," Solomon said, but knew from Henryk that *rasha* do not experience this dream world side effect.

"Lucky you," she said and smiled. "I thought I was going through early menopause."

"Is it too much for you? Would you like to take a break?"

A smile danced on her lips as she said, "Are you kidding me? I can't wait for next time."

He lifted an eyebrow, and asked, "Tonight?"

Rebecca's eyes sparkled, and she replied, "Yes, tonight."

Chapter 77

"Hello Agnes, it's good to hear from you," Arnold said, cradling the phone receiver to his ear and leaning back in his chair.

"Listen, Arnold, I only have a few minutes."

"What is it? Is everything all right?"

"I eavesdropped on a conversation between Myron and his father Solomon."

"What did they say?"

"With Mickey Coppola dead, Myron thinks it's time to take control of the entire city."

"He already has control. He's the damn mayor for god's sake."

"Not that kind of control. He wants to run the building contracts, the trash pickup, the parking lots—you know, mob stuff."

"He can't do that, and be mayor at the same time," Arnold said.

"That's why Solomon's coming to speak with you about. They want you to run the businesses until Myron is out of office."

"Solomon did call me. He left me a message asking if I wanted to be a wealthy man. I answered truthfully. After all, who doesn't?"

"You should have said no. When are you speaking to him?"

"He's coming today, this afternoon."

"What are you going to do?" Agnes said.

"At this point, I guess I'm going to speak to the man. But why would they want me, of all people, to run their businesses?"

"Solomon said it's because you're honest and trustworthy."

Arnold laughed. "That's a good one. Those mobsters want a Boy Scout as a partner."

"Apparently so," Agnes said with a chuckle.

Arnold walked down the aisle of his beautiful theater. It truly was an architectural wonder. But beyond the pride he had in owning such a property, the movie business hardly covered the mortgage, payroll, taxes and the maintenance.

The words from Solomon about making him a wealthy man sounded like music to his hears. Sure, he would talk to the old man, and see what he had to say.

"Ah, there you are." A voice came from a set of double swinging doors.

Arnold turned from the stage and saw Solomon enter the theater.

"Mr. Blass, wait, I'll come to you," Arnold said.

Arnold walked up the sloping aisle to where Solomon stood. "Do you mind talking here?" he said gesturing to the last row of chairs in the theater. "I don't want you to have to climb the stairs to my office, since the elevator is still out."

Solomon hobbled across a few seats, hooked his cane on the back of one in front of him, and sat down. Arnold took the aisle seat, leaving an empty seat in between himself and Solomon.

"I have to say that I was surprised by your phone call. The last time I saw you was when you were here during the campaign event for our former mayor, where I had a few unflattering comments about you and your son during my introduction."

"That you did. But no harm done. Myron won, your guy lost, and you lost your job as councilman," Solomon said, with a slight lift of his eyebrows.

Arnold sighed. "Why are you here?"

Solomon looked around at the elaborate details of the theater. "This is a beautiful place."

"You didn't come here for a tour," Arnold said impatiently.

Solomon nodded and said, "Okay, I'll get to the point." He grabbed his cane and rested his hands on top. "I can only imagine that you're not going to become a rich man running a movie theater, even one as luxurious as the Paradise."

Arnold nodded and said, "This is true. The upkeep for this place is four times the cost of a regular cinema, and we still charge the same price for a movie ticket."

"That's what I thought," Solomon said with a smirk.

"Are you proposing to buy me out?"

Solomon scratched his chin. "That's not what I came here for, but perhaps that may be possible."

This remark caused Arnold to sit up in his chair and ask, "Then what is it?"

"I'm sure you know what happened to Mickey Coppola."

Arnold nodded. "I read the papers."

"Well, with Mickey and that scumbag Carmine Rizzo gone, there's opportunity."

Here it comes, Arnold thought.

"We want to set you up in the business," Solomon said.

"The business? What does that mean?"

Solomon grunted and said, "Do I have to spell it out for you?"

Arnold stood up and took a few steps down the aisle and turned around. He put a finger to his lips, trying to act surprised, and then pointed at Solomon. "You're talking about organized crime."

"I'm talking about making more money than you could ever imagine. Plus you'll have the protection that the other bosses don't have. The risk is minimal."

"I'm assuming you're referring to your son, when you say protection?"

Solomon nodded. "Of course. With the power of the mayor's office behind him, he can squash any troublesome investigations."

"You know I was planning to run for mayor in two years?"

"That's the funny thing about making plans, they always seem to be changing," Solomon said, as he pushed himself to standing with his cane and made his way toward the double swinging doors. "You think about it, Arnold. I'll be back to discuss the details with you in a few days."

Arnold watched the doors swing closed as Solomon passed through them. He sat back down in the seat and stared at the painted clouds and stars on the ceiling.

Plans do change. Twenty minutes ago I was convinced that I was going to kick Solomon out of here with such a crazy offer of working with him and Myron. But perhaps the offer is something I can take advantage of. I need to talk to Agnes.

Arnold put his hands behind his head and smiled.

Chapter 78

"Come in, Moshe, I've been waiting for you," said Noa.

Moshe entered her apartment and saw Sammy sleeping on the sofa.

"Will he be here tonight?" Moshe whispered.

"Don't worry about waking him. Once he's out, nothing wakes him up," she said, as the E train pulled into the station, rattling the apartment windows in their frames and nearly shaking the potted plants off the window sills.

"Why do you live here, Noa? It's so noisy."

"The rent is cheap, and I'm used to it. And you know, Moshe, in my dream world, my life is quite luxurious," she said with a smile.

"I suppose it is," Moshe said, putting down his small valise.

"Come, let's sit by the window and talk."

Moshe sat down by the open window, while Noa filled a glass of water from the kitchen sink tap.

"Can I get you a nosh?" Noa asked, handing the glass to Moshe.

"No, I ate with Leah. I think she's getting suspicious of these overnights. I'm running out of excuses. I told her that I was going to sleep at the shop since I needed to work late."

"That would sound suspicious to me too," Noa said, as she took a seat across from him.

"I know. That's why I'm getting tired of this. I hope tonight I can put an end to the sneaking around, and the constant sweating. My customers are constantly asking if I'm sick and it's hard to work without sweat dripping on the shoes. After tonight, I'm done with this dream world."

Noa patted Moshe's hand resting on the table. "That's the plan. Tonight you're going to find the *rasha* and take him to Gehenna."

"You think I'm ready? The dream world still seems to take me places I can't control. How will I be able to take Solomon somewhere against his will?"

Noa nodded and opened the window a little more than a crack, allowing the winter air to cool them down. "Your previous encounters have prepared you for this. You told me how you burned his arm when you touched him."

Moshe nodded. "It was like my hand was a hot iron," he said holding up his palm.

"That is how you will take him. Grab him somewhere on his flesh."

"But he can fight back. He hurt me with his cane," he said pointing to his leg.

Noa nodded. "It won't be easy, but it must be done, Moshe."

"But Solomon will have something to say, or think about this too."

"Moshe, don't forget the most important asset you have, that makes you uniquely qualified."

Moshe exhaled and said, "That I'm *tzaddik*?"

Noa nodded. "That's right. The Almighty has chosen you to be his hand among us. You will need to call upon this gift and see this done."

Moshe nodded and said, "I understand."

"Good, let's eat something, and get you into bed."

"I told you, I already ate."

"You need to eat what I prepared for you. It will help you dream."

Noa served Moshe a plate filled with walnuts, almonds, cheese and tuna fish. She also gave him a glass filled with cherry juice.

Moshe gestured to the food and asked, "This will help me dream?"

"Yes, it's what we eat and drink when we want to go deep in the dream world. I think Sammy was picking at it before you came. That's why he's in such a deep sleep," she said pointing to him sprawled out on the couch with an arm dangling off the side.

After Moshe finished eating he made his way to the bedroom. He removed his clothes and climbed into bed. He could hear the E train pulling into the station. After a while, as the noises of the city blended together, his eyes turned heavy, and he fell asleep.

"Moshe, stop hiding and come out. We need to go home now, it's almost Shabbos," Clara said.

"Here I am, Mama," he said, popping out from under a wagon, where he and his friend Max were playing.

"Good Shabbos, Mrs. Potasznik," Max said.

"Come, Max, we will take you home."

"Can Max do Shabbos with us?" Moshe asked.

"If it's all right with his mother."

Moshe and Max looked at each other and laughed.

As the three walked out of the market square, a booming voice stopped them.

"One moment please, Mrs. Potasznik. Those boys need to come with me."

Clara and the boys turned and saw Captain Berbecki marching toward them. His gloved hand was pointing at the boys. "They were stealing again. Isn't that right, Moshe?"

Moshe looked up to his mother and said, "No, Mama, we weren't stealing."

The captain grabbed the boys by the coat collars and dragged them away.

"Let go of me." Moshe struggled, and reached around and touched the captain's arm.

The captain yelled and released the boys. His bulging eyes looked at his arm and saw the sleeve of his coat was burned away and his flesh was scalded. "What did you do to me?"

Moshe backed away as the captain pulled his club from his belt and swung it at Moshe, barely missing striking his shoulder.

The captain stared at his seared arm again and said, "I will kill you."

When he looked up, he was no longer the captain, it was Solomon walking toward him with his cane held high, ready to strike. Moshe, who was no longer a child, stood his ground. Solomon swung and struck him hard on his arm, knocking him down.

Moshe struggled to get to his feet. He tried to lift his arm but couldn't. The pain was too severe, it felt like the bone was broken. He reached out with his good arm and grabbed Solomon by the neck. He could feel the skin burn at his touch.

Solomon screamed, dropped his cane and tried to dislodge Moshe's grip upon his throat.

"Let me go," Solomon insisted.

Moshe looked at Solomon, his left hand welded to his skin, and said, "It is time for your soul to be extinguished into the fires of Gehenna."

As the words were spoken, darkness enveloped the tzaddik and the rasha. The earth beneath their feet vanished. They floated within a black void.

"Why are you doing this to me, Moshe? I am an old man. My time is at an end. Let me die peacefully."

"Solomon will die, but the soul of the rasha will live on unless it is brought to Gehanna," Moshe said.

"I am not rasha, Moshe. I'm just a man who wants to make a life for himself and his family. Why am I being punished?"

"For your wickedness upon those too weak to fight back."

A streak of lightning flashed across the darkness for a moment, just enough to see the ashen face and bulging eyes of Solomon.

A cool wind rushed by. They were moving. A flicker of light appeared in the distance. The light grew brighter, the coolness turned warm.

Moshe dragged Solomon by his neck toward the light. The light expanded into a red glow. Below them hung black and gray clouds, charged with bolts of lightning. The clouds parted, exposing the curdling river of blood of Gehanna.

Solomon's eyes filled with tears and he pleaded, "Don't do this, Moshe. You're a good man."

"I do this not as Moshe, but as tzaddik."

"Please spare me. I've fallen in love with a beautiful young woman. She has changed me," he said, with tears welling up.

Moshe looked down at the hordes of flesh eaters swimming in the river of blood. Their skinless arms reached toward them, begging for the new soul to be dropped in.

"I just want to die a natural death. I am not rasha, my soul is good."

The Righteous One 325

"You are rasha. Your soul must be extinguished."

Solomon's face turned young. He looked handsome and bright. "You are the hand of Hashem, tzaddik. You have the power to forgive. Offer me redemption. Let me prove to you in the few years I have left that your forgiveness will change me."

Moshe felt himself softening. Maybe Solomon truly was just a man, and not this bizarre amalgamation of some evil force. He turned to Solomon. and pulled him in close. "I am the hand of Hashem, and by his grace, you are forgiven, for now. You must show me that you are not rasha, or we will be back here, and I will release you into the cauldron below."

Moshe woke up screaming in pain. He opened his eyes and looked around, confused. *Ah, I'm at Noa's,* he remembered. He tried to push himself up from the bed, but the pain returned like a knife was cutting through his left arm. He pulled back the blanket and saw a bruise that stained his upper arm in colors ranging from pink to purple to black.

The bedroom door swung open and Noa ran in. "What is it?" Noa yelled.

"It's my arm. I think it's broken."

"Did the *rasha* do this?" asked Sammy.

Moshe nodded as he tried to stand up.

"Let me help you, Moshe," Noa said.

"Is it done?" Noa asked.

Moshe shrugged, shook his head, and said softly, "I offered him forgiveness."

Noa shook her head quickly, back and forth. "What are you saying, you offered him forgiveness?"

"What if he is not the *rasha*? What if he's just a man who wants to die, like everyone else."

Noa dropped her head into her hands and said, "What have you done, Moshe?"

Chapter 79

Myron jabbed his finger into Frank's chest and said, "I want you to send some muscle to each of those knuckleheads and tell them to find a new career."

Frank nodded, looking at the list of lieutenants that reported to Mickey Coppola. "I know these men. They will try to assert some control, but none of them have what it takes. Once they know there's nothing here for them, they will probably head to Queens or Brooklyn."

"They're next. I want the remaining families taken down, Frank. There will be a clean sweep of mob control in this city."

Frank smiled and said, "I have to say, Myron, that I never thought you had the will to do this."

"This will be my legacy, as well as my assurance of winning a second term," he said with a smile.

"What's this I hear about Arnold Lieberman withdrawing his name from the race?"

"It's true. Now that he's not an adversary, I'm going to offer him a position as my advisor. He can be a useful addition to the team."

Frank nodded. "Arnold Lieberman is a good man. I'm just a little surprised at his change in attitude. He certainly was not fond of you, or your father."

"Let's just say he has had an epiphany after the death of Mickey Coppola. Like many people did, or soon will," Myron said with a smirk.

"Well, I'd better get back to work. There's a lot to do."

Frank and Myron rose from their chairs and walked together toward the office door and shook hands.

"Thank you, Frank," Myron said and opened the door. They stepped into reception, where Agnes was typing.

"Thank you, Mr. Mayor," Frank said.

Myron patted Frank on his back and saw Niko sitting on one of the chairs lined up against the wall, reading a magazine. Her legs were crossed, with her right foot dangling one of her black patent leather Mary Jane shoes off her toes.

She is certainly easy on the eyes was Myron's first thought. He swallowed hard and his next thought was, *I'm not ready for this?*

"Niko, I didn't know you were here," he said, feeling his heart start to race as if he had sprinted up a staircase.

"I'll be going," Frank said, and exited out into the hallway.

Niko stood up and took a step toward Myron's office. "Do you have some time for me?"

Myron rubbed the sweat off the top of his lip with the back of his hand. He looked over to Agnes, stretched his eyes wide to express his surprise, turned back to Niko, offered a weak smile and said, "Please come in."

Myron closed the door to his office. Niko was already standing by the large window overlooking City Hall Park.

"Can I take your coat?"

"Sure," she said slipping it off and handing it to Myron.

Myron had not seen her for a few weeks. The one time he called her was right before her father's funeral.

"How have you been?" he asked.

"I'm feeling a little better. This hasn't been easy," she said, as tears welled up.

Myron took a breath. *Stay strong*, he told himself. "I'm sorry about your father. You know I had nothing to do with it. The FBI never told me about their surveillance."

"You really think I believe that?"

"I swear it's true. You can ask the commissioner," he said pointing to the door, where Frank was just standing a few minutes earlier.

Niko shook her head. "I don't believe you. But that's not why I came here."

"Oh, why did you come?"

"I came to tell you what's going to happen now."

Myron cocked his head. "Please tell me."

"You think I don't know what's going on, just because I'm a girl?"

"I don't know what to think," he said truthfully.

"Myron, I grew up watching Daddy run his organization. I know what he did and how he did it, and I know you, Myron. If you think that you're going to take over his business interests, without any pushback from me, you're mistaken," she said, with one hand on her hip and the other thrusting a finger at him.

Myron rubbed the top of his head. He had never seen this side of Niko before. "You want to be my business partner?"

"Not just your partner, I also want to be your wife. I think we'll make a formidable team."

Myron's mouth was wide open, with no words coming out.

"What do you have to say?" Niko asked.

"Are you serious? You want to be my business partner and my wife?"

She nodded and said, "What's so hard to understand?"

"Niko, you betrayed me at the Stork Club! You chose your father over me!"

"I was protecting him, Myron. You would have done the same if it had been your father and I'd been the one secretly recording our conversations for the FBI."

Myron nodded. *This is true*, he thought. "I can't argue with that. But why does that mean I should trust you again?"

"You're right to be skeptical, Myron. But you know that my father was everything to me," she said brushing away a tear. "I won't apologize for my devotion."

Myron took a breath, not sure how to react. He admired her unwavering loyalty but wondered if this was a justifiable excuse for her betrayal.

As if she knew what he was thinking, Niko squinted, pointed a finger at him and said, "Understand me now, Myron, with Father gone, you are my number one."

Myron smiled. "Wow, that's quite a statement Niko," he said.

"It is, but I mean every word of it. So, Mr. Mayor, what do you have to say?"

Myron looked into Niko's green eyes and felt his resistance melting away. He had loved her deeply before her betrayal—shouldn't that be enough to give her a second chance? He smiled and took a step toward her, put his hands around her waist, and pulled her in tight. "What do I have to say?" he asked.

She looked up to him, her green eyes sparkling, and she nodded.

"Niko, will you marry me?"

Chapter 80

S olomon waited an hour to see a doctor in the Lebanon Hospital emergency room.

"I've never seen a wound like this before. It looks like a hand print that was burned into your skin. How did this happen?" said the emergency room doctor, applying a salve to the fresh burn.

Solomon felt like telling him that a *tzaddik* burned his throat with his bare hand when he was being dragged to Gehenna. But that would probably get him committed to Bellevue for psychiatric care. Instead he just told him that it was a cooking accident.

With gauze wrapped around his neck like an Egyptian mummy, Solomon stepped out onto the street and hailed a cab. During the ride back home to City Island, he had a moment to think about how close he came to burning in the fiery river of Gehenna.

Moshe the cobbler had, after all, proven to be the lightweight Solomon thought he was when he first met him. But he was surprised how easy it was to convince him to offer his forgiveness.

Solomon was aware that he disturbed the balance in the dream world with his beliefs in Kabbalah's dark side. On top of that, there were his sexual exploits with Rebecca, which brought ominous warnings from the spirit, Francesa Sarah. But he had escaped eternal damnation, freeing his soul to carry on after his death.

Now that he had put the existential threat of the *tzaddik* behind him, he could focus on spending his remaining years in the dream world, making love as a young man, with Rebecca.

When the taxi pulled up to his home he opened the door and used his cane to push himself up to his feet. The cabbie thanked him for the tip and drove off.

Solomon entered the home and smelled aromas of someone cooking. Then he heard the clanking of pots.

"Is someone here?" he shouted as he walked toward the kitchen.

"You're back," the voice said.

Solomon stepped into the kitchen and saw Rebecca preparing something over the stove.

"What are you doing?" asked Solomon.

"What does it look like? I'm making you dinner," she said without looking up.

Solomon looked over to the kitchen table, where a bottle of wine and two place settings were neatly arranged.

"This is a surprise," he said.

Rebecca put down the wooden spoon and looked up and saw Solomon's neck wound.

"Oh my god, Solomon. What happened to your neck?" she said and hurried over to his side for a closer look.

"It's fine. Just an accident with some boiling water. I'm not too good in the kitchen."

She gently touched the bandage and said, "Does it hurt?"

"It's starting to itch now, which is a good sign. That means it's healing."

"It seems I came just in time. You're going to need someone to take care of you. So go relax, I'm making us dinner, and afterwards we'll sleep together in your bed and see what happens in the dream world."

Solomon scratched the top of his head, not sure the words he was hearing were actually being spoken. "You're staying the night?"

Rebecca looked up from the sauce she was stirring in the pot and asked, "Don't you want me to?"

Solomon nodded. "I do, yes. I'm just surprised to see you."

"Now go sit down and read your paper. Dinner will be ready in a few minutes."

Later that same evening, after a dinner of spaghetti and meatballs with garlic bread and wine, Solomon and Rebecca lay side by side in his bed. She leaned over and gave him a gentle kiss on his cheek and said, "Good night, Solomon. Can you turn off the light, I'm sleepy now."

Minutes later, as Solomon heard Rebecca's breathing deepen, he smiled to himself, thinking, *I can't believe my great fortune in having found Rebecca at this stage of my life.* Of course it would have been wonderful if he would have met her as a young man. But he could at least be with her in the dream world as the thirty-year-old version of himself.

He could barely keep his eyes open. Sleep seemed to take hold. *Maybe it was the wine,* he thought, as he fell into a deep slumber.

"That's ten girls," Leo Gorpatsch said, patting Solomon on his back. "Our largest delivery so far."

Solomon looked at the bills in his hand. "This is the most money I've ever had."

"We will be rich men one day, Solomon," Leo said.

As the wagon was pulling away from the curb, one of the girls turned and looked at Solomon.

Solomon stared back and pointed. "It's Rebecca, wait."

The man holding on to the reins pulled back and brought the horses to a slow stop.

Solomon ran over, reached into the wagon and lifted her out and onto the ground.

"Who is that?" Leo asked.

The man driving the wagon yelled, "Hey, you've been paid. Put her back."

Solomon reached into his pocket and handed him a few bills.

"That should more than cover it. Come with me, Rebecca, I have a wonderful place we can be alone together."

"Where are you taking me?" Rebecca asked.

"Up there," he said, pointing to a balcony at the top of the Great Synagogue of Warsaw.

He grabbed her hand and they flew upwards and landed like birds upon the decking of the balcony. "You can see all of the city from here."

Rebecca squeezed herself close to Solomon, resting her head on his chest.

"It's beautiful, Solomon."

"I used to live in that house right over there, with my uncle," he said pointing to a small cottage.

"Take me there," she said.

They held hands and floated back down to the street. Solomon turned the doorknob and they entered.

"It's smaller than I remember," he said.

"Take me to the bedroom," Rebecca whispered.

Memories flooded back at the sounds of their footsteps resounded off the wooden floorboards. He remembered being a child and playing in the cottage, while his uncle was out building what was to be the largest synagogue in all of Europe at the time.

The bedroom had a small bed, pushed up against the wall. A pair of red plaid curtains hung over the window. Rebecca took Solomon by the hand and brought him to the bed. She sat him down and leaned into him and offered her lips.

They kissed and slowly lowered themselves down to the straw-stuffed mattress. Solomon lost himself in her embrace.

"Do you trust me?" Rebecca asked.

"Of course."

"I want to take you somewhere. Will you come with me?"

"Anywhere you want to go, I will follow."

Solomon found himself being pulled along by Rebecca's hand through the darkness. A strange familiarity flooded his mind.

"Where are you taking me?"

"Patience, my love, we will be there soon," she said.

Solomon felt a rush of fear that extinguished his lust. He foresaw a vision of himself drowning in a sea of boiling blood. He tried to release Rebecca's hand, but her grip was unbreakable.

"It's too late, Solomon. You have agreed to follow me anywhere. This gives me the power to bring you to the eternal fires of Gehenna."

With those words, the darkness was split open by a red streak below them. Solomon recognized the desperate arms of the damned reaching skyward.

"You deceived me," he shouted.

"You were right about the cobbler. He was not strong enough. But I am."

"Who are you?"

"I am a descendant of Francesa Sarah of Safed—the last in her line. Solomon Blass, rasha, your soul ends here."

Chapter 81

Benjamin pulled up to Solomon's home and even before the car came to a complete stop, Myron threw open the car door, jumped out, and ran in through the unlocked front door. Finding it unlocked was not unusual. Solomon never locked his doors. "There's nothing to steal," he would say.

"Pops, are you here?" he shouted and walked out the back door and toward the dock. *He's probably fishing*, he thought. His old battered chair was there, as well as a fishing rod, but no Pops.

Myron walked back into the house and went into his father's bedroom.

"There you are, Pops. I've been calling you for a day and a half. Is the phone out of order?"

Solomon did not answer. Myron leaned in for a closer look. His father's eyes stared forward, not moving or blinking. Solomon's skin looked like the color of an overcast gray sky. Myron shook him. There was no response. The gauze around his neck wound seemed loose, like his body had started to shrink.

"Pops, what happened?"

Still no response came. Myron leaned over and gently shook Solomon's shoulder. Still nothing. "Pops. *Pops!*"

He pulled up a small wooden chair that stood against the wall, sat down alongside his father and stared at him, still hoping he would suddenly wake up. When he finally resigned himself to the realization that Solomon was dead, tears exploded from his eyes and gushed down his face, and strong heaves rocked his body.

He choked out the words, "I don't understand. I just saw you two days ago, and you seemed fine. Pops, I came to tell you that Niko and I are getting married and I wanted you to be my best man. But now you're gone. What am I going to do without you?"

Two days later Myron and Niko stood alongside the hole in the ground that his father's casket was lowered into. A rabbi recited the prayer to honor those who had passed. When it was over, Myron picked up the shovel, scooped up some dirt and tossed it onto the coffin.

Niki held onto Myron's arm as they walked back to the car.

"How come no one came to his funeral? Didn't he have any friends?" Niko asked.

Myron shook his head. "His only friend was the rabbi, who was given the electric chair last month for killing that Gray fellow."

"I'm sorry, Myron. We've both lost our fathers now. At least we have each other."

Myron nodded and opened the car door for Niko. "Yes, that's true. We certainly do."

Chapter 82

With the Solomon episode behind him, Moshe got right back to work. He realized he had screwed up, but he could never kill another person, or worse, terminate their eternal soul. It was just something he would have to live with.

"Thank you, Mrs. Rothman. Yes, I'll have your shoes ready by five today. Goodbye," Moshe said, and hung up the phone.

He turned to go back to his work table when the front door bells jangled.

Moshe walked up front and without giving his visitors a thorough look said, "Good afternoon, ladies, how may I be of service?"

"Moshe it's me, Noa," one woman said.

He put his hand to his mouth, and said, "Oh, sorry, Noa. I never expected to see you walking into my shop."

"That's fine, Moshe."

"Who is this lovely young lady?" Moshe asked.

"This is Rebecca, my daughter."

"Your daughter? You told me that you were last in the line of women, going back to Francesa Sarah."

"I'm not, but Rebecca is. For now. Hopefully one day she will find a nice man and get married and give me a granddaughter."

Moshe turned to Rebecca. "It is a pleasure to meet you."

Rebecca smiled and said, "I've heard many wonderful things about you."

Moshe smiled.

"I think you should lock the door, Moshe. Trust me, what I am about to tell you cannot be interrupted by a customer," Noa said, pointing to the door.

"So what happened?" Moshe said, as they stood around his work table.

Noa gestured toward her daughter. "The reason you didn't know about Rebecca was because no one knew about her. It's how we keep the lineage intact. When I was born, my mother hid me from view. At birth I did the same to Rebecca. She was given to a woman who comes from a lineage of women who took secret care of the daughters of Francesa Sarah. It's how we preserved the continuation of the line."

"That's interesting. So you can go into the dream world like your mother?"

Rebecca smiled and said, "I can."

"Then why are you not sweating?"

"It's been over a week. The sweats usually stop if you don't go into the dream world for that amount of time," Rebecca said.

"What were you doing in the dream world?"

"That's why we're here, Moshe," Noa said.

Moshe lifted his hands and asked, "So tell me."

Noa took a breath and said, "After your, um, incident with the *rasha*, you left us no choice but to go with our second option."

"Your second option?"

"Yes, Rebecca. She did what you couldn't do."

"What do you mean?"

"The *rasha* is gone. His soul has been extinguished into the flames of Gehenna."

"You took him there?"

Rebecca nodded.

"I had my doubts about you, Moshe. You're too good a man. After all, you're *tzaddik,* the righteous one. But you did provide a good distraction for Rebecca's seduction. Men are so predictable, no matter the age."

Moshe shook his head. "What are you saying?"

Noa explained to Moshe how Rebecca had been developing a relationship with Solomon in both the dream world and the awakened world.

"A *tzaddik* does not need permission to bring a *rasha* to Gehenna. So that meant if Rebecca was to succeed, she would need Solomon's consent."

Moshe looked at Rebecca.

She smiled and said, "He agreed to follow me anywhere."

Moshe's jaw hung open. "Solomon is really gone?"

Both Noa and Rebecca nodded, and Noa said gently, "Truly. The *rasha* is no more."

Chapter 83

Myron stared at the ceiling. The only sound he heard was Niko's rhythmic breathing as she slept. All he could think about was his father and the void he had left behind. The man who had guided him his entire life was gone.

He glanced over at Niko, curled up under the blanket, her face buried deep in her pillow, and wondered if a similar emptiness from the loss of her own father was finding a place in her consciousness.

A sudden noise from within the mansion stirred his attention. It was more than the squeaking of a water pipe or some other indistinguishable house sound; it was the sound of someone entering the mayor's headquarters.

When Myron heard multiple muffled voices, he rose quickly rose from his bed and reached for his pants. Just as he buckled them, loud sounds of footsteps charging up the staircase shook the floor. "What the fuck?" he said.

"What's going on?" Niko muttered as she awoke.

Heavy knocks pounded upon the bedroom door. "FBI! Open the door, Mr. Mayor."

"Myron, why is the FBI here?" Niko asked, now leaning against the headboard, the bedspread pulled up to her neck.

"I don't know," he said. "But I should open the door before they break it down."

"Myron, it's Agent Malone. Open the door now."

"I'm coming, one second."

The next time Myron saw Niko was when she came to visit him at the Metropolitan Correctional facility in lower Manhattan while he awaited trial.

He picked up the phone in the visitor's booth and said, "You look well, and very professional." Sitting across from him on the other side of the plexiglass window separating them, Niko wore a black suit jacket and crisp white shirt, tailored perfectly to her slender frame. In stark contrast, Myron greeted her in his federal prison uniform: the plain gray shirt and pants that all the inmates wore.

He put his hand against the glass, and Niko mirrored his gesture.

"Your lawyer told me that the judge decided against bail," she said, furrowing her eyebrows.

Myron nodded. "They consider me a flight risk," he said, and looked around before he whispered, "and they're probably right."

"Oh, Myron," Niko said, as her eyes welled with tears, "you'll be sent away for years."

"I'm afraid that I'll be an old man if I ever make it out of here."

"Is there anything I can do?" Niko asked, the tears now streaming down her cheeks.

Myron swallowed hard before he said, "Forget about me, Niko. You're young and shouldn't waste your life waiting for me."

Niko placed both hands on the glass and sobbed. "I'm so sorry, Myron."

Later that day, as Myron stood against the wall of his cell looking out through the bars and onto two prison guards having a conversation, his mind raced through his regrets.

Perhaps it's a good thing that my father is not here to see the shame I have brought upon our family name.

The more he thought about his father, the more he wondered what would happen to him after death. He remembered how his father had consoled him when his mother had died, more than twenty years earlier. "Your mother's soul will continue and she will eventually be reborn," Solomon had told his son as they stood by her grave the day she was laid to rest.

Myron sat down on the edge of his bed, stared at the lime green cement wall in front of him, and sighed. As much as he tried to imagine his father's soul taking a similar path, he had this unresolved doubt that lingered in his mind. He wondered, *Perhaps this Kabbalah wisdom was just nonsense, and when we die, that's it—it's all over.*

Chapter 84

"We got him, Agnes. He'll be locked up for years," Arnold said. "Frank gave all the tapes to the FBI. Myron is being charged with using the office of the mayor for illegal activities, linked to organized crime. There has never been a case like this before. The FBI is treading carefully so they don't screw it up," Arnold said.

Agnes stood up from the chair, walked over to the window, and looked out onto the Grand Concourse. "Well, it's done. Solomon is dead, and his son will spend a good portion of the rest of his life in prison."

Arnold nodded. "It seems so."

"What about Mickey's daughter, Niko?" Agnes asked.

"There was nothing the District Attorney could charge her with that would stick."

"I hear the city council has announced a special election for mayor. Perhaps you may run?" Agnes said, smiling broadly.

"How did you know?"

"I think I might know you even better than your wife does, Arnold."

Arnold nodded. "I'm going to run. And how would you feel about going back to work in City Hall for the new mayor?"

"You have to win first," she said.

"You always know how to keep my head out of the clouds, Agnes."

Chapter 85

"Moshe, it's good to see you," Arnold said, seeing Moshe sitting in a booth at the Fordham Diner.

Moshe placed his coffee cup down and waved Arnold over.

"How are Leah and the rest of your family?" Arnold asked, as he sat down in Moshe's booth.

"Thank god, everyone is well."

"That's good to hear."

"So what's this I hear you're running for mayor?"

"It's true. The election is next week. I hope I have your vote."

"Of course, it's good to have a friend in high places," Moshe said. "I read in the paper how you fooled Myron into thinking you were working for him. That was very clever."

"Between Agnes and me, and of course the commissioner, we had him surrounded. Plus Myron was a ticking time bomb. He would have self-destructed anyway had we not expedited his demise."

"So you got what you wanted. The *rasha* is gone and so is his gangster son."

"It's been quite a ride. How's your arm?" Arnold said, pointing to the cast.

"It's coming off next week. Being a one-armed cobbler is not easy." Moshe laughed.

"That's funny, Moshe. It's good to see you. I have to run. Campaigning is exhausting. Let's stay in touch," Arnold said, following his campaign manager out the door of the diner and into his waiting car.

As Moshe watched through the window, he sighed. *All's well that ends well*, he thought. But he really didn't believe it. He had failed at his task. All he had to do was release the *rasha* into the fiery pit of Gehenna, but he couldn't do it.

If and when the day came, and he was face to face with Hashem, what would he say? Moshe sighed and thought, *After all, isn't killing a sin? And who knows how I would be judged for terminating a soul?*

That night, when he got home, Leah had dinner waiting for him.

"Come, Moshe, and eat. I'm starving."

"It's a little hard these days doing things with one arm."

"The cast is coming off soon, and you'll be as good as new."

"I hope so."

"By the way, I've been meaning to ask you. You stopped sweating. I guess you got over whatever that was."

Moshe rubbed his forehead and nodded. "Yes, Leah, no more sweats."

Her comment reminded him that the last time he visited the dream world was when he brought Solomon to Gehenna. He wanted no part of that experience again, but he wouldn't mind experiencing something pleasurable.

Sammy told him that the only place he had any fun was in the dream world. The pleasantness of these thoughts allowed Moshe to quickly drift off to sleep that night.

He awoke in the dream world upon a rocky cliff, overlooking a churning seashore. From his vantage point, Moshe could see a long stretch of a desolate beach, shaded overhead by a front of dark clouds. He found and followed an array of chiseled stones that offered a stairway down to the beach.

As he stepped upon the firm sand, the clouds parted and rays of sunlight shone down upon him. Moshe closed his eyes and lifted his face to welcome its warmth. When he opened his eyes, he saw three people huddled around a fire, talking and laughing. Moshe smiled and called out, "Hello."

The people turned and waved at Moshe to join them. The clouds were now gone and only a flock of gulls filled the blue sky.

A man broke away from the group and was walking toward him. Moshe rubbed his eyes, to make sure what he was seeing was really there. But there was no denying his vision, the man walking to him was Gray.

"Greetings, Moshe, we've been waiting for you," Gray said with open arms.

Moshe accepted the embrace and grasped Gray by the shoulders and looked into his gray eyes. "Is it really you?"

"It's me, Moshe."

"But you're dead. I was at your funeral."

Gray nodded and smiled. "My soul lives on. That is until I am able to move on to another incarnation."

"I can visit you in the dream world?"

"Yes, for all of those whose souls who haven't yet been called. We were just discussing how, with your help, the soul of the rasha no longer exists," Gray said pointing to the two people standing by the fire.

"Solomon may be gone, but not because of me. I was unable to complete the task. If it hadn't been for Noa's daughter, Rebecca, the rasha would have survived."

Gray shook his head. "No, Moshe, what you don't understand is that we all knew that you couldn't do it. You're tzaddik, you're too kind. What you did was what was expected. Our ruse worked."

Moshe shook his head and said, "This was planned. I didn't screw up?"

Gray put his arm around Moshe's shoulder. "Noa is brilliant and you did great. Now come and see who is here. You have friends who are waiting for you."

Moshe and Gray walked toward the campfire. A young blond man greeted Moshe first.

"Hello, Moshe, it is good to see you again."

It wasn't until Moshe looked deeply into the man's blue eyes that he realized that this strapping youth was his former assistant. "Jack McCoy? Is that you?"

Jack nodded and smiled.

"It is wonderful to see you, Jack."

Another man who was facing the fire turned around, and Moshe immediately recognized the long white beard. "Rabbi Shapira?"

"Shalom, Moshe."

"Rabbi, how is this all possible?"

"It's possible because you make it so."

"Is this real?" Moshe said, looking at Gray and Jack.

"What does that word mean?"

Moshe shrugged. "I do not know, Rabbi."

"We are here now. You can touch my arm," he said, reaching his arm toward Moshe. "Do I not feel real. You want to tug on my beard?" he said pulling his beard.

Moshe smiled. "I suppose this is real. But when I wake up, this will all be gone. No one will know about it but me."

Gray and Jack stood next to the rabbi, who said, "We will be here for you, Moshe, to visit at any time you want. That is, until our time comes to move on."

"Come now, Moshe, let's sit by the fire and talk," Gray said.

He awoke to Leah shaking him. "Moshe, you're going to be late," she said.

Moshe opened his eyes and rubbed them to adjust to the sunlight streaming in through the window. He pushed himself to sitting with his good arm and stood up and made his way into the bathroom to prepare himself for the day.

"Can you help me dress, please?"

As Leah buttoned Moshe's shirt she stared at him with great intent. "Are you sweating again?"

Moshe touched his forehead with his good arm and smiled. "I suppose I am."

"The sweats are back. That's it, I'm taking you to the doctor today."

Moshe smiled, and took Leah's hand. "Come sit with me. I want to tell you about this wonderful place where we can experience things you would never believe was possible," Moshe said, softly stroking Leah's cheek.

"I know that look, Moshe. What are you talking about?"

"Leah, imagine we are both thirty years younger, and in love."

Leah squinted her eyes and offered a sly smile and answered, "Moshe Potasznik, have you lost your mind?"

The End

Acknowledgments

The Righteous One is a sequel to *A Cobbler's Tale*, which was drawn from the true story of my great-grandparents, Pincus and Clara Rubenfeld, and their son Moshe, my grandfather.

While Moshe Rubenfeld was not *a tzaddik*, he did have a unique ability to bring joy to his children, grandchildren, friends, and the many people he interacted with in his fruit and vegetable store on Manhattan's Upper West Side.

I would be amiss not to mention Leah Rubenfeld, Moshe's wife and my beloved grandmother who also played an inspirational part in *The Righteous One*.

About the Author

Neil Perry Gordon achieved his goal of an author of historical-fiction with his first novel – *A Cobbler's Tale*, published in the fall of 2018. With dozens of reviews praising his writing style, he released his second novel – *Moon Flower* the following year.

His creative writing methods and inspiration has been described as organic, meaning that he works with a general storyline for his characters and plot, without a formal, detailed outline. This encourages his writing to offer surprising twists and unexpected outcomes, which readers have celebrated.

Neil Perry Gordon's novels also have the attributes of being driven by an equal balance between character development and face-paced action scenes, which moves the stories along at a page-turning pace.

Both of these previous novels have encouraged Neil's shift in genre into the realm of metaphysical-fiction with his new novel *The Righteous One*. According to the author, this genre explores the possibilities of magic realism, where the supernatural is part of our tangible reality.

The author has attributed his love for the creative process from his education from his formative years spent learning-to-learn at the Green Meadow Waldorf School.

Readers can learn more about Neil Perry Gordon by visiting his website and blog at:

https://www.neilperrygordon.com/

0

CPSIA information can be obtained
at www.ICGtesting.com
Printed in the USA
BVHW081001270819
556808BV00003B/286/P